Who Your Friends Are

Susan Day

First Published in 2015 by Susan Day
Written by Susan Day
Editing by Anne Grange at Wild Rosemary
Writing Services
Copyright © Susan Day 2015

ISBN-13:
978-1512296068

ISBN-10:
1512296066

You will have seen Rita, dancing behind Cathy McGowan. In those days she was still Rita, just starting out and only glamorous enough to impress girls her own age. That was before she left her job, left home, did this, did that, met Paul McCartney, met lots of other people too, lots of men; got married, got divorced, made a lot of money, got mildly famous. You will have seen her, if you were alive then and watching television – ITV, Friday nights: Ready Steady Go.

Lovely Rita

Rita met Paul McCartney at a party – a child's party on a wet Saturday afternoon somewhere in West London, she never did know exactly where – and she saw him as soon as she came into the room, standing, talking to a young woman who was the mother of the child whose birthday it was. At least Rita surmised this because she was holding a large oval silver tray with pieces of birthday cake on it, but thinking about it later, she could just as well have been an aunt, or the au pair.

The party was coming to an end. Parents were arriving to collect children, standing around talking to each other, being offered drinks of wine. (At a child's party! Rita had never heard of that before.)

Most of the children were in another room; there was the noise of some sort of organised game, but the organisation of it was beginning to break up and at least one small child came in tears to look for their mother, or at least an adult to hide behind.

Rita had come into the house walking behind Howard and Brian, wishing she had not come – she would have stayed in the car if she had not been desperate to find a bathroom.

When she saw Paul McCartney, she knew him instantly, and felt relief (though she was still looking for a bathroom) that here was at least someone – even if he didn't know her – who she knew, who somehow made the whole day fall into place.

Because it started with Howard knocking on the door of her study-bedroom, saying he was going to London for the day, did she want to come?

'London?' she said, wrinkling her nose as if he'd just offered her something nastily incomprehensible to eat, like beetroot ice cream, say, as if she'd only vaguely heard of London, instead of telling anyone who asked that it was where she came from.

'Yes, you know, London.'

'Whereabouts?' As if it made a difference. She didn't know why she was so reluctant.

'I want to see a bloke at I.C. I think, Clapham, I think he lives.'

'I don't know where that is.'

'I'm not asking you to find it. We've got an A to Z. Borrowed it off Dave. Do you want to come?'

'By train?'

'By car. Brian's car. He won't mind if you come.'

She sat in the back of the Ford Prefect, behind Brian, where she had a view of Howard's profile, but mostly watched the Saturday traffic on the A12. Howard and Brian smoked ('Does she?'

'No.' So they didn't bother to turn round and offer her one.) and dropped names to each other.

'Andy Fairweather Lowe? My mate knows his drummer.'

'We can't afford him. We can't count on selling more than five hundred. The place is too small, that's the trouble.'

Rita had told him that herself, when he complained that the Entertainments Committee wasn't making any money. Howard, in between studying Politics, though not Economics, was in charge, in that no one else was doing it, of booking bands for the University.

'The Flowerpot Men?'

'Finished.'

'I know.'

Rita did not contribute, not because she knew nothing but because they didn't ask her. Howard had not taken an interest in her for her knowledge of music, but because he was, though younger than her, cocky enough to think it natural that he could pull the best-looking girl of the new freshers.

She had finished with her home boyfriend, on principle, believing that University was a new start that would not get off the ground carrying the weight of old boyfriends, old friends, old habits, and that space had to be made for the new, but so far that space had not been filled by anyone. The girls she had met were silly and tearful, and too young for her. Howard, at least, was refreshingly off-hand, and didn't appear to be scared of her, and she accepted that the normal state of affairs was that she was there for the look of the thing.

When they passed Chelmsford and she saw the signs to Ongar and Epping, she felt a small pang at the thought of the ex-boyfriend, and also of her best friend and their outings, occasionally as a four, to the Forest on summer Sundays. As with the boyfriend, she'd made even her best friend understand that things were going to change.

'I will miss you,' she'd said, but they agreed that they would be leading different lives from each other, and from the ones they had been leading, each of them on the edge of something new. She told her parents and her aunt Ginny that she wouldn't be seeing them again until Christmas.

London took forever to cross and none of it was familiar to Rita, not surprisingly, since she had always used public transport herself, bus or train to Liverpool Street, and the Tube for anything beyond that. She had never been south of the river before.

The two boys, she could swear, had forgotten she existed, and when they arrived at the door of a house in Peckham, she stayed in the car while they knocked, stood on the doorstep and were directed elsewhere. They utilised Dave's A to Z to reach Chiswick, in the process visiting houses in Streatham, Clapham and Richmond, where the bloke from I.C. might have been but wasn't.

At Richmond, she decided that she needed a pee, and that she would have to do something about it. The house looked respectable – actually it looked big and imposing and this indicated to Rita that the toilet would be clean, and she had hopes of a cup of tea too.

'I'll come in with you,' she said. Brian almost jumped, he had forgotten her so completely.

Howard said, 'Come on then.'

When the door opened though and she glimpsed the darkness of the flat, and smelled the smell of dirt, a smell both forgotten and familiar, she changed her mind. 'I'll wait here,' she said. In Rita's mother's house, if it didn't smell of Harpic, then it smelled of dirt.

At Chiswick, she stayed in the car, unwilling to try again without the protection of more make-up and some attention to her hair, things that she would not have thought of doing in front of the boys - they should never know that any effort went into how she looked. And at the last house, dubious as she was, she climbed out of the car inelegantly via the driver's door, and stood in her very short skirt and new brown boots, gathering her resolve not to show shock whatever should be on the other side of the shiny red door.

And what there was there besides Paul McCartney, she could hardly say, or she could, but it wasn't important. She felt that nothing else in the room, or in the rest of the afternoon, remained in her memory like the sight of Paul did. 'I can't explain it,' she said later to her friend. 'He was just so real.'

Howard did find the elusive bloke from I.C. who, however, did not have on his person the address of the person who could get Tyrannosaurus Rex to come and play at the University. 'But I tell you what, there's a bloke I know works in the box office at the Marquee.'

Having come out of the bathroom (which had a vase of flowers on its windowsill, how amazing), Rita stood by the door, partly because she didn't want Howard and Brian to go out and forget her, partly because she thought that Paul might not stay long and he would have to pass close to her on his way out. He had no children, everyone knew that, so it was not clear why he was there. He might stay all evening, or he might leave as soon as some undefined thing had happened. None of these people - grown-ups as she thought of them - let themselves appear impressed by being in the same room as a Beatle.

When he did turn and move towards the door, she moved out of the way, but slowly, so that he passed close by her. He smiled. She smiled back, crinkling her eyes as she'd practised rather than stretching her mouth and showing her teeth, which were slightly askew and tended to make her self-conscious. He spoke to her, though she could never recall precisely what he said, it was about her boots. He stretched out his foot and showed her his plimsolls, though he called them "pumps" – she always remembered that.

Then Howard came pushing through, knocking over a small child who was standing inoffensively in his way.

'Rita!' He pretended to be surprised at seeing Paul McCartney.

'Hello, Paul,' he shouted, and put out his hand as if they knew each other.

'Got to go,' said Paul McCartney. And he went.

Howard shrugged and grinned at Rita. Rita knew that she was blushing with shame. 'You – twerp,' she said, but he had already turned to Brian and was grabbing his arm. 'Did you see that? Did you see who that was?'

Rita left the house – not to follow Paul, she would not have dreamed of that, but to get away from Howard and Brian, and the feeling of being ashamed of how pathetic they were – and managed to find her way, by bus, because buses were what she trusted, from St John's Wood to Liverpool Street, where she picked up a 279; fifty minutes later she surprised her aunt and uncle with an unscheduled visit. After an evening of tea and television, she went to bed in her old room, and surprised herself by finding that as she lay under her old eiderdown, she cried quietly and steadily, like drizzle, until she fell asleep.

I'm Pat. It was me who wrote that about Rita and Paul McCartney, and although it sounds like fiction, it was true. Rita told me about it.

'I wish I'd been there,' I said.

'I wish that cretin hadn't come and interrupted,' said Rita, and then, 'I wish it had been John.'

You will have seen her, if you were alive then and watching television. I was her best friend and I used to sit at home, with my boyfriend, after work on a Friday and catch this magic glimpse of a tiny prancing person I only had to walk down the road to see as large as life.

She had, actually, been within spitting distance of The Who, and The Rolling Stones, and plenty of others, on Ready Steady Go, but she'd missed the times when the Beatles were on and had only been under the same roof as them at the Finsbury Park Astoria, with me and a thousand others.

Now, this many years later, I never see her, except, now I'm not working, occasionally on daytime TV, or on Youtube, since Zoe, on her last visit and between arguments, showed me how.

When they made me leave my job, I made a list of all the things I would do. I don't claim that it was an interesting list. Sort out sideboards. Empty loft. Measure all windows and all curtains. Throw away useless curtains. Matthew's room. Kezia's room. Clean windows. Stuff to Oxfam. Clean lampshades. Clear shed. Clear carport. CLEAN HOUSE. Tidy garden. Something like that anyway.

Maybe I asked too much of myself, maybe the list was too long and the jobs too big. I would look at it after Don had gone to work and wonder which one I felt up to doing. Some days I decided on one, and sometimes I opened a cupboard and looked at the stuff inside but I never got further than that. Then I would go back to the kitchen and wash up the breakfast dishes, maybe go and make the bed, have a cup of tea, see what's on TV, have lunch early. Afternoons I would go and buy something for the evening, walking down to Sainsbury's, or Asda if I felt like going further, and that would be the day gone.

Evenings, Don was home. It was summer, and the days were long and passed, not quickly, but they passed. Don and I went to Torquay for a week, as usual, calling in to see Katie and the boys on our way home. When I got home, I found my list underneath a cut glass bowl on a sideboard (Auntie Peggy's) and threw it in the bin without looking at it.

Then I made another list. It said: Move house. Go to Italy. Then I stopped because I couldn't think of anything else. I crossed out Move House because I knew that Don would say it was paid for and it was an appreciating asset and he would move when he couldn't manage to get up the two steps to the front door. I almost crossed out Go to Italy but the thought of having no ambitions at all stopped me. Change hairstyle. Join a gym. Have makeover. Do a course. Walk the Pennine Way. Look up old friends. Learn to ice skate. I was amazed suddenly at how easy it could be to think of things other people might care for but I didn't.

Eventually though, I did sign up for a course in Creative Writing.

I don't know where I thought would be a fitting place for a Writers' Group, maybe shabby and old-fashioned is the right thing, but whatever I expected, it is a small room in the community centre, with First Aid posters on the wall and the Brownies' toadstool upside down in the corner.

I arrive early, and find a seemingly jovial man in corduroy trousers setting out a circle of wooden chairs, the sort with a compartment on the back for a hymn book.

There's an element of surprise in his welcome and after he's invited me to sit down, he clearly can't think of anything else to say, and manages to keep himself busy reading the posters about the Heimlich Manoeuvre. To his relief and mine, other people begin to arrive, chatting to each other like old friends and joking with corduroy man. No one alludes to the fact that I'm there, but at twenty-five to eight it seems that we are ready to start and Jerry – I've heard them call him that – with a visible effort, acknowledges me, a new recruit. 'So I'm going to ask everyone to introduce themselves.'

When you've spent a working life in social services, you are used to going round a table or a room saying your name. These people seem never to have introduced themselves to a group in their entire lives; they shuffle about and giggle and with a great deal of modesty (not much of it false), facetiousness and embarrassment, they manage to tell me who they are. There is John, tall and gaunt and old in a tweed sports jacket, and Jim, small and gaunt and very very old in a tweed sports jacket with leather elbow patches. The women are a bit younger. There is Joan, who adds that she writes poems, Jean who looks as if she could have been left there since the last Brownie meeting, Jocelyn - rather posh, and Jean's daughter Julia, who has dreadlocks and a multi-layered, multi-coloured approach to clothing.

'And you are...?'

I wish I could say Jane or Jennifer but the truth sticks to my tongue and I say 'Pat.'

'What we do,' says Jerry, 'people read out their work and we can all comment on it if we want, and then I take it away with me – that's what I'm paid to do – and go through it, make corrections and so forth, and bring it back to you the following week. OK?'

'Do you – I thought you would set subjects, or...tasks?'

'Oh no, we gave that up years ago. Whatever you pick never suits everyone – sometimes suited no one,' – he laughs and they all laugh – 'so now we just do our own thing. You'll find out.'

He begins giving back sheaves of paper to people – 'Janet not here this week?' – and waits for someone to begin. 'How about you, Julia?'

'I'll go last,' she whispers. 'If there's time at the end.'

'Up to you, my dear. But don't say I never offered. Joan?'

Joan reads a humorous poem about her duvet. Jerry chortles and John says, 'We can always rely on Jean.'

'Joan,' she corrects him.

'Now then,' says Jerry. 'What about Jocelyn? Jocelyn's book is coming along quite nicely.' She is shuffling a stack of at least twenty pages. 'Fascinating. I don't think we'll have time to hear it all today.'

'I've got some more here,' she offers. 'For next week.'

'Lovely,' says Jerry. 'And you'll read us some now.'

'Of course.' Jocelyn's book is a combination of a memoir of her parents, and a travel book about all the places they had ever lived and worked, and which she has visited since their deaths. Today's bit is about Singapore and her own arrival in the world.

'Fascinating,' says Jerry again.

'So you were actually born in Singapore?' says Joan. 'How exotic. And when you went back, was it how you remembered it?'

'That's in the next chapter,' says Jocelyn.

'Coffee,' says John, unfolding himself like a collapsible walking stick and hastening to the kitchen. He rattles open the hatch and we can hear him filling a teapot from the urn.

'Twenty-five p,' he says to me as I take a cup from the counter. 'Tea all right? We've got coffee.' But everyone is drinking tea as if they know something about the use-by date on the coffee jar. Except for Julia, and she drinks water.

'Do you write?' she whispers to me.

'Well, not much, yet.' I was expecting this question,

though I expected it to come from Jerry. 'But I used to,' – a lie – 'and I thought I'd try to get started again.'

She looks disappointed. 'No one here is a real writer,' she says. 'At least, not the ones here tonight.'

'There are other people then?'

'Oh yes. There's Judy, she's quite talented, but she writes so slowly you see, that we only ever get about half a page from her. It is good though. And there's a man called Jeff, he writes crime stuff. I don't like it but he has sold some stories so he's like a proper writer.'

'What do you write then?' She is about the age of my son and there is a long blue thread trailing from her jumper and sticking to her stripy tights. I expect her to say 'poems,' or something about dragons and swords but she doesn't.

'I do sort of...' – she gulps with embarrassment – 'sort of descriptive pieces. My – someone – told me to look, really look, at what's there, and I started to write it down, and then Mum dragged me to this class.'

'Does your mum write?'

'She says she does but she doesn't. Sometimes she does, like, a little story or something, because she feels she has to, but she only comes really to keep me company.'

I put my cup back on the hatch. John is counting up the £1.75 and writing it in a notebook, and Joan and Jocelyn are washing up the cups.

'Settling in alright?' asks John. 'They're a good crowd, a good crowd.'

I smile. 'What do you write?' I ask, feigning interest.

'Me? Oh nothing, nothing. Not really, you know. But I make myself useful.' He gestures to the teacups. 'We have a rota for washing up, you know.'

After the break, Jim reads from his work in progress, which is his autobiography. He has an amazing memory for detail.

'So,' says John, very animated, 'you went to Raynham Road. I've known you all these years and I never knew that. I went to Brettenham Road. Not a stone's throw away.'

'My dad went to Brettenham Road,' says Jean.

'Amazing,' says John. 'Amazing.'

I hang behind at the end, wanting to get my money's worth, and ask Jerry for an idea for something to write. He looks hunted.

'Whatever you like. We're very eclectic.'

'But I need some tips. If I was writing a short story, how should I start? I don't have any ideas.'

'What about...' – he is looking longingly at the door – 'pick three objects, let's say a – a Rolls Royce, or any sort of car you like and a – a birthday cake and a bloke called – em – Harold. Or Howard. It's just a practice – write a story with those three things in. Give it a go. We won't be hard on you.'

I can believe that because they haven't been hard on anybody.

Before I even open my front door, I can hear the sound Don singing along to the Beatles.

'OK?' he says, though he does not look up from his

Sudoku.

'OK,' I say, and I make a cup of tea and tell him about it, and – this is a nice thing about Don – he listens as if he's interested, even though I know he's not, and then he tells me about some stuff on the news, and then I wonder when we can go down to Bristol and see Katie again. He doesn't answer, and I ask him if he could fix the outside light, and he says he will, and when it's eleven o'clock, we bolt the front door, and turn all the sockets off and go to bed.

I saw her standing there

'He wants what?'

'Photograph me.'

'What, like...?'

'Like a model, I suppose.'

'What did you say?'

'Said I would. If you'll come too.'

'Well I'm not letting you go without me.'

The young man – boy maybe – who had approached Rita, was waiting by the door of the shop to see what she would do. He wore black only – jeans, turtleneck sweater – and his hair was black too, his eyes dark in a thin, pointed face. He was more scruffy, and looked more gentle, than the boys Rita usually liked.

'Where's he going to take this photo? Where's his camera?'

'Back at his studio.'

'Bedroom, more likely.'

'Come on,' said Rita. 'What harm can it do? He might snap you as well.'

'Crack his camera, that would.'

'It'll be a laugh.' Although Rita was not laughing; her lips were set together and tiny spasms in her jaws gave away that she was clenching her teeth. She was wearing white knee socks like Marianne Faithfull.

'All right then.'

Unsurprisingly, the studio did turn out to be

his bedroom, but surprisingly, it was kitted out with an elaborate-looking camera on a tripod and two industrial-looking lamps which were directed to shine at an area hung with a white sheet and strips of foil which the girls could see had clearly come out of a Bacofoil box – the box was in full view, on the floor. This struck them as funny, but they were also somehow reassured by it. He was called Colin, he said, and he was an art student. He showed them where he developed his photos – 'not a darkroom exactly, just a dark cupboard.'

He said he was sorry he had nothing to offer them to drink or smoke: photography was expensive, and his grant for the term was nearly all spent. It was still weeks until Easter when he would go back to his parents. He showed them some of his pictures, to prove maybe that he was a real artist. He probably was, because the girls were not very impressed by them.

'Is this the first time you've taken people?'

'Well, not quite,' he said, perhaps a little hurt, who could tell? 'But I need to get some portraits in my portfolio. It's all the same, you know, whatever your subject is – getting the light right, that's the biggest thing.'

'And pointing the camera in the right direction,' suggested the friend, but he didn't find that funny, and began setting up his equipment.

'Start with her,' said Rita.

So the friend sat on a stool draped with a blanket, and the camera clicked away.

'Did you notice any flash?' she asked Rita later. 'When he was taking me, I mean.'

'I can't remember,' said Rita.

Then he fussed around Rita, getting her in position, and looking through the viewfinder and fiddling with the reflecting strips, and took a number of shots, some of them from very close to her face. Rita sat calm and clear-eyed through it all, not apparently either enjoying or disliking the process.

'Now,' he said. 'Just go down the hall to the bathroom and take your sweater off. I'll give you this sheet – look, it's clean, honestly – and I want you to put it round you so that your shoulders show.' Rita took the sheet, without arguing – 'No bra straps,' he called after her.

He never said 'please' or 'I'd like you to', just 'do this', 'do that,' but Rita did as she was told, posing with bare shoulders, looking like Natalie Wood, while her friend sat watchful and slightly bored.

When they left, after giving him their addresses so that he could post copies to them – this was the deal – and came out into the street, the icy air prickled on their faces and got up under their skirts. They were in an unfamiliar suburb of London and it was dark, but they found a bus stop and worked out a way home.

The two of them sat contentedly on the top deck of the bus from Finsbury Park, smiling at each other occasionally, but mostly looking at their reflections in the dark bus windows.

Of course, the friend was me, but I don't tell the group that. I didn't know, while I was writing that, how to include me. I didn't want to identify myself, but couldn't bring myself to give me a different name.

But it all happened as I've written. I can't remember what shop we were in, or what part of London, or why we'd gone there. I can't remember exactly what we were wearing, or where the boy lived. I just remember the cold when we came out of that house, and the icy wind round our legs – we were wearing skirts of course, and I could feel my skin above the stockings turning blue.

The writing group are polite but haven't much to say. Nobody tells me I'm an undiscovered talent. Judy has turned up this week, and she has the effect of livening proceedings, being louder than the rest and keen on being heard. She takes no notice of me though and tends to monopolise the attention of everyone else. Suddenly, on only my third week, I'm no longer a novelty, and my story is brushed aside. Dull, and long ago.

It worked out well, though, that boy and his camera. He sent us some photos, only two of me (if only I could find them), so it proved he'd had his flash on at least some of the time, and they were the nicest photos I've ever had taken. He sent Rita a whole pile and she – I had no idea she was thinking of this – picked out the best, set them out in an old album and took them to a model agency, and the agency signed her up.

So she became a model, and her face was in magazine adverts and on knitting patterns, and even once on the cover of a magazine, though it was only Camping and Caravanning Monthly. She didn't do fashion because she wasn't tall enough, and she never became famous, but she made money, and after a year or so she left her job at the bank and lived on modelling so that she had – though she kept it secret at the time – more time to study for her A-levels. That was another plan I knew nothing about, and I don't think anyone else did either.

The other thing about that day which sticks in my head is that when we got to her Auntie Ginny's house, we heard that Kay had had her baby.

'Little girl,' said Aunt Ginny. 'Deborah. *That's* fancy, if you like.'

Rita shrugged, but I thought I could see that though she always tried to act cool, this time she was actually a little bit emotional.

'Will you go and see her?' I asked.

'Probably. You'll come too, won't you?'

And when I got home, mum told me that my Aunt Peggy had been round to say that Theresa had had her baby too. Same day. A boy. You can feel the plot thickening, can't you?

Another thing about that day – how significantly events cluster together, or seem to, in our teenage years – it was the day I started going out with Don.

I'd known Don all my life, just about, we all had. He lived on the council estate near Rita, while mum and I, and Aunt Peggy and Leslie, lived in smaller, older houses that we rented privately. But we all mixed and used to hang around together, in the park when we were younger, and then at the youth club.

Don was at school with Les, on the fringe of the same group. He was a tall, shy boy, with a long, quite good-looking face and brown eyes that seemed to slant downwards, giving him a rather bloodhound puppy look. His ears stuck out. He was never at the centre of a group and never spoke if more than one person was listening. But he was quite clever and was apprenticed to be an electrician; he had a motor scooter that he went to work on. He was known mainly for his record collection.

'Going out tonight?' asked mum.

'Well, I was going to, but Rita's not going now, she's staying in with Val and Tony while her mum and dad go to the hospital.'

She hadn't suggested that I should go round and sit with her, and I didn't want to be pushy – since all the trouble with her family, Rita seemed to want my company less and less often, only when it suited her, and it was making me feel as if I had to be careful not to do anything wrong.

'You can come round to Peggy's with me, then,' said mum, as if it was a treat. 'I've got a present for the baby.'

I could see she had been going through some of the bags she kept at the bottom of her wardrobe – the settee was covered in balls of wool, bits of material, ribbons, bags of stuffing, empty cotton reels, a pair of shoulder pads, a pair of braces which it was unlikely she would ever need, and assorted children's clothes, none of them new. She held up a pair of blue woolly mittens.

'Your Nan knitted these for you before you were born, she was so convinced you'd be a boy.' She continued scuffling through the bags until she pulled out a pair of bootees in roughly the same colour wool.

'She'll be sending a big parcel, if I know Peg,' said mum. 'She might as well put these in with it.' Mum was always careful with money.

Auntie Peggy was sitting by the fire with her friend Edie. She was pleased to see us, so that she could repeat to me the brief conversation she'd had with Leslie – 'He couldn't say much, he was in a phone box.' Then they thought they might have a drink to wet the baby's head and Peggy got up and fetched her purse.

'Pop round the off-licence, lovey,' she said, sitting down again, out of breath, 'and get us three bottles of Mackeson.' Obviously I was not going to be included.

Anyway, while I was there in the shop, Don came in for a packet of cigs, and because he knew Les, I told him the news. We had a conversation – the first I'd ever had with him on his own – standing on the corner in the freezing cold, and he asked me if I wanted to go to the pictures with him next Thursday, when he got paid.

I'm looking through you

That Saturday morning, Rita woke with Tim in her bed. She was twenty-three. Tim was stroking her bottom in a vague sort of way, but as soon as she could be seen to be awake, he became more active and began kneading bits of her more urgently.

After they had made love, Tim got up to make tea. Rita lay in bed and watched him. Neat was what Tim was. Neat body, neat movements, neat moustache and beard – the right amount of facial hair for those times, but neat. When he came out of the kitchen area with two mugs, she turned her eyes away from looking directly at him; it was what she would have wanted him to do if she was walking around naked.

'What are you doing this weekend?' It was Easter.

'I don't know. Nothing special.'

'Not going to see your family?' Tim had not known Rita long.

'I don't think so. I might go and see my friend. She's just had a baby.' She did not mention the Easter eggs she would take to Val and Tony, and the ones she would leave at her mother's for Kay's children. She felt maybe that Tim (one sister two years younger than him) might find her family slightly distasteful.

'Tomorrow is the day to do that,' said Tim. 'I

have to make family visits tomorrow, but today I can please myself. As indeed –' he stroked her shoulder with the hand that was not holding his tea, 'I have just done.' He leaned towards her. 'And I hope it pleased you as well.'

Rita did not like to talk about sex, though she liked doing it. 'Yes, thanks,' she said shortly.

'I don't call that good enough,' he said, taking her mug of tea from her hand and putting it, with his, neatly, under the bed, where they would not kick them over. 'I think we may have to try again, for a more positive response.'

It was different every time with Tim, as if he was ticking off items in his I-Spy Book of Sexual Positions, but by the time the knock came at the door, they were up and dressed. Music was playing; they were planning what to do with the afternoon. Rita went to the door and there found Si. He smiled, as Si did, twitching one corner of his mouth. She had spent the last eighteen months being in love with Si, without getting anywhere.

'How did you get in?' said Rita, irritably. He gestured vaguely down the stairs and walked into her flat. It was the sort of flat that is really a bedsit, one big room with a rudimentary kitchen area and a bathroom. The bed could be hidden behind a curtain, but it wasn't at the moment. Rita felt that if Si looked at it – as he surely would – he would see the imprint of Tim and her, and see heat rising from it.

I should be past this sort of thing, she thought, by which she meant that she should be safely married and settled down with one of the men who impinged on her life. It almost didn't matter who.

Si looked around amiably, then went to the kitchen, and they could see him boiling the kettle and searching through cupboards.

Tim looked at her for an explanation but Rita said nothing because she could think of nothing to say which would not make matters worse with one or the other of them, or both. Si brought in three mugs of coffee on a tray.

'Beautiful day,' he said in his soft Bristol voice. Rita loved his voice. Tim's voice immediately sounded harsh and pompous and he dropped down the scale of what it was to be the right sort of man – not the perfect man, but the right sort of man.

'Going to go out, were you?' asked Si.

'We thought of doing so,' said Tim. 'I've got a car.' Even Rita could tell that it was a very unsubtle attempt at one-upmanship; he dropped further down the scale.

'Nice car?' enquired Si, apparently interested.

'Very nice,' said Rita sharply, perversely moved to be on Tim's side. Si's smile twitched once more.

'You haven't introduced us,' said Tim. He, in

turn, seemed to feel the need to say something critical to show her that she didn't need to defend him.

'He's Tim, he's Si,' she said, not looking at either of them.

'So, Tim,' said Si. 'Tell me about yourself. What do you do, and how long have you known Rita, and all that sort of thing.'

'Rita and I work together,' said Tim, still defensive.

'You into these machines then, these IBM thingies?'

'No, that's not my bit of it. I'm more on the artistic side myself.'

Si looked over the rim of his mug at Rita, but spoke to Tim.

'Interesting girl, our Rita. I've never understood what she's all about. Beautiful, I'm sure you'll agree.'

Tim agreed.

'But all these numbers, and punch cards and big machines that do what?'

Rita said nothing but Si continued as if she had said what he expected her to say.

'Well they can do all sorts of things, can't they, but do we need it? Do we need to know Pi to three thousand decimal points, or do we need another thousand prime numbers? I know I don't. Do you, Tim?'

Rita went to the bathroom. She needed to go

anyway, but once there, she found she had no wish to come out, to be awarded to the winner of whatever competition was going on.

She turned on the bath taps, although she had already washed, and the noise of the water stopped her hearing the men talking. When the bath was full enough, though, they were still there. She heard Tim laugh, shortly, and Si's voice continued. She got into the bath, making sure first that the door was bolted. After twenty minutes or so the water was going cold, so she ran some more. Tim and Si seemed to be getting on well, judging by the laughter that came from the room. She wondered if they had noticed she had gone. She stayed where she was.

She stayed there until they left.

First Tim, after calling to her through the door.

'Come out please, I need a slash, what are you doing in there? Are you all right?'

And after he'd gone and she still didn't come out, Si left too, without saying goodbye.

I'm afraid the group is not altogether positive about the Rita stories. I thought they would be quite uncritical – and so they are, to each other – but towards me, because I'm new I suppose, they are not so protective.

'It's a very downbeat ending,' says Jocelyn.

'Sort of tails off really,' says Jean.

Joan thought I should make my stories more dramatic.

'More dramatic than meeting Paul McCartney?'

'Well,' she says. 'What I mean is, you don't make the most of it. If he had asked her out, or written a song about her...'

John thought the men were unconvincing.

'It seems to me you're falling between realism and fantasy,' Jerry says. 'But keep going, you need to practise. More detail. You'll find your style eventually.'

'I tried to put in detail,' I say. I want to say that I put in everything I knew and added bits as well; I want to ask him how to put in more detail. Where does it go? I open my mouth to speak but Jerry is looking at his watch to avoid me. He knows he should be professional and give me some guidance, but Jeff is there tonight and he really wants to get on with something more masculine.

'I liked your story, though,' whispers Julia at coffee break. Her style has changed; her dreadlocks have been cut off and she's wearing tracksuit bottoms and trainers.

'Have you written anything?' I ask her.

'Oh yes, I do some every day. But I don't want him,' –

she twitches her head in Jerry's direction – 'to have the chance to patronise me.'

'Why do you come then?'

'Just to keep mum quiet, really. She likes me to get out and do stuff.'

Jocelyn has thought of something else to say.

'I have a problem with your central character,' she says, as we wash the tea cups. 'I just can't get a sense of her. She doesn't seem,' – in spite of the tea towel, she does that speech marks thing with her fingers – 'real.'

'Ah,' I say. But I don't say, Actually she is real, not "real" but really real. I've known her all my life, just about. Those things happened. Her boyfriend – the one she went to London with – wasn't really called Howard, but apart from that, it all happened. She told me about it. I don't say this to Jocelyn, because I know, and I heard it for myself when I was reading out loud, that I haven't put Rita on paper. I wanted to show how glamorous she was, how all the men were after her, what an interesting life she had, but I've made her ordinary, and she was not ordinary. Back then she was extraordinarily beautiful and extraordinarily clever, and I was her best friend.

From the age of six, Rita and I were best friends. She was pretty then, in the way that makes some girls popular, but she was also clever and that put other girls off. She could be bossy too, though more so at home than at school. I could cope with it – sometimes I would do what she wanted, other times we'd have a row, and I

34

might win, or I might just do what I wanted anyway.

As we grew older I knew, of course I knew, that boys looked at her more than they looked at me. Aged thirteen or fourteen or fifteen, I cried myself to sleep probably once a month because the boy that I fancied, fancied her. When we began actually going out with boys, of course she had more offers, but she never got serious about them and they never lasted long. She never got to the stage we would have called 'courting' which was where you had a boyfriend who came to your house on the same nights every week, who sat in your front room with your parents – in my case, just my mum – and watched telly, and once a week took you to the pictures. Rita would go to the pictures with a boy, or to a dance, and maybe see them again once or twice, but she kept them at a distance and didn't invite them home, not before and certainly not after the big row.

She's the only person I know, or ever knew, who was ever in the same room as one of the Beatles. We loved them so much, even though we were quite grown up – sixteen – when we first heard them. My favourite was George, but Rita always preferred John. She liked the suggestion of surliness; she liked his spikiness and his quickness and the smile that lit up and made you think you could change him if he'd only let you love him.

When he sang *Anna* she wanted to be that girl so much that she told me she'd like to change her name to Anna. She liked his voice better than Paul's. But it was Paul she met. After Sergeant Pepper, after the death of Brian Epstein, before they all went off to India, in that last little space where they were still, we believed, in touch with us, when there were so many things we didn't know, before we knew how the story was going to end.

Now they appear as historical figures in documentaries about the sixties, so many documentaries that Don and I don't always bother to watch. Sometimes I almost forget which two are dead and which two are not. Sometimes I almost forget whether it was Paul that Rita met, or John.

I don't know why I persevered with Don. People said to me that he wasn't my type – Rita said he was a twin to Alan who lived next door to her, but she was just being mean. It's true I was his first girlfriend and he was a long way from being my first boyfriend, and it's true he was quiet and people thought I was noisy and a bit domineering. But I was eighteen. Other girls I knew were getting engaged, Rita's younger sisters were married. I was looking, even if I didn't quite know it, for someone to settle down with. And Don was just right. He was docile, and domesticated. He got on well with his mum and dad and I think he would have stayed at home for ever if it hadn't been for his sexual urges, which puzzled him until he got together with me. He used to say things like 'You see people kissing in films but I never saw the point until I did it with you', and 'I never understood why people would want to get married.'

Other boys went out with me because I was their

level in terms of looks, but they really wanted someone prettier, and so did I quite often, but Don had no idea that Rita was better looking than me, he just knew he was nervous around her, and he wasn't nervous with me.

So really I do know why we stayed together. I wanted him and he needed me. He mumbled, and he still does, but I could put up with that. He wanted to be married and have a house and some children and live as his parents did, and he had no ambitions to go abroad, or dreams to be a millionaire, and that suited me fine. It wouldn't have suited Rita, and that's why she didn't understand.

The writing group, only once a week as it is, is helping to fill up the space left by having no job. I try not to think about my old desk and its files and papers and memos and empty cups. I look forward to Tuesdays. Jocelyn I like best, and Julia. She is an innocent, a sort of damaged flower fairy. I realise that she's had some sort of breakdown – I imagine to do with drugs – and that her mother is protecting her as powerfully as she can (which is not very), from the world and from herself. They all ask me about myself, where do I live, how many children, do I work, stuff like that, and I tell them bits and pieces, like you do. It's not really interesting to others who don't know them, is it? – that Katie lives in Bristol, or that Zoe is vegetarian and has a little girl, but it keeps the coffee break ticking over. I tell them I'm retired, but fudge round what I used to do.

But I'm getting less and less input about my stories. If I ask them, they think I want them to tell me they're good; by becoming a member of the group I've become protected against their real opinions.

Even Jerry, who is paid to be critical, just mutters: 'Coming along, coming along.'

I do my writing in the mornings, after Don has gone to work. I turn the radio off and sit at the kitchen table – I believe this is the way that women writers do it. My first story I wrote in an old school book of Matthew's, that I fished out of his cupboard, but then I became a bit more grand, and went to Stationery Box and bought some (some! more than one! a commitment!) A4 ruled pads. I keep the one I'm using, and the finished pieces, in an old cardboard folder from work (labelled Child Protection, and I wonder why I don't tear the label off, or even better, throw the whole folder away and buy a new one) and I keep it out of sight when I'm not using it by parking it among the stuff in what used to be Katie's room, where no one ever goes now. I find that the morning goes by quite satisfactorily this way, and it means that things I haven't done – washing up, shopping, houseworky sort of things – have to be crammed into the afternoon, so that feels busy and goes quickly. It may not be what they call "living life to the full".

Don knows all about it – it's not a secret, but he would be embarrassed if I ever asked him to read anything I'd written. He wouldn't know what to say, so I keep it to myself; a small private pastime, like picking my nose, or looking on Google Earth at Katie's house.

Rita's wedding

After the ceremony, which was brief, Rita hugged, briefly, her mother and her Aunt Ginny, looked around at the other guests – family only – as if she couldn't remember why they were there, and then, and only then, smiled, and took Peter's arm to go outside for the photographs.

Rita's wedding

'He's not as tall as I thought he'd be,' said Aunt Ginny.

'Well, you only see him sitting down on telly,' said Rita's mum, as if it made sense.

Rita's wedding

It was cold for May, and viciously windy, so that the hat that the groom's mother – unwisely – had chosen had to be held on by hand, which gave her the look of someone impersonating a teapot.

I spent a long time trying to put Rita's wedding on paper, but nothing would come. I was there. It was an awful day that I find hard to think about. Don will never talk about it at all. But while I was there, in those days before mobile phones, I didn't know what was happening at home.

When I heard what was planned I was embarrassed about what my wedding had been like. From being the day that we spent so long planning and arranging, it turned into such a church hall affair, so dull.

Rita's was a small do, sophisticated it seemed, family only except for me, registry office in Hampstead, lunch in a restaurant, no speeches or dancing. Of course her family were quite put out and thought it was cheap and that she must be pregnant. Her dad had died the previous year so he wasn't there, noticed more for not being there than he would have been if he was. Val was there, wearing hot pants, and Kay with Malcolm, but not the little girls. Tony stayed away and Theresa was not invited. Peter's family were there, just as bemused as Mrs D. and Aunt Ginny, just as excited and scared of having their photos taken – though pointlessly, because only Peter ("Teen Idol") and Rita ("Pretty Secretary" or in some that had done more research, "Model") appeared in the papers, the picture editors having sacrificed the wide shot of self-conscious family members for the full length shot which could include Rita's thighs. I read the Sunday papers next day while I waited at the hospital and I thought how happy Rita was and how miserable I was.

Of course they weren't happy, or not for long. Peter was away a lot, touring with the band. Then Peter left that band and was at home; he wanted to leave the big flat in Hampstead and move to the country, but Rita would not move out of London because she was hoping to get started in TV, having taken Pete's surname of course, so that people, Don among them, always thought that was what she married him for. And she wouldn't get involved in drinking or drugs or parties and in fact wasn't very interested in his music at all. She said to me that it was only for teenagers. Irreconcilable musical differences. So they split, and Peter played with some other bands, and now, so Zoe who reads magazines tells me, lives in the West Country with a second (or third?) wife and a yacht called the "Lovely Rita".

Rita moved back east to Finchley, where she's been ever since. I remember that flat when she first moved into it, tall windows and wooden shutters inside that shut the evening out.

It wasn't evening when I went there last, but a dark wet afternoon. It must have been a weekend because Rita was never at home on weekdays – even on Saturdays and Sundays she was hard to pin down in that workaholic post-divorce phase which never seemed to go away. But if it was a weekend, I don't know why I took two children with me instead of leaving them with Don. It was just before Christmas, must have been because I remember coming back through cold wet streets, glittering with the reflections of Christmas trees.

If I sit here now, at the table, and look at my hand holding the pen, I mean my sixty year old hand and this blue Bic, then nothing is sure, or I am sure about nothing. Was it her birthday? Did I take a present? How come that information, which would have been securely in my brain for a week before – thinking, deciding, choosing, buying – could I afford it? – wrapping, carrying – and for weeks afterwards, has gone? Once I knew it, now I don't. What was I wearing? What were Katie and Zoe wearing? How did I get there? By bus? Or did I walk all the way with a double pushchair? (I never had a foldable buggy till Kezia was born, when the big double pushchair had disintegrated under the weight of Katie who wasn't really, until she was four, able to walk a useful distance.)

I stop looking at my hand and look out of the window instead. This is the window I've looked out of every day, hands in the washing up bowl, since 1969. So, the back of the house opposite says to me, you took two children, in a pushchair, so Kezia wasn't yet born? That's right, we still had only two, the miracle that was Kezia was yet to arrive, and if it was December – and I'm sure it was now – then I was pregnant, but didn't know it for sure. Only a queasy feeling, and a restlessness, and a wondering – could it be true? And if it was, would we cope? That's why I didn't go on a bus, I thought I might be sick with the heat and the smell of people and wet coats. But I had to go because it was Rita's birthday. Or it had been the day before.

Don gave us a lift – our car was new, new to us that is

– and he was taking it to his brother's so that they could service it, or adjust the tappets, or grommets or something. So he dropped us off and I unfolded the pushchair out of the boot and Zoe wanted to walk and we set off, but then she wanted to sit, or maybe I wanted her to and we had a bit of a shouting episode in the street. She had quite a command of language, Zoe, and she wanted to go into the shops and see the bright colours and touch the tinsel. Katie was quiet and tired that day – I always felt she had a tiring life, overcoming her problems and struggling to keep up with a younger sister.

Rita was expecting us, and I'd thought she would have been prepared, but it was clear as soon as we were through the door that there was going to be trouble. Zoe went for the birthday cards which were on a low table and swept them off it. Katie went for the heavy glass ashtray, I took it away from her; she wailed a bit but was distracted by a bunch of roses in a vase on a low shelf by the fireplace. Everything was low, everything was breakable, or precious, or both. Everything was attractive and pretty and threw me into panic and confusion. ('Sorry. Sorry.')

I scrabbled in my bag for something to distract them, but of course they had seen their old crayons and colouring books before, and their soft toys. Their favourite things, with bells and whistles and twirly bits, I'd left at home – too big, too noisy and distracting for me and Rita while we had our friendly chat. Wrong decision.

I gave Rita her present – I don't remember doing it but I must have done – and she brought out orange squash and chocolate Santas for the girls. I tried to insist, looking at the cream shag pile on her floor, that we should sit in the kitchen, but though glossy and smart, it was tiny and had nothing to sit on, so we each took a child and held them on our laps, talking past their heads, Rita uncomfortable with Zoe – though she had nieces of her own, she should have been used to it – and me with Katie, uncomfortable because she was such a big girl and I felt embarrassed that she needed to sit on me at her age. It wasn't a satisfactory talk – I can't remember what we tried to talk about but I know we failed.

Then they both wet their knickers. They were still being toilet trained and I'd put them in training pants with a plastic outer layer, but this was the seventies and nappy technology wasn't what it is now. And then it got worse – though thankfully in the bathroom – because as soon as Katie had her clean ones on she did a poo in them, and Zoe, with me and her sister in a bathroom twice the size of the kitchen but carpeted with the same cream as the sitting room, waited till they were on the floor and I was struggling with Katie's smelly bottom and then jumped on the dirty pants, getting it all over her socks and then spreading it generously about.

Rita took us home in her car. We heaved the push-chair into the boot and she put newspaper on the back seats and we all three sat there, crackling slightly. When we were outside our house – she wouldn't come in –

she smiled and there seemed to be something different about her.

'Thanks for the lift, Reet,' I said.

She said: 'I'm not Rita anymore,' and she told me her new name. Strangely, that hurt me more than anything else, not that she would change her name but that she would do it without telling me first.

I thought of the evening we would have had once upon a time, deciding on a new name for her, but she'd done it all on her own, or worse, with some new friend who I didn't know. Then I realised that she'd smiled to show her teeth – had been doing all afternoon in fact – and that she'd had them straightened.

I remember now what I gave her for her birthday. It was two coffee mugs that I would have liked to keep for myself, not bought in the market like the ones we had, but in a posh shop in Enfield. And I'd gone there specially, it being a shop that we used to look in together when we both worked nearby, and not the sort of shop you'd go in every day of the week. I think they were turquoise blue on the inside, like the bottom of a swimming pool, and brown on the outside, shiny but a bit knobbly. Maybe I'm remembering another pair of mugs, long gone, but in any case, as soon as I saw them in the context of her flat I realised that they were wrong. They didn't go. We used them for a cup of tea, and she thanked me, of course, but I knew. And I know now, that was the moment when I realised I didn't know Rita any more.

Rita apparently tried to get into television, and

worked for a while for Rediffusion as a trainee announcer, but it didn't seem to be going anywhere, and she hit upon the idea of helping young people in the music business with their finances. After all, she had experience at the bank, she was savvy about percentages and generally numerate, and she knew people from when she worked for the record company, and through Pete.

So she became probably one of the first independent financial advisors, not to ordinary people like me and Don, but to people who sometimes later became famous and passed her name to other kids who were making a start in that bewildering world. And much later, when daytime television started, who better to sit on the sofas and tell the world what was an ISA, and how to get the best out of their energy tariff? She was still lovely, Rita, and well preserved, and she spoke calmly and authoritatively, but you could still hear the London in her voice (that was why she never got on as an announcer) and people felt she was one of them.

So it all came around, from being in the crowd on Ready Steady Go, to being part of the Richard and Judy show, or Good Morning.

But still, I haven't put her on paper, and it occurs to me that maybe I should start at a different point, with the time of her life when I was a daily part of it, when her details were my details, and we heard the same stories from our parents, about the war and the rationing and the bombs, and we went to the same school and knew the same people and our lives had not diverged.

'Write what you know,' Jim advised me, one coffee break after entertaining us almost to death with an exhaustive description of every family in his street circa 1930. He is a cheerful old man, merry you might say, and he doesn't seem to mind being old at all, even though you can tell from the way he eases himself in and out of chairs that his knees are stiff and giving him gyp. He has heavily wrinkled pouches above and below each eye, and his eyes themselves are as dark as raisins; when he smiles, which he does more than strictly necessary, you can see that there aren't many useful teeth left in there. I don't know what he has, beyond toiling away at a piece of writing that we all find tediously detailed, to make him happy, and surely he knows that we're just being kind to him when we sit through it.

'Start with something you know inside out,' he says again. He is being kind to me, and I have to think that maybe he's right. Back to the beginning.

Lady Madonna

There was some discussion about what name to give the baby. The father, being away in the army, had not much say in the matter, though he'd previously expressed a preference for Mary if it was a girl.

'Maybe Marie,' thought the mother, but she didn't say anything. She thought all along that it would be a boy: Tony or Michael or Roy, she would go along with any of those.

Once the baby was born, and was cleaned and wrapped and tucked up and only allowed to be held at certain times, and once the hugeness and sheer strangeness of the experience was beginning to recede a little, she – the mother, Kath – began to receive visitors, sitting up in the double bed that almost filled the room where she used to sleep in her single bed, leaning back against feather pillows and feeling her own body unfamiliar to her.

Neighbours, mostly, popped in. 'I'm just popping in, dear, to say hello and have a little look.'

They brought things, cast-off clothes or a pair of knitted bootees, or an egg or an orange or a magazine. 'Just an egg for your tea, you need to keep your strength up.'

Ted's brother came, with his wife and their child, and he – the brother – looked so much like Ted that Kath nearly cried, because she missed him and because in all the excitement and pain, she had almost forgotten about him.

'What's her name, then?'

'I haven't really thought. I want Ted to be here so we can decide.'

The brother's wife looked sideways at her husband.

'I never let him have any say in it. I think it's the least they can do, after what we've been through, if they let us choose.'

Kath hadn't thought of it that way before, and would have agreed but didn't want it to get back to Ted.

When they went, her mother said, 'I don't think Ted would mind if we went ahead and named the baby. It's not as if it was a boy.'

'There's no harm in thinking of a name,' agreed Kath.

'Have you thought of any?'

She hesitated, because she knew what sort of reaction it might produce, but if that was to be her name, it had to be said, there was no other way.

'I like Jacqueline,' she said.

Her mother seemed to think for a long time – seemed to – Kath knew she was only waiting till all her objections were in place before she spoke.

'Jacqueline,' she said, pronouncing it with a "W" in the middle, as if she had never heard it before. 'It's more modern than I thought you'd like.'

'I'd like something a bit modern,' said Kath.

'It's French.'

'Yes if you say so. It's more modern than I think Ted would like.'

That's right, thought Kath, more modern than Mary.

'Ted will like it,' she said.

'And it's very long,' said her mother. 'People won't use her proper name. They'll call her Jackie or something like that.'

'That's quite nice though.'

'Jackie is a boy's name.'

'I've never known a boy called Jackie.'

'In Ireland they are, dear. And it doesn't go with your surname.'

'What do you mean?'

'Listen to it. Jacqueline Doughty. You know I'm very fond of Ted, but Doughty's not a pretty name.'

'Neither is Swallow.'

'I have to disagree with you there. Nobody can help their name, I know, for good or bad, but Doughty. Doughty. It sounds like someone who's not sure of himself, and if you write it down it looks like something to do with baking.'

'I don't think it matters. Jacqueline will go with anything.'

'Then again, you see, Jacqueline is a very long

50

name. Suppose she's not a good speller when she gets to school.'

'Oh mum, we don't have to think about school yet.'

'We have to think about everything. Naming a baby is a responsibility. Once it's done that's it, she's stuck with it. You have to look at it from all angles. Look where we went wrong with your sister.'

Kath's sister had been christened Jane, but had always been known, in the family and out, as Ginny. Mrs Swallow hadn't minded too much when she was a child but nowadays, twenty-three and not in a hurry to settle down, Ginny seemed to be having too good a time, and the first three letters of her name were maybe forming too much of the basis for her personality.

'What do you think, then?' Kath was tired and leaned her head back against the headboard.

'Rita.'

'Why Rita?' She didn't absolutely dislike it, but it wasn't how she saw her child. Rita was a woman's name.

'Why not? Nice neat name. Modern, if you like modern. Can't be shortened. Rita Doughty. Sounds right. Don't you think? Or what about…Enid? You had a great aunt Enid, a good woman, never married though, kept chickens, I think we took you to see her once. Or Vera, that's nice. I wouldn't ask you to call her after me,' – Mrs Swallow's name was Maud – 'I don't think it would be fair on her, my name's a bit old-fashioned, though at the time I'm sure my mother thought it was a good idea.'

The baby had been stirring and whimpering, and now began to cry in a more organised way. The grandmother went to the crib. 'Will you look at that now, she's got her arm right out of her shawl. You wouldn't credit it, only two days old. There'll be no tying you down, young lady, I'm sure.' She picked her up and the baby quietened. 'She's a beautiful one, yes you are, and what are we going to call you? What's it to be then, do you think, Kath?'

'I'll think about it,' said Kath, but she knew that it would be Rita. So Rita it was, and as long as her grandmother was alive, she told ever more frequently how she always knew she'd be an independent one, ever since she struggled out of her shawl before she'd properly got her eyes open.

When the next baby came, things were different. The war was further away in the past; Ted was home and so was Kath's brother Billy, which had made it difficult for them to continue living at the Swallows'. So they were staying with Ted's mum, who was on her own, and though the house was smaller, there were fewer people in it. It was winter again, after Christmas this time, instead of before, but even colder, if that were possible.

The fire was lit again in the bedroom and Theresa was born by the light of a paraffin lamp because there was a power cut. There was no talk of calling her Jacqueline. Mrs Swallow may not have approved of her name, but she said nothing. The new baby was placid and well behaved; she lay much of the time with her eyes shut, even if she wasn't asleep, which worried Kath. 'Babies ought to be looking around them,' she said, but Ted's mother wasn't much interested.

'She'll be all right,' said Ted, and by and large, for the space of her childhood, she was.

The third baby was born less than a year later. 'I'm sure it's a boy this time,' said Kath. 'It feels like he's got ruddy football boots on.' But it was another girl. 'That's it,' said Kath. 'I'm not having no more, not to please no one.'

'It's just you fall so easy,' said her friends. By now they had a house, and lived next door to people Kath and Ted had been at school with.

'I can't help it,' said Kath. 'But he'll have to do something. I've got my hands full as it is, without having any more.'

So for a few years that was it, just the three girls: Rita, Theresa and Kay, as nice as you could hope for: Rita and Theresa with their mother's black hair and serious blue eyes, and Kay stouter and fairer, with wide grey eyes and a loud assertive voice.

I know as I'm reading it that I've let Mrs Swallow come across as too prim and posh, but never mind, the group likes that one.

I've noticed that about people, that they can talk for ages about names and stories to do with names. 'Oh, I had an Aunt Fanny,' they'll go. 'I was going to be called Hermione but my dad put his foot down.' All that sort of thing.

I never liked being called Pat. It sounded like a name for lard or margarine. My nan, my dad's mum that is, named me, apparently on the grounds that she'd always wanted a girl and never had one, and she always called me by the full three syllables. 'Pat*ree*sha,' she said it, with the stress on the middle one, and that's probably why I never use my full name.

And, except for Julia, who was too young, they all liked the gas lights and the feather beds. 'My grandma lived in a house like that.' 'We were all born at home in those days.' 'Three under three, no wonder she wanted to stop there.' 'My grandma had eight.'

'I do want to know what's going to happen to those little girls,' says Joan. 'Are you going to write some more?'

I leave the group feeling like Catherine Cookson. I will take my characters and follow them through their lives, with their domestic details and their sisterly rivalries, and a great novel of the twentieth century (second half of) will emerge. They will interview me on Woman's Hour.

It's quiet when I open the door: the silence between

discs.

'You're back,' says Don. 'Zoe's been on the phone,' and then adds, 'Crying.'

Oh Zoe. Always some drama or other, to make me feel guilty. Zoe, the best-looking of the three, the cleverest, the most hard-working, the most conforming and the least likeable. I should be more tolerant, I know. I should put more effort into her and her sisters and her brother, and sometimes I try, but it never seems to work out right.

I know what she would say now – 'You think more about that Rita and her sisters than you do about us,' but it's not true, I don't. It's just that they were the only other family I ever knew properly and I do find myself comparing my children with them. 'But Mum, that was years ago,' my kids say, and it is, far away in time, but I was almost part of that family. Of course I can't help remembering.

'What about Matthew?' I say to Don. 'I texted him, asking him to ring.'

Don makes a noise which expresses that Matthew hasn't been in touch, and also that he knows I'm worried, and so is he, but can we please not talk about it.

I ring Zoe in Liverpool, who is upset because Grace is having at least one tantrum a day. 'It can't be good for her Mum,' she moans. 'Holding her breath like that has got to be bad for her brain.'

'Well you did it,' I say, though I can't remember if she did or not. One of them did.

'Did I? But Mum, it's driving me insane. I want to slap her.'

I think of Mrs Doughty dealing out slaps left and right like someone out of Oliver Twist and think, but don't say, 'It won't do her any harm.' To think that not so long ago I was a social worker. But not a good one.

'Zoe, love,' I say. 'It's normal. Kids are like that. She'll be fine. It's a phase.' And I think to myself that I was often tempted to slap Zoe, more than any of the others, through all the years of her little-childhood, and even into her teenage years, and even, I have to admit, until she left home. Because she was a pain, cried for nothing, and some things she did, like food fads, have even lasted to this day. Zoe and her bloody food fads. Banana strings. She liked bananas, but if there was one scrap of those stringy bits along the side she would scream as if they were about to detach themselves and come and get her by the throat. Even now, she shudders. We tried mashing her bananas but she was suspicious and insisted on watching as we peeled the skin off to make sure we weren't trying to poison her. 'There's a bit.' That was the start of it, and then came suspicion of all vegetables if they were presented in irregular shapes, because the bit that was cut out could have been – well, usually had been – a soggy bit, or a green bit on a potato, or an eye or whatever. There would be more screaming.

I swear, if Grace behaved like her mother used to, her feet wouldn't touch the ground on the way to the child psychiatrist. And as they got older, Kezia used to tease her, looking at her dinner and going 'Urgh, what's that?'

'What? Where?' Zoe would panic.

'Leave her alone,' I'd say.

'Sorry, can't tell you. Mum says I've got to leave you alone,' and there'd be Zoe, poking anxiously round her plate for foreign bodies or evidence of rot and corruption.

I can't remember a time when I didn't know Rita. My mum used to go to work, so after school and in the school holidays, I was mostly round their house, like another daughter. Theresa's friend, also called Pat, was usually there too, and maybe someone of Kay's, and later on, little children knocking on the door for Val and Tony.

When we were little, we played in the street, not only us, but all the kids from up and down. We played chasing games and hiding games: 'What's the time Mr Wolf?' and 'Queenie-I' and 'Please Mr Crocodile', and when we got older, some of us had roller skates and there were a few with bikes that we all learned to ride on.

Or we might play in the back garden, making a den or making perfume from flower petals. Rita liked playing schools and would line up her sisters and anyone else, be the teacher and ask them to count up to a million and slap their hand as soon as they hesitated. I refused to be one of her pupils but she wouldn't let me be a teacher because she said I would be no good at it, so I was the headmistress and gave out the milk.

If it rained a lot, we would pile inside. At my house, the front room had the good furniture in it. It was cold and we used it at Christmas, but at the Doughtys' it was different – bare, but the kids could go in there. It was still cold though. There was a bit of old lino on the concrete floor, and what we'd now call a sofa-bed, but which was then called a Put-U-Up, covered in slippery hard green stuff, and the rest was toys. There was usually a clothes horse full of clothes because Mrs D washed twice a week and ironed every day, and the windows were usually running with condensation. And there were all these toys, because it seemed that no one in the family had anything that belonged personally to them. A doll was the family doll, its pram was anyone's to push. If a visiting child left anything behind it was the devil's own job to get it back. You had to find it for a start, in amongst the heaps of broken and unbroken, and then you had to get away from the three girls who would gang up and insist that it was theirs, they'd always had it, their nan gave it them for Christmas etc., so unless you could show your name on it, or you could get your mum to go round, you'd had it. And then they'd say 'Well we've got one just like it.'

It didn't bother me. A lot of my toys were there be-cause that was where I played, and I soon learned to keep anything precious at home and out of their reach.

Mrs Doughty never touched the toys. I saw her push them all into the corner with a broom so she could sweep the floor, but she never tidied or sorted or had anything to do with them; there were hard old apple cores and shredded bits of old comics in with them. Except when she was ironing, she kept to the kitchen, which was cosy and had the wireless on and a smell of boiling water, boiling either with Daz, or with carrots and onions for soup.

My mother never made soup. Soup was tomato and came out of a tin. My mother only ever cooked out of tins and packets. I was the first person I knew to have a Vesta curry. Mum didn't get home till a quarter to six, so I would be at the Doughtys' till then, but I can't remember any contact between my mum and Rita's house.

Though there must have been, because I remember now that she came round once while I was there to give them a box of pears from the tree in our garden. (They were tough and woody, and we never ate them, but mum guessed rightly that the Doughtys would be less fussy. She never liked things to go to waste, mum.) I peeped through the front room door with Rita and Theresa and felt unsure as to who I belonged to.

I knew them all. Because I was Rita's friend, I was superior to Theresa and Kay. We were not only older, but cleverer. Kay had lots of different friends – she was popular because she was lively, but she was also quarrelsome, so friends came and went. Theresa had a best and only friend, a girl so small and quiet that Theresa could almost be said to be the dominant one of the two. She was Theresa's Pat and I was Rita's Pat. Val calls me that to this day, on her Christmas card.

So Rita was the cleverest, Kay was the noisiest and

Theresa was the prettiest, even prettier than Rita.

I never got on with Theresa, and she didn't like me. I thought she was empty-headed – well she was, there never was a head with less in it, if you could judge by what came out of her mouth. I think she was jealous because I was close to her sister. Actually I think she was jealous of everyone, of Rita, of Kay, of me, of Pat, of any of Kay's friends. I think Theresa looked at anyone, anyone, and thought 'That person's better than me' and felt disgruntled because of it. So her pretty face would make you notice her but fairly soon you'd realise that she had nothing much to say.

Her main characteristic seemed to be passivity, even then as a little girl, she would let anyone borrow her things or do her hair; she would always take any part or do as she was told in any game, not cheerfully, but grudgingly, but she couldn't argue because she never had an idea of her own. I think of her sometimes.

After the class, it is customary, so I've gradually come to realise, for the men to go to the pub. The women are not invited, or if they are, it is a jokey affair that presumes that they will not take up the invitation. But this night when the chairs are being pushed back to the walls and Jerry is stuffing various people's work into a Lidl bag, I catch Jocelyn's eye.

'I will if you will,' she says. 'Don't see why we should let the men get away with it.'

Joan blushes and fumbles with her gloves and says she has to get home before...

Jean says a decided 'No', but I see Julia's face lighten a little at the idea. That girl is over twenty-one – she can make her own decision about having a half of lager in a pub. Maybe next week.

Judy, a youngish, fat, clever woman agrees that a drink would be 'most welcome,' in a tone of voice that means 'absolutely bloody necessary,' so when Jerry says in his facetious way, 'Right chaps, shall we adjourn? Ladies?' we: Judy, Jocelyn and I, stand up and follow the men out of the hall and along the road through the swirling litter to the Rose.

There's an awkwardness while the men wonder how to include us in their drink-buying ritual. Jim and John are poor and Jim buys John a half – you can see it's his turn this week; Jerry and Jeff are not poor and Jeff buys Jerry a pint – you can see it will be Jerry's turn in about half an hour.

They are slow about offering to include us in case we ask for something like a gin and tonic, and never get our round in.

'It's all right,' says Judy, in an actressy sort of way. 'We'll buy our own.' She turns to us, playing the part. 'What can I get you?' But we take our drinks to the same table as the men, who are by now quite pleased to see us.

I listen to Jocelyn telling Judy about the Patagonian plains.

'Was it a package tour?' I ask naively. She's not even offended, almost embarrassed rather.

'No Pat, I just go, pretty much.'

'Isn't it dangerous?'

'Sometimes, though, you know, these things are never as dangerous as people think.'

'Probability low, severity high, though,' says Judy.

'Oh I wouldn't argue with that, but you could say that about walking home through Edmonton Green. And, I say to myself, no one cares about you, Joss old thing, so if any harm comes to you, it won't hurt anyone else, and if I don't do it, well I won't have lived as I want to, will I?'

She's quite small, round-faced like an old-fashioned wooden doll. She dresses in clothes from charity shops and cuts her own hair. Her voice is the poshest one you would hear around these streets. And she travels the world on her own, fending off village dogs with her walking poles and checking her sleeping bag for snakes – she didn't say those things, but that's what I imagine. And I sit in my house evening after evening and try to persuade Don to go as far as Bristol with me.

Roses of Picardy

Ted would sometimes take his daughters to football matches. He went by himself to first team matches, but when it was the reserves playing, and he was supposed to stay home and be useful about the house, he sometimes felt the most useful thing he could do was to take one of the older ones to the Spurs. Sometimes he took two, Rita and Theresa, or Rita and her friend, but he complained that he couldn't watch two children and keep an eye on the game. For reserve matches the terraces were next to empty. Children could skip and run from the top to the bottom and back again, swing on the crush barriers, and even run all the way round, looking from the far side to try to spot their dad, ignoring the grunts and thuds of the match in between.

Mostly, Rita never watched the match. Occasionally the men on the terraces would cheer or shout and she'd stop and turn and look at the field going 'What?' and see that they'd stopped running and were walking back to their starting places, or gathering around a fallen player, like mourning elephants. It was in the days before substitutions, so you might see the injured one get up and hobble about miserably, try and run and pull up with a grimace. If he really couldn't run, he might change jerseys with the goalie and go in the net, wincing and hardly jumping at all. But with all the running about and a bag of Percy Dalton's peanuts to get out of their shells, Rita would miss any exciting bits that might have happened.

Ted played football as well, on Sunday mornings in the park. He didn't get picked every week, because, he explained to Kath, he was not the nippy winger he'd once been. 'Getting old,' he said.

'Getting fat more like,' Kath said. She was a woman who believed in bluntness as a virtue and thought that compliments were a sign of insincerity. She could neither take one nor give one, but she was not shy if it came to criticising someone, in their hearing or not, or if it came to defending herself against criticism, even if there was none.

'Milk's gone off,' Ted might say, during a hot spell, before they had a fridge.

'You try keeping it cold. It's been standing in water, it's been in the shade. What do you expect me to do, stand and fan it? And it's Co-op milk, so it hasn't got no cream on it.'

Ted would pretend that he hadn't spoken and she hadn't replied, and that would be the end of it, except that one of her words would snag in his mind and unravel a few minutes later as a song, Fanlight Fanny maybe, or You're the Cream in my Coffee.

Kath sang too, all the time when she was on her own, but sometimes with Ted. They hardly talked to each other beyond: 'Shall I put the kettle on?' – 'Where's my?' – 'Hold this while I...' – 'Give us your plate' – sort of conversations, but they would sing together.

If they were washing up, Kath with her hands in the water, Ted with the tea towel, the little girls putting away, taking the knives and forks one by one as he put them, dry, on the table and jostling to put them in the drawer, Ted would start the singing, usually a comic or music hall song, Yes We Have no Bananas, started by humming, and would build up by including a word here and there until it was proper singing. This was to get Kath to start. She wouldn't sing on her own if he was in the house. But once he started, she couldn't stop herself.

She would start with maybe Clang Clang Clang Went the Trolley, and Rita would at once see in her mind the trolley buses that ran along the High Street, which however, though they bumped and shook a bit, didn't clang so much as buzz. After a few preliminaries, a sort of comic warm-up, the parents would go for their favourites.

Some Enchanted Evening, Oh How We Danced On the Night We Were Wed, Bye Bye Blackbird, You'll Never Walk Alone.

Even now, that song of the terraces says to

66

Rita – not Liverpool, not even football, not Carousel, not Gerry Marsden – but her mother scouring saucepans after Sunday dinner, in water gone brown and scummy at the end of the washing up, and her dad hanging the sodden tea towel on the fireguard, both of them lifting their voices to assert that there would be a golden sky at the end of the storm.

As the girls grew older and learned the words, they began to join in. Kay was the best singer of the three.

'As good as her mother,' Ted said, but actually, she was better. She sang all the time whether anyone was listening or not, in bed before going to sleep, as she got up in the morning, while playing, on her way to school, anywhere. She knew all the old songs, but as a teenager she sang pop songs. Hear it twice and she would know it.

At school, she was told to be quiet, but she couldn't do it, and so she got into trouble and spent, altogether, many hours outside the classroom door.

Only once, she sang in public, and even then it was only family. It was when Kath's mother died.

Rita demanded to be allowed to go to the funeral, not because she really wanted to, but because she felt that at fifteen, she should go.

Then Theresa wanted to go, and she was the

one who had been closest to their nana, and then Kay refused to be left out, so they had to borrow three sets of black clothes and three black scarves for their heads. 'We look like nuns,' said Kay, and Rita laughed while Theresa looked anxiously in a mirror.

Afterwards, when everyone was round at Aunt Ginny's, with all the relatives and a few neighbours sitting round drinking tea, talk turned to songs and what had been Maud Swallow's favourite.

'Knees up Mother Brown,' whispered Rita to Theresa, but Theresa didn't ever get jokes and just frowned and shook her head. It seemed that Roses of Picardy had been her favourite.

'She used to sing it when we were kids,' said Ginny. 'She had a lovely voice.'

'Kay's got a lovely voice,' said Ted, for something to say, he explained afterwards. 'She'll sing it for you.'

'I can't,' said Kay, but she wasn't shy, so after a false start when she started laughing – 'Don't look at us,' said Kath, 'Look out the window' – she stood in Ginny's front room, looking at the summer evening sky through the bay window, and sang.

By the time she got to 'Roses may die in the summertime and our roads may be far apart', the women were crying, and by the time she ended, the men were looking into their teacups and clearing their throats. Only Rita and Theresa had no tears.

Kay finished on a soft trembling note and looked round the room. Ginny was sobbing loudly – 'That sister of yours can turn the waterworks on,' said Ted afterwards – and the women were gathered round her, patting and offering handkerchiefs and tea.

The men were looking at things, anything that wouldn't look back. Kay went slightly red and slid back into her place with her sisters. She never spoke about the performance, ever, and neither did anyone else.

At the same time, on the other side of London, Paul McCartney's singing was being put to the test by Parlophone. Of course what happened to Paul and the rest of them after that is history, and what happened to Kay is only a story, or maybe not even that. I wanted to put that into my story but I couldn't get it to fit in. Still, it seems important to me.

We go to the pub again and this time Jean and Julia join us. It turns out that last week they couldn't come because their husband/father picks them up in the car at the end of the class. It turns out too that they live very near me and I am offered, and accept, a lift home.

I'm sitting next to John as he slowly sips his half pint. 'Are you married?' he asks. 'I can see you're wearing a ring, but many widows...'

I assure him that I am married, to an electrician, and that I have four grown up children and three grandchildren. When I've said that, I find, as always, that there is nothing left to say.

'Ah grandchildren,' he says. 'Lovely when they're little, aren't they? Then they grow up and they don't want to know you.'

'They have their own lives,' I say to him, thinking of Jay and saying the thing I myself most need to understand.

He tells me about his wife who is now in a care home, about his children who are 'very good,' but live too far away for him to see often; his grandson who is a university student. 'Brunel,' he says. 'Wouldn't hurt him to pop over here on a Sunday. See his grandma, say hello.'

'Not an easy journey, across London,' I say, now feeling that the poor young man needs to have excuses made for him.

'He should have a bike,' says John. 'I always had a bike, got me all over the place. I rode to Devon once, slept in barns, that sort of thing, marvellous.' He sips again. 'Funny thing, I never went to see my grandparents. Saw them every week till I started work – I was fourteen, worked in a timber yard, stopped going round there for my Sunday tea – never saw them again, never. Died within a month of each other, a month.'

'Often happens that way,' I say.

'Wonder what they said about me though, not going to see them.'

'They won't have held it against you,' I say, professionally soothing. 'They will have understood.'

'You didn't know them,' he said gloomily, as if, after much pondering, my words had brought him to an opposite conclusion.

'I liked your description of that family,' says Jeff to me. He has a boyish air but seen close to is quite wrinkled. Apparently he once wrote a crime novel that won a prize, but never found a publisher, so he is what passes for a celebrity in the group. 'I liked the singing, but I think you went on a bit too long about it. You need the telling detail, and then no more. Edit, that's the trick.' He gulps his pint. 'If we can only do it.'

It's very nice being picked up from the pub in the car belonging to the paterfamilias of Julia and Jean. I sit in the back with Jean, and the car, a large soft one smelling of newness, swishes through the rainy streets. The man driving – I'm never introduced – asks what road I live in, and insists on dropping me at my door, even though this means he has to turn round in the road between the parked cars. I wave from the front door and Jean waves back, but Julia isn't looking.

Don is listening to Cliff Richard's early hits, which is so unusual that I ask if he's died or something.

'You'd be surprised what I listen to sometimes.' Well I would and I wouldn't. I know that in the opinion of one side of Don, 1960s Good, anything since Bad, a sort of historical specialism; but there's another side of him that can't help liking some later stuff and grants it a sort of honorary 1960s status. Cliff Richard comes into the historical category.

'The bulb's gone in the hall now,' I say. 'That's two. Will you change them or shall I?'

'I'll do it,' he says. 'There's not room in that hall to put a ladder up and I'm not having you standing on the sideboard.'

At the weekend, we have an unexpected visit from Matthew. Hair dyed black, eye sockets bruised black with tiredness. My beautiful boy. His yellow fingertips are scabbed and bloody where he has bitten and pulled at the skin. Even that annoys me, before he's even spoken.

'Hello darling,' I say, and it's not the way I normally talk. 'How nice to see you. Are you eating with us?

Would you like a bath? Coffee?'

I know he won't stay long, and I don't want him to. I don't want the inevitable irritation that will make me criticise him, or the inevitable argument when I do. And I'm thinking, please don't ask for money because I'll have to give you some, though I've agreed with your dad that we won't fund you.

'Mum,' he says, not looking at me. 'I don't want you to go to that writing group again.'

I'm so surprised that I almost feel guilty. What does he know about it? How does he know about it?

'What writing group?' I didn't know I was going to deny it until I heard myself.

'Don't you go to a, you know, a writing group?'

'Of course I don't.'

'A sort of, like, evening class?'

'I don't know what you're talking about.' I've almost convinced myself, and just hope Don doesn't come home and join in. I rush on before he can think of anything else. 'Where have you been? We haven't seen you for ages.'

'Sheffield,' he says. He picks at his thumb, the sight of the sliver of skin pulling away from him makes my throat tickle, as if I'm going to be sick, and I'm irritated again.

'Sheffield? Whatever made you go there?'

'Been to stay with Jake's mum.'

'Did you like it?'

He shrugs.

'I've got a cousin in Sheffield, with quite a large family. If I'd known, I could have –'

'Don't want to see your cousin.'

'No I don't suppose you do. But it's lovely to see you, Matt. Have you got any washing you'd like to put into the machine?'

'No. Is dad in?'

'He's just nipped out down the record shop. He's got something ordered and it's come in. I don't know how long he'll be.'

'All right, is he?'

'He's fine. You'll see him when he gets back.'

''m going now.' He's going before we've had an argument, and I feel let down, somehow. I give him a £20 note "for food", before he turns and slouches off, and I watch him from the door until he's gone.

Of course when Tuesday comes, I go to the group as usual, hardly even remembering what Matthew said.

The young ones

Theresa, on Easter Monday, sitting on the train to Southend-on-Sea, smiling with excitement, breathless like the others from running across the bridges at Liverpool Street Station, and with a small, cold, detached wonder hovering above her head.

'We're going to the seaside,' sang Kay, and Theresa thought, I'm here, Kay is my sister and Rita is my sister and Pat is my friend and we're here. And Rita's Pat.

The compartment was full, and the five of them were squashed between other people (two couples, grand-parent-aged), but Kay still managed to bounce on her bit of seat, and wave as they passed the back gardens of East London, though no one was in them to wave back.

Kay was the youngest: the smallest, plumpest, nosiest and noisiest, the most annoying of sisters. She was here because she had nagged and pleaded and wept, and their dad had given in. It was Theresa and Pat's day out, their idea, their plan and they had saved up since Christmas. They didn't want Kay. But she's all right, thought Theresa. Now she's here it's all right.

She did go on though.

'Let me come.'

'No.'

'Why not?'

'You're not old enough.'

'Am.'

'Not.'

'Let me.'

'NO.'

'I'll tell dad.'

'Go on then. Tell him.'

'He'll let me.'

'Not his business.'

It was only that Rita said she would come too, and her friend Pat, and they would look after Kay and keep her out of trouble – they said to mum and dad. Mum and dad didn't know what Kay was like.

Theresa nudged her Pat, and they smiled at each other and wriggled a little with anticipation.

'Your mum,' said Pat, 'trying to make us bring sandwiches.'

'Rain hats,' agreed Theresa. They giggled, but quietly.

Flat Essex countryside went by: bare trees, daffodils in gardens, shining big clouds.

'If it rains, I don't care,' said Kay. 'I wouldn't wear a rain hat. I'd rather die.'

'I'd rather wear a rain hat,' said Rita. 'If no one could see me, than mess up my hair. Rain makes it go all frizzy.'

'It doesn't,' said Rita's Pat loyally. 'You've got lovely hair.' This was true, and it was the result of effort as well as luck.

'I don't care about my hair,' said Kay, and this was true too. She never bothered much about what she looked like. She just put on some clothes, or some of her sisters' clothes and combed her hair like a little girl, with a parting, and hardly ever wore make-up, and went out, singing usually, to have a good time.

She wouldn't wear a roll-on either, though Rita, who did, said it would improve her figure. But Kay wouldn't even wear stockings. Her legs, shades of pink and mauve and blue in winter, off-white in summer, came bare out of her skirt and went bare into her shoes. She was almost – no not almost, she *was* – what their mother called slummocky.

Theresa and Rita were not slummocky. They had new stockings on, and Rita also carried a bottle of nail varnish to stop any snags from becoming ladders: clear varnish, because pink – in blobs on your legs – was sluttish.

Kay sang. She sang 'Bobby's Girl' in a clear strong voice, making the dust rise from the seats as she thumped them at the appropriate places. The elderly women smiled indulgently, the men rolled their day's supply of cigarettes with a little pop-up machine and didn't speak or look at anyone.

It didn't rain. The day warmed up and became like spring should be. The expanse of shallow sea glittered and a couple of unsupervised children splashed in it along the muddy shore. The girls wrinkled their noses at the slimy sand and set off along the pier. 'Walk out, train back,' said Rita's Pat.

Each time the train passed, they waved, looking to see if there were any nice boys. Kay whooped as well as waved, trying to do a wolf-whistle.

'Who was that to?'

'Anyone,' said Kay, climbing on to seats (pulling her skirt up and showing a lot of leg) and jumping off.

'Kay,' said Rita. 'Don't show yourself up.'

'No one knows me,' said Kay.

The end of the pier was cold and not very exciting, apart from being a long way into the North Sea.

'At Clacton,' said Theresa's Pat, 'They've got a Big Dipper on the pier.'

'But they haven't got the Kursaal.'

'Let's go there,' shouted Kay, causing a near-by woman to jump involuntarily.

'Later,' said Rita's Pat. 'We'll have our dinner first. It'll be cheaper outside than in there.' She thought she was always right, and she often was, though she still deferred to Rita most of the time. Theresa and Kay didn't like her much, and when Rita wasn't around they made fun out of Pat's pointy nose and the way her hair turned neatly under at the sides, but stuck out at the back, and her big hips, like a parsnip.

Rita had brought their dad's camera, and they passed it round, taking pictures of each other – Theresa and Pat, Rita and Pat, and the three sisters together. They rode back to the promenade on the little train, waving and giggling.

On the Golden Mile, Kay wanted Rita to lend her the money to buy a cowboy hat with 'Kiss me slow' painted on it, but Rita wouldn't. She didn't mind people having fun, but she knew where the lines were drawn between respectable and common. Kay didn't.

They bought rock novelties to take home for Val and Tony, and Rita's Pat bought an ashtray for her nan who was in hospital. The shops, though, didn't distract them too much from looking at the people and nudging each other and pointing at anyone remarkable. Old people they laughed at, except a lady in a wheelchair, whom they made way for, making sympathetic noises. They cooed at babies and dogs, and looked girls of their own age up and down with an unsmiling stare, whispering together after they'd gone about the price of their dress or the cut of their hair. Kay would say, 'She's a tart,' and though Rita shushed her at first, they all began to say it, about anyone. It became the catchphrase of the day, and all five of them, whenever they heard it said, in all their lives, would smile, even if they didn't remember why.

A group of boys walked towards them and, except for Kay, they sobered themselves and walked demurely on, looking round as they passed. They were shocked to see Kay, still snorting with laughter, approach one of the boys, and more shocked to see him reach into his pocket and bring out a lighter. At this point Kay ran, shrieking, to catch up her sisters.

Theresa stood and looked at the boy. How nice-looking he was, with floppy fair hair like John Leyton. She smiled, but he only looked bewildered and then walked after his mates.

'What did you do that for?'

'Felt like it.'

They ate egg and chips in a café and then continued along the prom to the Kursaal. They paid, impatient, and went in. They saw couples in dinghies hurtling down a slide and into water, screaming.

'Shall we?' said Theresa's Pat.

'I'll come with you,' said Theresa.

'I'm not,' said Rita. 'My hair will be all over the place after that.'

'Let's go on the Waltzer,' said Rita's Pat. 'Come with us, Kay.'

'I'll wait for these,' said Kay.

The two oldest made to walk away. 'If we don't see you before,' said Rita, 'meet back here at five o'clock.'

Theresa and Pat screamed a bit, splashed

down, a man with a hook pulled them to the side and they climbed out of their dinghy, inspecting their wet clothes.

'I'm never doing that again.'

'I don't know. With a nice boy, maybe.'

'With his arm round you.' She was thinking of the nice boy on the prom.

'Where's Kay?'

'Must have gone with Rita.'

'Shall we go on the Chair-o-planes?'

'Dry us off a bit.'

Chair-o-planes. A lovely feeling, thought Theresa. Not so fast that you feel sick, but easy and cool, and just fast enough to make you laugh. She worried that a shoe might come off, as Kay's had once at a local fairground, and she couldn't find it; and they'd all had to go home with her hopping and squawking, and all of them had been told off, even though it was only Kay who had been reckless, and had to be bought a new pair.

Ghost Train. 'I don't like it,' said Pat as soon as they went through the curtain and before anything frightening happened. 'Nor do I,' lied Theresa. Pat hid her face in Theresa's shoulder, but Theresa kept her eyes open through the lurching of the cars and the sudden jumps and screeches. 'That was awful,' said Pat. 'Awful,' agreed Theresa, but she thought, Nothing to be afraid of at all. But if you were with a boy, you'd have to pretend to be scared.

Big Wheel. Most of the chairs had couples in them, the boys lounging confidently with their arms along the backs of the seats, and the girls ready to scream. Theresa and Pat looked for Kay and Rita as the chairs swung upwards, one at a time. When it got going you couldn't see anything except the sea in the distance, and the pier; looking down just made you gasp and scream. Pat screamed a bit.

They bought strawberry Mivvis, and ate them on the bumper cars. They paid to go into the Wall of Death but found it boring. They went on the Waltzer and flirted with a skinny dark-haired boy who paid them special attention, spinning them to make them beg him to stop. Pat begged him obligingly, and he seemed quite keen on her, but Theresa didn't like his narrow gypsy face and resolved not to beg, however sick and dizzy he made her feel.

They ate candy floss, though neither of them liked it. They went from ride to ride, listening to the different music from each of them, songs a year or two old, that made them nostalgic for the time – so long ago it seemed, though it was only a week – when they were still at school.

'Shall we have a hot dog?'

'We might be sick.'

'What's the time?'

'I'll ask.'

They made their way back to the entrance. Rita and Pat were there, accompanied by two young men.

Theresa could see that Rita was quite taken with hers, in a sports jacket, slightly chinless, but polite. Rita wasn't intimidated by boys who talked posh and maybe lived in detached houses.

'Where's Kay?'

'Isn't she with you?'

They looked about them, as if she must be where they had seen her last, four and a quarter hours ago.

'Tell you what,' said Rita's Pat. 'We'll wait here with Roger and Roy,' – they all four smirked – 'You two go and look for Kay. Meet back here at half past.'

Theresa and Pat plunged back into the fair. It was getting busier, and though it wasn't yet dark, the lights had a new intensity as the sun went down behind the enclosing fence.

'I'll kill her.'

'I'll help you.'

'What if we miss the train?'

'Loads of time.'

They wandered past rides, scanning faces. After half an hour, they went back to the entrance. Rita seemed to have acquired new airs.

'What a nuisance she is. What do you think we should do, Roger?'

'Give it another half hour,' he suggested. 'We'll wait here.'

'It doesn't take four of you to wait here,' said Theresa. 'Come and help us look.'

'If she not back here by six,' said Rita, 'we'll all look for her.'

'If she's not back by six,' said Rita's Pat, 'I'm going. She's your sister.'

'As you wish,' said Rita serenely.

At quarter past six, Roy and Roger politely declined the offer of the chance to search for the kid sister of the (however delectable) Rita. The two Pats, having calculated train times and connections, decided they would go home. Rita, grumpy now, and Theresa, more grumpy, set off to search again.

'Hello,' said a voice next to Theresa, as she stood waiting for the Big Wheel cars to move round. 'I saw you earlier.'

It was the nice-looking boy with the floppy fair hair. 'Want to go on with me?'

'Come on,' shouted Rita.

'I can't. I've got to look for my sister.'

'See you later then.'

'Did you look round the back of the Ghost Train?'

'No.'

'Why on earth not?'

They stepped over cables and were out of the lights. The music competed now with the heavy hum of generators. Theresa had stopped believing they would find Kay, but she was there, with her blouse undone and a boy's hand up her skirt.

'Kay Doughty.' Rita's voice, though she tried to sound authoritative, came out rather shrill. 'Wait till I tell mum.'

Theresa said nothing, but she pulled Kay, by the hair and resisting, out into the light.

'Do you know what time it is?'

'We'll have to get going.'

They ran through the darkening, thronged streets, under the coloured strings of lights, all the way to the station, carrying their shoes in their hands.

On the train, they got their breath back.

'Just you wait.'

'Mum'll kill you.'

'What have I done? We've caught it. We'll be home in time.'

'She doesn't care.'

'We spent hours looking.'

'She spoilt our day.'

'She's a tart,' said Theresa.

Kay spluttered into laughter.

Rita looked severe. 'She's a slut.'

Kay looked hurt for about three seconds.

'Listen what I can do. Kenny taught me.' She put her little fingers in the sides of her mouth and regardless of a carriage full of people, produced a wolf-whistle, piercing and perfect.

That's what Kay was like. She didn't care. And now look at her. I remember that day so well, but when I once spoke to Rita about it, a long time ago now, she looked slightly alarmed and claimed she didn't remember a thing.

All that bickering: alternate bickering and giggling that went on between the sisters that Theresa's Pat and I didn't need or bother to get involved in, all that 'I'll tell mum', 'Dad'll kill you' stuff that came out of their mouths as easy as breathing, and then laughing together at something that even I had no idea about, hadn't even noticed, holding on to each other and screaming with laughter, even Rita sometimes; even Theresa who never understood a joke.

Difficult to believe now, that there was ever that unholy closeness between them. Sometimes. But at other times, there was bad feeling. Theresa and Kay thought that Rita tried to be something she wasn't and they called her 'Lady Muck' behind her back.

Rita was bothered that the rest of her family wasn't very clever and had little interest in her ambitions. And she was tortured by the idea that Theresa was prettier than she was. She used to ask me all the time, 'What do you think of Theresa's dress? Does that jumper suit her? Does that colour look better on her or on me? Who's better looking, her or me?' It was like being the mirror in Snow White.

It is only when I start reading that story aloud that I realise that I've put myself in it, with my own name, but the group don't seem to notice. They have plenty to say about Southend though, except Jocelyn and Judy who are not Londoners and have never been there.

'Now then,' says Jerry. 'The Christmas bash.' People exchange pleased glances.

The first part of the evening is to be a poetry competition – we are all asked to bring a poem on the theme of Christmas and the one judged – by Jerry – to be the best, wins a tin of biscuits. That is scheduled to take one hour only – 'No need for me to bring milk then?' confirms John – and then we will go for a meal at the Italian restaurant down the road.

Joan gets quite excited, and even I feel a twinge of pleasure at the thought of an evening of undemanding chat with people I don't know very well. It's not rock and roll, I know, but neither is watching telly with Don.

A couple of days later, there is a message from Matthew on the answering machine to say that he is coming round on Tuesday evening.

'What does he want?' wonders Don.

'Money for Christmas. Christmas presents. A place to go. Just money.'

'You know what we said though.'

I do. We agreed we would not give him money – at least Don put forward sensible reasons, and I said OK. I'm not ashamed to admit – yes, I am ashamed, but I have to admit – that I would rather pay Matthew to stay away from us.

If it meant I didn't have to see him as he is now, I would stoically hand over cash; if it saved me from even having to know what he is now, I would probably re-mortgage the house. Yet he's not a murderer or even a criminal, except for a bit of shop-lifting when he needs to; he's not a drug addict, though he's not a stranger to a fair amount of different substances. He's not violent, as far as I know, though he is usually bad-tempered. He's just a grubby, shambling, work-shy, gap-toothed layabout who moans and whines and feels sorry for himself.

Sometime around ten years ago, more than that even, something malevolent got into the soul of our bright-eyed, popular, promising boy, and bit by bit, month by month, we lost him.

It was at that point, I suppose, that Don stopped looking like a bloodhound puppy and started sagging like a grown up dog. And by now, I must say, sagging is the right word for him. His ears have got longer and every line of his face runs downwards. He looks, as they say, like I feel.

'But I'll be out. It's the day I go to writing class. In fact, I'll be late back, because we're going for a meal.'

'He seems to want to see you. Listen.'

'Mum, I need to see you on Tuesday. I'll be round about six-thirty.'

It's puzzling because it's a more focussed message than we've come to expect, and it shows him thinking at least five days in advance.

'He'll probably never turn up. He'll forget by Tuesday. But I can leave something for you both – you can have a better evening without me.'

I say it with relief, and a consciousness of wriggling out of an obligation, but it's true, Don gets on better with him than I do. We mention it more than once during the evening, pondering what can be going on, and then leave it, to see what will happen.

Of course I go to the writing group. The idea of staying in for Matthew is laughable, because he won't come anyway. I volunteer to be the first to read my poem, because I know it's awful and I want to get it over with and give them time to forget it.

'Christmas morning, bells ring out.

Hear the little children shout.

First to wake is little Grace,

Chocolate buttons round her face.

Alfie isn't far behind,

Power Rangers on his mind.

My oldest grandson, lovely Jay

Would rather stay in bed all day.'

And so on, through the family. I notice, when I've got to Don ('never feeling put upon') that I've missed out Matthew, but it doesn't matter, especially as I've deliberately never owned up here to having a son.

'Lovely,' says Jean. 'How lovely to have all those grandchildren.' Her eyes are filled with tears.

'Where's Julia?' I ask, to change the subject. I saw her earlier, dressed like a fairy, in silver.

Jean shakes her head sadly. 'She changed her mind about the meal. I don't know why. She went out to phone her dad to come and get her. She left me her poem to read.'

I wonder why a girl her age can't get a bus at eight o'clock on a Tuesday evening, but on second thoughts, maybe the fairy outfit would make her a bit conspicuous.

It's quite a jolly meeting, with no criticism at all. Jocelyn's poem is about Christmas in Kuala Lumpur, and Judy's is a haiku. Jean's is if anything worse than mine, but maybe more based in fact.

She reads Julia's out in her absence, a sad little piece in free verse, though Jerry said we had to rhyme. It begins 'I remember when Christmas was magic.' Don't we all?

When I get home, Don is listening to the Everly Brothers, singing along to 'Poor Jenny.' He stops when I come in the room.

'Well, he came,' he says.

'Who?'

'Matt.'

'Oh. What did he want?'

'I don't know. Came late, about half seven. Said where were you? Then got a text message and went.'

'Didn't eat his meal?'

'Took it with him. Lucky he never put the gravy on.'

'Didn't say what he wanted?'

'No.'

The mystery lingers.

I throw my Christmas poem in the bin. Our Christmas isn't going to be like that.

I know what I want out of Christmas. I want the

children at home, with partners and grandchildren, I want harmony and peace and pleasantness. I want to look around, tired but happy, at the end of the day and feel the love coming from them as they pick idly at nuts and mince pies, I want the grandchildren sitting on my knee and talking confidentially to me. It has never happened. It has nearly happened, but nearly only makes it worse.

What usually happens these days is that Don and I stay at home, phone everyone on Christmas morning, exchange presents, watch a film on TV, eat and drink and go to bed. What can spoil it is that Matthew might put in an appearance.

And when it's over, I think 'was that it?' and reflect that even Linda Dickinson, the mother of the worst family in Haringey, manages to get her tribe (those of them who are not in prison) around her, feeds them and loves them and gives them all piles of presents. If she can do it, why can't I?

Last year, Zoe and Philip and Grace came for Christmas, and Kez managed to tear up for the day from somewhere in the Midlands. It was horrible. Grace was just one and had a terrible wheezy cough that kept everyone awake all night. Philip doesn't drink, and Zoe criticised most things I did, from the tree to the cooking to Grace's presents (how I'd looked forward to that bit!) to the washing up, to the choice of film, and added some comments about the state of my house while she was at it. Then Kez managed ("managed?" It wasn't difficult!) to upset Zoe by suggesting that antibiotics might not be necessary for 'a bit of a cold', then the two of them got into a snarky 'so sorry, you're the expert of course' sort of thing until Don had to barricade me in the kitchen to stop me telling Zoe to leave.

It would have been worse if Katie had been there too. Zoe and Katie never got along. We could think of all sorts of reasons for it, and tried all sorts of schemes to try and make them behave like sisters, but as they grew older, it grew worse. I remember some long-ago argument – what it was about I don't remember – when Katie even tried to apologise.

She said, 'I apologise unreservedly.' She was like that, she liked words but sometimes they didn't come out quite in the right way.

It made Zoe livid. 'Now you are just taking the piss.' But she wasn't, she was trying, for once, to put it right. I had to be on Katie's side, mostly, and I think that's what turned me against Zoe, who always had to have things her way.

This year Kez can't or won't, get home, Katie never will. Matthew won't commit himself, so we have been invited – summoned even – Don and I, to Liverpool for the event. Zoe has to do everything right. She is the least rebellious of the children, worked hard at school, behaved well too, went to university, got qualified, worked hard. She has a good job, and a good man with a good job, a nice house bought with the savings of both of them; had a wedding and a baby in the proper order. Now she wants a proper Christmas, and that means grandparents. Philip's are at home in Hong Kong, so it's down to us. Zoe will do everything by the book. Don hates being away from home, and struggles to make us reject the invitation, but there is no escape, it's our duty and we have to, and secretly, I'd rather do anything than stay at home, in the house for three days, for another year.

Until we get there. It is as I suspected it would be. Don is depressed because he's a long way from home, the food is vegetarian and he can't listen to any music – Zoe has Radio 4 on. Philip is a dear man, and is doing his best, but is under orders to Zoe and a bit out of his depth.

Grace calls me Granma. Why Granma? I want to say to Zoe – and do, in fact. *She* never had a Granma. *I* never had one. Nan was good enough for us, Nanna if you were feeling posh. Where's all this Granma come from all of a sudden? Jay and Alfie call me Nan, why should Grace be different. 'Leave it,' advises Don.

On Christmas Eve, I take out our battered copy of Raymond Briggs' Father Christmas, much loved by all my children. Even when the girls were teenagers, they would still sit quiet with me when I read it to Matthew and Jay the night before Christmas. I never managed to establish many family traditions, but that was one of the few and I want, now that she's old enough, to offer it to Grace. When Katie finally left home with Jay, I bought her a copy to take with her, and when I gave it to her she hugged me. I remember that.

I wave the book at Grace and try to entice her onto my knee.

'Oh lovely,' cries Zoe and picks up Grace and dumps her in my lap. She wriggles down again.

'Come and look at the book, darling,' goes Zoe.

'If she doesn't want to...' says Don.

'Maybe she's too young,' says Philip.

'It's only pictures,' I say.

'Don't make her, Zo,' warns Don, but she picks the child up again and lands her in my lap.

'Now,' she says sternly. 'Stay there with Granma and read that book. No getting down till it's finished.'

Grace turns a perfectly comprehending face from her mother to the book and I turn to the first page.

'Who's this? It's Father Christmas.'

'We call him Santa Claus,' calls Zoe from the kitchen. 'Don't confuse her, will you?'

'Cat,' says Grace, reaching out a hand and ripping the page. I take hold of her soft little hand to stop any further damage and she shrieks and puts her foot through the book. Weakened already by being more than thirty years old, it lands on the floor, except for the cover which stays in my hands for Grace to have another go at.

Zoe shrieks. 'Gracie, what have you done? That was mummy's book.' She seems really upset, but so am I and I say without thinking, 'It's not yours. It's a family book.' She huffs back to the kitchen. 'Family. What family?'

Grace is dancing on the pages while Philip tries to pick them up out of harm's way. 'We'll buy another one,' he says. 'A better one.' That's how much he understands, and Don, who could see if he wanted to, that I am ready to cry, pretends nothing at all is happening by raising the Radio Times (Double Christmas Edition) in front of his face.

When we are in bed (on a mattress on the floor, which can't be good for my back), I lie awake – not just not-quite-asleep, but so awake that if I was at home I would have got up and done something – and review all those thoughts that invade at the worst times. I am a bad grandmother, but that's nothing beside the fact that I was a bad mother. I was a bad mother and the proof is that my children stay away from me. I drove Katie away and so lost Jay as well, Zoe is someone who I don't like that much, and she only sees me because she is close to her dad. I could say much the same about Matthew; and Kezia, who I love the best, is always far away, lost to me as well, by being in a world I know nothing about.

Eventually I sleep, and dream about Matthew as a little boy.

One time when I was saying how the Doughty girls were like sisters to me, Don said, 'Why don't you see them, then?'

I couldn't argue. He sees his sister, and his brother, behaving as they're expected to behave. I haven't had anything to do with Theresa since she was sixteen. Val, though she always sends a Christmas card, not since Malcolm's funeral. Rita not since – I don't know. Yes I do know, Malcolm's funeral too, and she was a bit frosty with me.

Kay I have seen, once a year, between Boxing Day and New Year's Eve, every year. This started way back when Kay first had Debs, and I suppose I felt sorry for her so I called round with a present for the baby, and after that, they would invite me when they had their family party. When our kids were little, it used to be a welcome afternoon out in that dead time after Christmas. As the children grew up, they stopped coming with me – I think Don stopped well before that – but I carried on because, as much as anything, I didn't know how to stop. It was nice anyway, seeing Rita and listening to Malcolm's anecdotes, and eating and drinking in a warm and comfortable, if overstuffed, sitting room. After he died, of course, I couldn't stop going, even though there were no more parties.

Every year, Kay has grown fatter. She was sturdy as a child, chubby as a young mother, and as a widow, has steadily eaten herself huge. Chairs are not big enough to contain her, she wobbles when she moves, her clothes are like loose covers. I admit to being well-upholstered myself, but she makes me feel elegant.

This year, when the door opens, I find Val standing there, also a big woman, but one who carries it well, hair blonde and brushed, looking older, certainly, but looking nice, if a bit orange, a woman who looks after herself, who knows how to dress, who could be out enjoying herself, but who chooses to visit her sad sister. And we slip back into the way we were with no awkwardness or hesitation.

'Have you seen her lately?' I ask, and they know who

I'm talking about.

'She sent a card,' says Kay.

'I spoke to her on the phone,' says Val. 'I wanted her to come and celebrate her birthday with us – not on her birthday, but it was her sixtieth, I thought it would be nice for all of us.'

'We're not posh enough for her,' says Kay, as she always says.

'I thought,' says Val, ignoring her, 'that we might see more of her now she's retired, but no.'

'Retired?' I didn't know that.

'Apparently. Still owns the company, and all that, but taking a back seat, that's what she told me she was going to do. And she had some radio work coming up, she thought.'

'What about Theresa, have you heard from her?'

'She sent a card,' says Kay.

'I ring her now and again,' says Val. 'She's OK I think, as far as you can tell. One of these days we'll have to go and see her, won't we Kay? You'll come with me, won't you?'

'I don't know if I'd like it,' says Kay. 'It's a long way to go.'

'It's only a couple of hours up the M1 – we could do it in a day, there and back. Or we could stop somewhere.'

'I don't know.'

'I'll come with you,' I say. 'I could see how Leslie's getting on.'

Val looks embarrassed. 'I don't know if I want to see Les. I know he's your cousin, Pat, but I don't feel like he treats her very well.'

'Better than no husband at all,' says Kay, out of the blue but surprising no one. 'You wouldn't think, would you, that it would be Theresa who ended up the only one with a husband. And you too, Pat, of course.'

There is no answer to this. I can't say how comforted she should be by having her daughters, because Val is there, and Val, so I heard from Kay over the years, had the misfortune, stupidity, call it whichever, to marry twice, both times to alcoholics with a low sperm count, and to spend some wretched years wishing she had children. And I can't say what a good husband Malcolm was while she had him, because he wasn't really, and I can't say that having a husband isn't all it's cracked up to be when Kay is stuck in some mid-century fantasy about being the little woman to some all-protecting man.

'How are the girls?' I ask, to deflect her.

'Show her that photo of all of you,' suggests Val, sounding relieved, and Kay gets up heavily and goes out sighing.

'I don't know how you do it,' I say – it's just one of those things you say, isn't it? but I mean it.

'Do you know,' says Val, 'I feel like I might as well give up trying. I mean, I'm on my own too, but I get on with it, go out when I can, you know. But it makes me miserable for days after I've been here.'

'How often do you come?'

'Most weeks I come round for an evening. She won't come out, not to the pub, or for a meal, or to the pictures. You can talk till you're black and blue in the face, but no. She's younger than you, but it's like she's eighty. You'd go out, wouldn't you?'

'Oh I would. Don – you know what Don's like, doesn't mix – but I go out when I can, like you.' So much I could say, left unsaid.

Kay returns, not with one photo, as expected, but with three large biscuit tins, their lids warping against a strapping of elastic bands.

'I've brought them all,' she says. 'Save going out again.' By 'out', she means out of the room. If that's something to be avoided, goodness knows what "out of the house" would cause her to feel like. 'I've had these since mum died,' she explains. 'I didn't want to look at them by myself. I've dusted the tins though, every week.' As if we'd doubt that.

When the lids are off, the contents spill over. Val picks a photo off the floor and then looks disappointed.

'Who's that? I've never seen that person in my life. I hope they're not all like this.'

It's clear that no one has ever sorted, or probably even looked at these, for many years, before Kath died twenty or so years ago. I almost expect them to crumble into dust, but they seem more to spring into life, to take in air and light and ask to be looked at.

Each tin is a jumble – single dog-eared, tiny black-and-white snapshots; wedding pictures in white card frames embossed with silver; the odd packet pristine, as if just collected from Boots; a bundle with the traces of a long-perished rubber band round it; school photos in stiff card frames – 'there's you,' cries Val to Kay; a few with names and dates on the back – "Margie 1943".

We look through, randomly picking up, squinting at, turning over, laughing, commenting. 'Look at those glasses.' 'That could be...no, it isn't though.'

Kay is hesitant at first, as if the tins are haunted – well they are to her, I suppose – but she is beginning to unbend, I mean literally. She gets stiffly out of her chair and sits on the floor, stretching her feet towards the coal-effect gas fire.

'Tell you what,' says Val, after a few minutes of this. 'I've got a bottle of wine – let's open it and go through these properly. We need some paper and pens and – I tell you what Kay – have you got something like sandwich bags, or envelopes? Something to put them in.'

'What would I be doing with sandwich bags?' says Kay, but she goes off to fetch envelopes, and Val sees to glasses and bottle opener.

They are like voices, these photographs, like turning on a radio and hearing a song that you heard when you were seven and didn't understand. They show people together who I never even thought of as knowing each other – Ted's brother with his arm round Kath's sister, in a garden, Val saying: 'Is that my dad? No it's not, I never realised Uncle Eric was like him.'

They bring back ghosts, not just the old ones - Nana Swallow stately in a dropped waist dress and little hat, Nanny Doughty in a pinny, looking like a child dressed up to play house – but Tony, horrible, doomed Tony, and you look at him, squinting at the sun, digging on the beach, being carried, laughing, on Kay's back in the garden, and you think, was there something even then? Should we have known?

'Is there a picture of our house?' asks Kay, but no there isn't, only a corner of the coal shed in the garden. No pictures of inside either, for of course, ordinary people didn't use flash then. And no pictures of the street in front, where we mostly played. Photos, it seems, were only taken on your own turf, with your own people, in your garden, or on your bit of beach. And only of happy moments, because who is going to waste precious once-only film on a moment when kids are crying or sulking or pushing each other. That's not how you want to remember them.

It surprises me though, that Ted with his box Brownie, could find even this many happy moments to snap, because they weren't a cheerful family, not ones for smiling much. Tony, as I remember him, was downright sullen, pulling his eyebrows down so that he looked like a little gargoyle. I wish there was a picture of him like that, but instead he populates the photos, bigger and more often than his sisters – Ted must have got a new camera – laughing boyishly and doing boyish things: riding a trike, kicking a ball (very blurred), sitting in a blow-up paddling pool in a sunlit garden, a long time ago.

Val is looking through the school photos. Kath, I feel, wasn't very interested in the little snaps that Ted took, and just put them in a drawer, never to be looked at after the first time, but she used to have the school photos on display. Display that is, as far as she could go, which meant propped at the back of the dresser shelves, behind a jug or a pile of plates.

Val is laying them out in five columns, one for each of them, and in chronological order. It's an alarming sight, five children magnified by ten years of schooling, fifty smiles – because you had to smile. I remember the photographer. He made bad jokes, until you cracked, even Rita. Fifty pairs of eyes, and they all had nice steady eyes, not a squint among them, and except for Kay's, all blue. Five faces growing older, longer, bonier, more defined.

'There's two of this one, for some reason,' says Val.

'Can I have it?' I say it quietly, and tuck it into my bag quickly, like a secret trophy.

As Val and I leave, I notice Kay's Christmas tree, still wrapped in its netting, propped up beside the garage. Val sees me looking.

'Waste of money, wasn't it?' She lights a cigarette and inhales with big dramatic breaths. 'God Pat, you've never seen such a sad Christmas. I'm not doing it again, I tell you. And do you know – another thing – what's in that garage? Malcolm's car. Still there. Not even the girls can get her to look at it, never mind sell it. I'd take it off her hands if she'd let me.' She kicks gently at the back tyre of her old Fiat. 'Do you want to go for a drink?'

'I'm driving, and we've already –'

'So am I, but what the hell. Let's throw caution to the

windows.' She doesn't want to go home to her cold house; too early to go to bed, too late to put the heating on and settle in. Only ghastly Christmas programmes on TV; all friends and acquaintances trapped within their own families.

'I wouldn't mind a coffee.'

So we stop at a bar and have a coffee, and Val has a glass of wine as well. 'I can walk home from here.'

'Would you really go and see Theresa?'

'Why not? I might get more response.'

'She's depressed.' I'm meaning Kay. 'I wouldn't be surprised if she's agoraphobic.'

'Yeah, she's depressed. Rita's angry, she won't see Kay. Those daughters of hers are just too superior for words, that grand-daughter's a brat, Tony's away, Theresa's gone, where does that leave me?'

I wonder if she's had more to drink than I know, but hey, stop a minute, poor woman, poor brave Val, isn't it all true? She tries to keep a family together, or to reassemble it from its scattered shards, but it must be like trying to knit a spider's web. Yes, what she'd like to have is one of those close-meshed webs like you see in bushes, as cosy as cotton wool, but what she's got is like what I've got – one of those big autumn radial webs, and each one of her family is on the end of a radius, as far from the centre as they can get, and as far from each other.

'Do you hear from Tony?'

'Do I hear from Tony? We were good mates, me and Tony, after the girls left. You don't know what it was like, Pat, you never came to our house again. First Rita went, then Theresa about a week later, and I never saw her till mum's funeral, then Malcolm moved in and Kay had the baby, and then they moved out again and it was so quiet, except Mum never stopped going on about it all.'

'Val. You've done your best. Kay couldn't wish for a better sister.'

She sniffs into a tissue and sips her wine. 'Don't let me kid myself. I don't do it for Kay, I do it for me because she's all I've got.' I notice that she has a nervous blink of her eyes when you look straight at her.

'You've got friends.'

'I have. I've got good friends. And do you know what? They've all got families. And what comes first? Their children, their husbands and their mothers and their grandchildren. As mine would, to be fair, if I had any, but there's no one I can just go and see, just call round, just any time – only Kay, because she's always there. As far as I'm concerned, agoraphobia's a good thing because I don't have to ring her up and go 'Are you busy, will you be in?' She'll be in, I know she will, sitting there like death's doormat.'

I think of Don, always at home when I come in, always always there, and I feel a shiver of horror at the thought of him retiring and not even going out to work every morning. Three years till then.

'Val, you know I'm retired now, sort of. I'm quite free most evenings. Just let me know. You can even call in on the off-chance, if you like. I'd always be pleased to see you.' Which is true and it pleases her. Later, I remember that I should have said 'Not Tuesdays,' but I don't have any expectation that she'll do it, so it doesn't matter.

There were always people knocking at our door. The paper boy knocked for his money on Saturday mornings, the milkman on Friday evenings, the rent man on a Monday evening. The man from the Prudential came once a month; a woman I called Auntie Else delivered the Avon catalogue and came back with the delivery.

It wasn't like now, when it's all two clicks of a mouse and your money's gone you know not where. You knew what you'd had for your money: an Evening News every day, which we never read, and a News of the World on Sundays, which my mum took back to bed with her and read every word of, except for the football and racing pages. A pint of Grade A every day and six eggs on Fridays. Soap and talcum powder and little bottles of cream in fanciful packaging. For a long time, I didn't understand why we gave the insurance man money but mum explained it was to pay for our funerals if we died. 'What a waste of money,' I'm said to have said.

All those people used the knocker. Neighbours and family did that thing where they went 'Oo-oo', through the letter box, and then let themselves in. We didn't have much family, only Nan, and Auntie Peggy with Leslie in tow, but we had plenty of neighbours. Old ones with whiskery chins and gummy mouths – 'I'd have put me teeth in but I left 'em upstairs and me legs aren't what they used to be,' – who popped in to tell us who they'd seen round the shops, or what the Queen was doing.

Women more my mother's age would call in to scrounge a cigarette after they'd fed their kids, and before they had to start putting them to bed. They'd drop their voices to whispers when I was in the room but when I was outside the door, they told my mother all the bits of news she'd missed by being at work all day – usually babies born, or miscarried, or on the way, or husbands drunk or useless.

Male neighbours never came to the door, or only if there was an emergency, and even then, a sprint to the phone box was more appropriate.

Other kids came, of course, to see if I was coming out, and sometimes I was, but more often, I was going to Rita's. They knocked at the front door, except for Rita, who as my best friend had a privileged position, and came round the back, and opened the back door to talk to me directly.

One night, I was sitting with mum and we were listening to the radio. The 'Take it from Here' music had just finished and I knew she would start thinking about sending me to bed because it was school tomorrow. Knock at the door.

'Now who's that at this time of a Sunday?' It must have been winter, because when she opened the door, me standing behind her, it felt as if the dark and cold rushed in and filled up the hall.

It was Ivy Saunders from across the road, and that

was strange because she would normally have come right in, but then, she wouldn't normally have left her husband and children to come visiting on a Sunday evening. She saw me and rolled her eyes at mum to tell her to send me away. I crept back into the room and lay on the floor to listen at the crack under the door. Whispers.

'...hospital...save her...this afternoon...' More whispers.

Mum coming back into the room (me getting up hurriedly from behind the door), looking for her purse. When I saw her face, I was frightened. I followed her out into the hall again and saw that Ivy was crying, not like a child cries with noise and a screwed up face, but silently, just tears running down her face.

Mum gave her some money, and when she put it in her hand, she covered it with both of hers and held it. I had never seen anything like that before. Then she went.

Mum told me, of course. She could never keep anything from me for long. It was Ivy's next door neighbour, called Joyce, and she had died while having a baby. It was the first time I realised that a person as young as that could die. Although my father had been young when he died, I always imagined him as old. And grown-ups had feelings. I had not known that before.

When I went to bed, I thought of something else. If the insurance man paid for funerals, why did mum have to give Ivy money?

When I asked her, she made a noise that could have

been a laugh, or could have been a cough, and gave me one of her little pushes. 'There's more to death than funerals,' she said.

All Together Now

A new girl. A new girl. The six-year olds nudged and whispered to each other. The new girl stood with the headmistress, Miss Genower, at the door, looking at Mrs Croft, not at the other children.

The school was newly built, to serve the big new council estate. Outside the big square windows, a cold wind was tormenting the cherry blossom. The new girl was dressed in a skirt of red and yellow plaid with braces, and a fawn-coloured woollen jumper with a collar and three buttons at the neck, all done up. Her socks were fawn and pulled up to her knees so exactly that her legs were like doll's legs.

'This is Rita,' said the headmistress to Mrs Croft. 'I've shown her her coat peg, and she has paid her dinner money for the week. Will you have enough milk?' She waved her arm to the crate of small bottles by the door.

'We will today,' said Mrs Croft, 'because June Barnes is absent. But could Miss Horrocks order an extra one for tomorrow, just in case?'

'I'll be sure to tell her.' Miss Genower turned to the class and twinkled kindly. 'Be good boys and girls now. One or two of you must look after Rita until she gets used to us.' She turned again to Mrs Croft. 'She has a sister in the baby class and will need to collect her at the end of the day to take her home.' She pattered out of the room and down the corridor to her office, to continue plotting her retirement.

Many of the girls, and one boy, by now had their hands in the air, urgently wanting to look after Rita. Mrs Croft scanned the room in a harassed way. This would make thirty-eight in her class, and as she said in the staffroom on the rare occasions she managed to sit down for a few minutes, no one can even see that many children in one go.

'There dear, go and sit in that empty seat next to Linda.'

More whispering. There was a reason why the seat next to Linda was empty, and though Rita's expression didn't change – she was too careful for that – her nostrils expanded just a tiny bit.

'And quiet, everybody. Put up your hand if you have *not* finished your news. Well, you people, just finish your sentence and put a full stop,' – three of the children just put a full stop – 'and Mary will collect the books in. Maureen will give out the mental arithmetic books.'

Mrs Croft usually taught top infants. Her classroom management tended to founder on the lack of reading, and other, skills of these Class One children. Maureen struggled to hand out the books because she couldn't read the names, and a boy called David – the one who had put his hand up to have Rita next to him –

was called in to help.

At playtime the girls crowded round Rita. They found out where she lived ('over there'), what school she had been to before ('it had nuns'), what her sister was called, what her favourite colour was, and whether she owned a dolls' pram ('no'.) They established that she was not the tallest in the class, nor the smallest, and that her eyes were blue.

'And black hair,' said Maureen.

'No one has really black hair,' said Heather.

'I never said it was black,' said Rita. 'It was her.' She had got nine out of ten in mental arithmetic and was feeling on top of things. Also she was used to bossing her sisters around.

'Well, I think it's black,' said a girl with brown hair. She did not have a best friend and was ready to be impressed by Rita.

Then a teacher rang the bell, and they lined up and went inside. Rita sat next to Linda again but avoided looking at her, having quickly realised her status.

Mrs Croft gave her a reading book. Rita took it confidently and opened it.

'Come out here, dear,' called Mrs Croft. 'I'll listen to you first.'

Rita stood beside the big desk and set off. Those who bothered to look could see that Mrs Croft was stopping her, and turning to a different page, and stopping her again, and finally sending her back to her seat, where she sat looking down at her hands, without speaking or looking at anyone.

I read this out at the first meeting after Christmas. The photo of Rita that I took from Kay's house is propped up against the vase in the middle of the table, and all through the cold blowy days of January, I'm writing away obsessively while Don is at work. I have two more crowding into my head, two more, that is, about Kay and Malcolm, so that I wonder all of a sudden why I've made them into separate stories, instead of one long one.

Anyway, it's nice to be back with the group, though I never thought I'd say that. Jean and Julia aren't there though, and a little wisp of worry goes through me, wondering whether something has happened to Julia – certain however – how? – that nothing could ever go wrong with Jean.

Judy is unimpressed with my picture of how school was. 'I can't believe,' she says, 'that any child could get away with pretending to read.'

'That's how schools were,' I say, against the temptation to tell her that it was true, a true story – I was there – it was my best friend. 'There really were that many in a class.'

'Better behaved in those days, though,' says John.

I remember a boy called Derek taking his trousers down in the corridor, and a girl called Maureen – yes, the Maureen who couldn't give the books out – having soggy toilet paper thrown at her so that it stuck in her hair and she cried, and the shenanigans that used to go on when two children were sent to the sink to mix up the ink with powder and water, and it doesn't seem to me that we were that well-behaved.

'Might have been better at your school,' says Jim. 'They were rogues and scamps at mine.'

John grins; a cemetery of yellow teeth. 'We had our moments, it's true.'

Any minute now, they'll be off down memory lane with British Bulldog and soap box carts, and tying fireworks to people's doorknockers. I know, because I've heard it all from Don's dad, every Sunday when we visit him in the Home. I know his childhood, it seems to me, as well as I know my own.

I interrupt John all of a sudden to ask Jim: 'Did you ever know a boy called George Childs?'

He doesn't even have to think.

'I did. Lived over the back. Tall. Joined the redcaps in the war. Jeepers, we hated them. Never spoke to him again. Well, never saw him again, if truth be told, but I wouldn't have spoken to him if I had.'

'He's my father-in-law.'

Jerry calls a halt to all this, but I know Jim will get back to it in the pub, and I'm not wrong.

It was me who taught Rita to read. She honestly thought she could, because at her previous school, with the nuns, she had memorised the books as other children read them, but at our school we used different books. She'd changed schools, not because her parents had noticed that she couldn't read, but because Theresa had turned out to be scared of nuns and their mum had got fed up of the morning tantrums.

I don't even know, thinking about it now, whether my mum would have noticed if it was me – parents weren't like they are now, suspicious, and scared at every turn that their child will be sold short in some way. No, we were just sent to school and expected to pick up some rudiments and if we didn't, it was our own fault and we'd have to work in Woolworth's.

Anyway, when Rita stood at Mrs Croft's desk and jabbered on about Tip the dog in the garden, in spite of the pictures of a cat on a bed looking out of a window, she was – I don't know – mortified? Embarrassed?

Mrs Croft was puzzled but in a hurry. She gave Rita the book to take back to her place, and at the end of the day, told her to take it home and practise. I heard all this because I had fallen in love with Rita, and I was concentrating on her instead of colouring in my symmetrical pattern.

After school I caught up with her and her sister. They went a different way to me because I used to go to my nan's after school, but it turned out that they lived near where I did. Rita was carrying the book by the spine at arm's length, as if she had dropped it in dog poo.

'You can't read it, can you?' I didn't know any other way to come at it.

'I could at my other school. It's this book.' She twitched it and the pages fluttered.

'I can show you.' See, I could read.

'Go on then.'

I read the first page to her, and she repeated it, word perfect.

'See.' I turned the page and waited. The same words were there, but in a different order. She said nothing. Theresa started whining to go home – we were sitting on a hard garden wall in the sunshine and she was thirsty.

But when I was at home, I thought about it and I remembered – it was so long ago, more than a year – when I couldn't read, and how in the baby class with Miss Hodnott, there were wooden letter shapes you could make words with.

I don't know when I first went to Rita's house. It was early on in this process, because I remember sitting on that chilly concrete floor and writing the alphabet in the spaces around the pictures in a colouring book. That was the only sort of book they seemed to have. Rita and Theresa were there, but Theresa wasn't very quick to learn, or maybe I confused her, but Rita picked it up straight away. I don't know what I did that helped her – maybe she would have cottoned on anyway, but it cemented us together.

Together we made a very successful academic whole – my reading and writing, and her number skills. She taught me my tables in return, and some prayers which never came in very useful, and we sat together in class, leaving Linda on her own again. Best friends.

Everyone had a best friend. Maybe I did before Rita came on the scene but I can't remember who it might have been. But after that, we were inseparable, until we went to the grammar school where the first thing they did was separate us. We didn't always sit together. In

Miss Wilcox's class – and we had her for two years – girls had to sit next to boys, I don't know why, maybe to civilise them, but it seemed to have the perverse result of sexualising them. Or maybe that would have happened anyway.

Rita wasn't either particularly popular or unpopular. Some girls are popular just because they're pretty, as long as they're not too bumptious, but she stayed fairly much under the radar. She was bossy to me, and to her sisters, but reasonable with other girls, polite to teachers without being a teacher's pet, didn't tell tales or pass on rumours, didn't think she was better than other people, would take her turn at things like being first ender when we were skipping, didn't make a parade of her prettiness or her cleverness, never tried to be noticed or to be a leader at anything.

You never heard Rita come forward at school with the first suggestion of what to play. She even got on with Linda, and seemed to see something nice in her, but she did it without alienating the rest of us, for whom Linda was a permanent outcast. But maybe there was something about Rita that kept people from feeling warm towards her. I didn't need reasons to be her friend. I liked her because I liked her, because she was Rita, not because she was nice.

Our 11-plus results, or rather, the schools we had been allocated, came to our homes through the post, and that day, the first part of the school morning, instead of an arithmetic test, was given over to where we were all going. Rita and I were both going to the

118

same school, which we had picked together. One other girl, Heather, and a boy whose name I forget – was it Russell? – were going there too, but about half the class had 'passed' and were being shared out in the other grammar schools round and about.

The other half were going to secondary moderns.

We weren't even sitting in our seats at this time, it was all too interesting, and Miss Wilcox was so interested in our letters and in who was going where and with who, we were all clustered round her desk. At playtime, the boys went out, but the girls stayed there, talking to her – Maureen went to the staffroom and brought a cup of tea back to the classroom for her – and we watched Miss Wilcox drink her tea as if she was an ordinary person. It was May: we had two more months there, but it felt as if we were leaving already.

'What about Linda?'

No one had so far asked or thought of asking, and she hadn't said. Miss Wilcox had a special voice, kinder and more definite, for Linda, in case she should be thought to be picking on her and she used it now. 'Linda? Did you get your letter?'

Linda handed it over without a word. We all knew it would say Albany Road Secondary Modern. Miss Wilcox paused, then beamed at us all. 'Very good indeed, Linda. You did really well. Linda's going to the Girls' Grammar.'

We all looked at her, and at Maria and Pauline who were also going there. And I said – it's not the sort of thing I usually did, it just came out. I thought it, and then I found I'd said it: 'Well, she'll need to have a wash,' and everyone, including Miss Wilcox, pretended they hadn't heard.

Later at dinner time in the playground, Rita had a bit of a fight with Linda, not fists, just a bit of pushing, and that was because she was sticking up for me. But Linda never did go to the Grammar School. I heard she refused to let her mum buy the uniform, and that she turned up at Albany Road on the first day and they let her stay.

School's out

At the end of assembly, the fifth form girls were told to stay behind. When everyone else had filed out, smirking, they were told that they could sit on the chairs vacated by the sixth form, instead of sitting back down on the floor, or worse, left standing. Clearly then, this was not an investigation into graffiti in the toilets or a matter of someone being seen taking their beret off on a bus.

Rita sat next to her friend Barbara, feeling – probably alone of the whole group – aggrieved that she was missing Maths, and that the boys would be at this moment learning something extra and arcane that she would never now know.

The Deputy Head, in charge of girls' welfare and all things female, stood in front of them: tiny, monkey-faced, hair cut like a boy, to deliver her careers talk.

They were approaching a time of choices and decisions. The first of these was whether or not to stay on into the sixth form. Some people – she did not say 5C, who did a greater proportion of technical subjects, but she meant them – might not achieve sufficiently good O-Levels to be allowed to stay on: five O-Levels would be required. A few girls at this point stopped bothering to listen, so never heard that they shouldn't be discouraged.

If they would like to work with people, they could go into nursing. If they preferred to work with *things*, there were banks.

Rita was puzzled by the reference to *things*, which was making people snigger discreetly, but she knew that for herself, banks were far preferable to hospitals. She had visited a hospital quite recently, when her Nana was dying, and there could be nothing worse than working in one every day.

Banks, on the other hand, though neither she nor her parents had ever set foot inside one, had the glamour of money, though she realised that the most complicated piece of arithmetic involved would have to be compound interest, and she could do that easily, so it might be quite a dull place to work.

If however, girls were to stay on into the sixth form, they would have the additional option of becoming a teacher, although, if they wanted, in spite of having A-Levels, to work with *things*, there were other and better jobs in banks than those that would be being done by those girls with mere O-Levels.

'You must talk about it with your parents. After the Christmas holiday, I'll be asking you what your plans are.'

At break, they drank their milk in the hall – even those who didn't like it drank it – it stopped them being so hungry, and anyway, after ten years, they were used to the taste and the routine.

Rita and Barbara, with two girls from 5B, settled on a radiator, easing aside a group of third years who were singing 'Love me Do', quite competently as it happened.

'What do you think you'll do?' asked Merle.

Rita shrugged.

Barbara said: 'Stay on with me – I'm going to.'

'I might.' Wondering what her parents would say.

'She'll get enough O-Levels, easily,' said the other girl.

'Then we'll have to choose three A-Levels,' said Barbara. 'I'll do History, Geography, maybe French.'

'History's good,' said Merle. 'Maybe Biology.'

'Yah, just cos you like him.'

'No it's not.'

'What would you do, Reet?'

'Maths,' she said, stating the obvious. 'I think you can do two Maths A-Levels.' She felt exhilaration at the thought. Maybe Physics.'

'You'd be the only girl.'

'Maybe.'

'And would you be a teacher?' said Merle.

'Someone,' said Rita, and it was the first time she'd ever thought of this, 'must have to teach the teachers Maths. When they're training, I mean. They have to know more than their pupils, mustn't they? And so they have to know more than A-Level, so someone must have to teach them.'

The bell rang, which saved the other three from having to process this idea.

All through the Christmas holiday, Rita thought about it, about going to University and studying Maths and the idea grew and hardened and became more than an idea: it was an ambition, a plan, a future. Only she didn't speak to her parents about it.

Her sister would be leaving school at Easter and they were all discussing and wondering where she would get a job. From things that were said, it was clear that they assumed that Rita would be leaving school after her exams, and that she would need a job too.

Her next sister would be leaving the following Christmas, just after her fifteenth birthday, and how strange it will be, thought Rita, when they are out at work, bringing home wages, giving mum something for their keep, and she would be still at school, wearing uniform, doing home-work and looking towards three more years of learning after school.

She couldn't be sure how her mum would receive the idea, and if she said no, it would be like Cinderella being denied the chance to go to the ball; better to wait for the fairy godmother in the form of a set of brilliant O-Level results. She spent more time that holiday in reading and studying than she would normally have done.

Sitting next to Barbara in class, Rita could look past the rows of boys to the window and out to where the builders were putting up the new Science block. It was an unchangeable custom that the boys sat in the two rows nearest the windows, most powerful boys next to the radiators, and the girls sat in the rows between them and the door, most popular girls at the back.

A girl came into the room with a note.

'Rita,' said the teacher. 'Miss Playfair wants to see you in her room at the end of this lesson.'

Waiting outside the room, Rita felt a small curl of excitement that she was going to reveal her ambition to someone. Miss Playfair sat behind her desk and did not ask Rita to sit down.

'You have been talking to one of the building workers.'

Some of the fourth year girls did this, at lunchtime, hanging around the fence that separated the trenches and pipes from the part of the field that was still in use. Of course it was forbidden, and Rita would not have thought of doing it herself. Partly, she was obedient and conformist, and partly, she would think it was beneath her to be trying to be noticed by labourers at work.

'What?' she asked.

'This morning,' said Miss Playfair. 'You were seen, on the bus, talking to one of the building workers.'

Rita's fears cleared. 'No,' she said, not realising that it was possibly a worse crime. 'He's one of my family.'

Miss Playfair stiffened. 'Sit down,' she said. Rita sat.

'Now, my dear, explain to me precisely what relation this person is to you.'

Rita tried to find the term for the person, who was her mother's sister's husband's cousin's son, but there wasn't one. His name was Mick, and he was one of the youngest and definitely the best-looking of all the builders.

Miss Playfair didn't know it, but some of the female staff had spent their break times watching him from the staff room window, as he carried bricks up ladders. It was one of them, Miss Parry, a young Maths teacher, who had been on the same bus and had reported Rita.

'Explain,' prompted Miss Playfair.

'He's living with my Uncle Bernie and Aunt Ginny. He's related to Uncle Bernie. He's not from round here so he can't live at home.'

Miss Playfair had never had occasion to discipline Rita, and as she had never taught her, she knew nothing of her more than her name. Now she questioned her about her family, and her friends outside school.

It was clear to Rita that having two sisters at secondary modern was even more of an indictment than being on social terms with a common labourer.

'All I will say to you, my dear, is that in your position, as a pupil of a grammar school, and, if I look at your marks, a promising pupil, you have to be careful. In later years, your sisters may not be as well-educated as you would like them to be. You may find that you would wish them to be – improved. Your Uncle and Aunt and their young relative may appear altogether different to you in the future to the way they do now. Consider this a warning to you, to be careful with whom you associate yourself. You may go.'

Rita left the room, and went back to class, but her mind was not on her work, and when she was walking from the bus stop with her friend that afternoon, it became clear to her for the first time how angry she was, and how she would not stay at school a moment longer than she had to.

I didn't mind leaving school. I would have stayed if Rita had, but there was no point without her. All our secondary school life, we'd been in different classes and the idea of being together in the sixth form had some glamour, but the idea of being in the sixth form by myself had no appeal at all. My mum didn't mind either way, though I knew she'd be pleased about me bringing in some money and paying for my own stockings.

Rita wouldn't even go back for Speech Day to collect her GCE certificates, or her Maths prize. I don't think I had any idea why she was so angry – I knew she was, but I couldn't feel it with her, snobby was just the way school was, there was no point getting upset about it.

Now, when I think about it, I think that Rita's reinvention of herself had started long before she went to university, probably when she left junior school, and it was the feeling that she had almost got away with it and then her disguise had been sussed at the last hurdle, so to speak, that had enraged her. I didn't care about the Speech Day anyway. It was a Tuesday, and we had started going to the Royal at Tottenham, dancing.

I saw Linda Dickinson the other day, outside Marks and Spencers at Angel Road.

It had been that way since we were at primary school, I'd be down the shops, or at a dance, or on a bus, and there would be Linda, years apart sometimes, but always in the area, like me, never moving away. Or my mum, when she was alive and before she went off her legs and into the Home, would tell me that she'd seen

Linda in the fish shop or the doctor's waiting room and she was all right but looking her age, and she thought maybe, though Linda hadn't said as much, that one of her men – a husband, or later a son – was back in prison.

Poor Linda picked bad men. She had a couple of kids before she was twenty and then split up with their dad. Then she had a couple more sons when my kids were little, so we would both have pushchairs and shopping bags when we met. We never went for a coffee, or invited each other round, it was never like that. She was just an acquaintance that I'd known since I was five, and we passed the time of day.

So until recently, when I saw her looking in a shop window, I would have gone up and said hello and asked how she was, but this time I dodged into the shop through the nearest door so that she didn't see me.

He's so fine

That Saturday evening, the one that some people, if they knew, might say changed her life, Theresa walked to the church hall for the youth club dance with Alan from next door.

He carried his record player and Theresa carried the records, packed tightly and in order into a thick brown paper carrier with string handles. The handles cut into her fingers and she shifted the bag from hand to hand every few yards. Alan was nineteen. Though he had lived next door all Theresa's life, she had never spoken to him until a few weeks ago. He had gone to the boys' grammar school, and lived a different sort of life, travelling on the bus every day and carrying a briefcase.

When Theresa and her sisters looked in his windows at night, they could see him doing homework, or trying to play a guitar. He was a distant, shadowy, exotic neighbour, and his mother had a job and didn't talk over the fence.

Since Theresa had started to get to know him she'd had a sense of her world opening up: a sense of new possibilities, of horizons beyond those that she could see with her eyes.

'Where's your friend?'

'Out with her boyfriend.'

'Oh.'

Theresa found Alan hard to talk to but easy to

be with. He had gone to University – whatever that was – when he left school, but had come back after a few weeks. People said he'd had a nervous breakdown – whatever that was – and certainly he didn't go to work, or do anything much, nowadays, except sit in his room and compile his playlist for the next dance.

'Is Rita coming tonight?' It was obligatory to fancy Rita, although actually Alan was very afraid of her and preferred Theresa.

'She's gone to the bus stop to meet Pat and this boy they work with.'

'Oh.'

On dance evenings, the ping pong tables were folded and stacked behind the stage, members could bring non-members as guests, you could buy Coca Cola as well as orange squash, and it went on till half past ten. Mrs Howard and Sid the vicar took care over what the hall looked like. Chairs were placed neatly round the sides of the room and the curtains were drawn across the windows so that it was enclosed and private, and people standing at the bus stop couldn't look in as they did on ordinary club nights.

Theresa was sitting on the edge of the stage, talking to Sandra Dwyer when they both saw Rita and Pat come into the hall, escorting – and they were – they each had an arm through his, like prison warders, as if he might run away – a tall boy, with full lips and fair hair that fell over his forehead, and eyes that looked around the room ready for people to like him. He was wearing a Beatle jacket.

'Who's that?' said Sandra.

'Rita's brought him. He works at her place. I think he's called Malcolm.' Theresa did not take her eyes off him.

Kay came from the far end of the room, almost at a run. She spoke directly to Malcolm, ignoring Rita and Pat. Theresa couldn't hear her but knew what she'd be saying. 'What's your name? Do you like the Beatles?' She saw him smile at her.

'You want to tell your sister to be careful,' said Sandra. 'The boys say she's a scrubber.'

'She's not.'

'It's not me that's saying it. Mick told me. She's always snogging with boys out on the fire escape.'

'She's not.'

Sandra shrugged. 'Have it your own way.'

'Only if she's going out with them.'

'What, going out with four boys in one night?'

'What four?'

'Dave Pierce, Dave Gardner, Ray and the boy off the Corona lorry.'

And your Mick, thought Theresa, but she said loyally, 'She never went outside with Ray.'

'Three then,' said Sandra.

Four, thought Theresa.

Kay could be seen trying to bully Malcolm onto the dance floor. Not many boys danced, except for the slow songs, when they could run their hands up some girl's back, and if they were brave enough, down it. The Twist had been and mostly gone, but in this place at least, jiving lived on. Jiving was what girls were good at; they practised in their front rooms, always with their best friend, until their movements flowed precisely with each other's, like the neat unfolding of flowers. Rita and Pat were dancing to 'It's my party', their faces expressionless, unless one of them – nearly – made a mistake. Then they gave each other little professional smiles to show it was all right. Malcolm was not going to take the chance of showing himself up, but the next song was 'Anyone who had a heart', and Kay pulled him on to the floor, and moved close to him. Theresa watched and waited, and exchanged an occasional word with Alan as the records played.

As the song came to an end, Kay whispered to Malcolm and he smiled. Theresa went hot and cold. Anything, she thought, she would do anything to have him smile at her. Kay and Malcolm made their way to the side of the room and then slipped through the fire door. It was eight o'clock.

Rita and Pat had been talking about him for weeks, indulgently and patronisingly, as if he was a child, a pretty spoilt child whom you couldn't help but humour. Theresa felt she must talk about him. She went up to the group of older boys and girls where Rita and Pat were standing and laughing. Rita did not encourage her sisters to mix with her at the youth club. She only came now to the monthly dance, never the ordinary nights. Soon she would stop coming altogether and move into bigger, wilder, less old-fashioned nights out, where her sisters would not, because they could not, follow.

Theresa stood next to Pat. 'Where's Malcolm?'

Pat scanned the room. 'He was with Kay. I don't know where they've gone.'

'He's nice-looking.'

'Yes.' Pat smiled that tolerant smile. 'And he knows it. He's too big for his boots, you know. He thinks we're all after him. And –' she lowered her head to Theresa and whispered, 'he's got wandering hands.'

Theresa heard these words not with her ears, it seemed, but with her body. A shiver started – she couldn't have said where – and reached down her legs and up her back, and reverberated through her. At the same time, she saw as clear as if she was on the fire escape with them, Malcolm's hands wandering round Kay's willing body. She said loudly, 'Malcolm's taken Kay outside.'

Rita was annoyed to be interrupted, but she

couldn't ignore the remark. Taking her friend with her, she went – discreetly, because Rita was not vulgar – to the fire door. Theresa waited where she was and saw Kay being brought back in – thwarted but not chastened – and Malcolm following, looking a little pink but still smiling politely.

He stood uncertainly for a minute or two before walking nonchalantly to the stage and the record player and beginning a conversation with Alan. Theresa watched Alan duck his head to avoid looking Malcolm in the eye, but he answered, and they seemed to be talking about the records, Malcolm picking them up and looking at the B sides.

Theresa went back to her place on the stage and looked at him. She had never seen anyone in real life so gorgeous. Not as gorgeous as Paul McCartney, but unlike Paul, he was here and now and touchable. He smiled at her, across the little eight-piles of records, and continued to talk. Theresa could barely smile back. Having received a smile, which had been the ultimate she longed for, she wanted him to speak to her. At last he did.

'Are you Rita's sister?'

'Yes.'

'How old are you?'

'Sixteen.'

'Got a boyfriend?'

'Not at the moment.'

'Not?' he jerked his head at Alan.

'No.' Theresa was mortified that he might have thought she went out with Alan.

'Want to dance?'

'In a minute.'

She would not trust herself to jive, but hoped for a slow one to be next. They danced to 'Don't let the sun catch you crying'. This happens. You meet someone, you like them, they like you, it's easy, it's love. She had never believed it before. It was the peak of the evening. Somehow, after that, she and Malcolm became part of Rita's group. Theresa didn't like it; she didn't understand the jokes, though Malcolm seemed to, and she wanted to dance slow dances with him, not stand in a corner listening to the talk of people she hardly knew. She became scared. Was this what being in love would be like? She shrank and stopped trying to follow the talk and laughter.

Suddenly Malcolm wasn't there anymore. She looked and saw him dancing with Kay. She thought he liked her, but now she felt she must be wrong, so she didn't try any more to smile at him, or flirt, or be nice. Maybe that was what changed her life.

Rita and I worked in the office, you see, and Malcolm worked – or was employed – in the stores. On a Thursday evening, everyone was paid, so all the men from the stores, and the other bits of the shop, came upstairs, and Rita sat at a desk behind a little window and pushed their pay packets at them through the tray underneath. Of course you couldn't start a conversation in those circumstances, with fifteen blokes behind you wanting their money, but there were other occasions when we saw Malcolm.

We might – one or sometimes both of us – be sent down to the warehouse with a message, or a receipt that hadn't been signed properly, or we might be on the shop floor emptying a till when Malcolm would come out of the service lift with boxes on a sack barrow. And there were lunch times.

He was lovely to look at. His face managed both to have definition and be soft and boyish. His eyes were blue and he smiled a lot. He was only working there, he said, to get some experience, because he was going to be taken on in his dad's firm, just as soon as he knew a bit about shops. His dad, we were given to understand, owned a firm of shop-fitters which employed three men, which, in time, Malcolm would manage and, in time, own. Rita and I had never met anyone, apart from the window-cleaner, who owned their own firm. And who employed men. It was aristocracy.

Rita treated Malcolm as if he was slightly ridiculous, but I could never see him like that. He wasn't stuck up and he didn't brag about his prospects, just let it out as if he couldn't really understand how such luck could have happened to him. He fancied Rita like anything and there were soon all sorts of jokes and allusions going back and forth between them, and I think that was how he came to our youth club with us. It was to do with who would ask who to go out and who would decide where to go.

Rita told me she had no intention of going out with him but she didn't mind having him as a friend. That's what we said in those days, 'I just like him as a friend.' Well, I didn't. Given half a chance, I would have liked him as a lover. Even the unspoken word "lover" at that time would cause me to go pink and sweaty with lust, but I tried hard not to let anyone guess. I wasn't at all sure it was normal to feel what I felt.

Anyway it ended up that we – not just Rita but both of us – would take him to our Youth Club once-a-month Friday dance. Kids in those days used youth clubs longer than they do now – my kids used to roll their eyes when I told them about it. Worse, it was a church youth club. I'd been in the church (Sunday school, Brownies, confirmation, Girl Guides, Bible class, youth club, the whole lot) since I could walk, just about, because my mum, being on her own, thought it would be a good way for us to have a social life. Rita and her sisters didn't have anything to do with it until they hit their teens, and they moaned like anything about having to come to church, but there it was, it was the rule, and if you didn't turn up on a Sunday you'd be turned away at the door on a Friday.

And I don't know whether it was like that for Theresa, but I do know that night was when Malcolm met Rita's two younger sisters, and the thing that has always puzzled me – well, it comes later, and I think I could make it into a story.

They – the writing group that is – are not enthusiastic about the story, though at coffee break Jocelyn tells me how she remembers the music of those days, and how just the names of the songs can take her back.

'I was at boarding school you see, but we were allowed to go into town on Saturdays, and I used to buy a record with my pocket money. They were six and eightpence, do you remember? If I had a pound for my birthday, I would buy three. Then we used to play whatever I'd bought all evening on the record player in the Common Room. Only on Saturday evenings though, it was locked up all through the rest of the week.' She sighs wistfully. 'Happy days.'

'Have you still got them, your records?'

'I have but I can't play them. I'm just CDs these days.'

'If you ever want to sell them –' I'm thinking of Don, though why, when we cannot move in our house for records, I can't fathom.

She shakes her head, appalled, and I wish I hadn't asked her, because I wouldn't like it if I had to part with things that are so entangled with my life and who I am.

When I get home, Don is listening to Dylan. How strange we found that to begin with, how we struggled to like him; how young and innocent he sounds now, just a boy. I suppose it's us that's changed, not him.

I wouldn't want you to think that Don was only a boring man with a big record collection. He has many good points. He's loyal, and would never criticise me to anyone, in the family or out; even in private he's always fair. He sticks by the people and the things he loves, or is used to; he visits his dad, keeps up with his sister and brother, sends birthday cards to his nephews and nieces, and his uncles and aunts, without being reminded. He was a good dad when our children were little, patient and sympathetic, and he's even better now, much better than I am, I know it.

He does things in the house, though he does moan about not being able to have room to manoeuvre while he's doing them, and he does hang back when it's an electrical thing, though you'd think he could knock them off without thinking, as it's his job. He can cook too, and we've always taken turns at doing the evening meal, until recently when I finished work and it seemed silly not to do it myself. He's not quiet within the family, he's chatty and cheerful and encouraging, and if his reluctance to go anywhere and see anyone is a frustration to me, I do love him, though I don't know what I mean by that. I want to protect him, I feel I have to defend him.

Anyway, I'm missing a week of the writing class because Kezia is coming home for a few days and I don't want to miss any of her. To think that there was a time when Kez was the one we worried about. Would she ever learn to read? Why couldn't she concentrate?

Suppose she didn't get any GCSEs? Her teachers loved her, and no wonder, because she was sunny and obliging then, just as she is now. 'She'll be fine,' they said. 'She's not academic but she's not stupid.'

It didn't make sense to me. Katie, though physically clumsy, had come through with her mental abilities intact; Zoe was demonstrably very bright; Matthew, though only a baby when Kezia was going to secondary school, seemed to be a quick learner. We were the stupid ones, Don and me, for worrying, but we just wanted her, more than the others even, to be perfect. Wasn't she the symbol of the damage we had overcome? After three grim years of hostility and discontent, hadn't we made up, got back on track, all by ourselves without counsellors or marriage guidance, and had this perfect golden baby. Why then couldn't she learn to read?

And then late on Sunday, she rings to say she's not coming. She doesn't say why. Don shrugs and says nothing but I can tell how disappointed he is from the way he swallows hard, as if something is stuck in his throat. He goes into the front room and puts on Buddy Holly.

I begin putting the extra food I've prepared – lasagne, her favourite, and rhubarb crumble – into the freezer and begin a mental interrogation of her. 'What's the matter? Is it me? Has something upset you? Why can't you tell us why? Have we done something? Have we said something? Is it because you're gay?' (She's never said she is, but I think she might be. Don doesn't.)

But even inside my head, she doesn't answer and I put the kettle on with a heavy heart and think how right that phrase is, because something in my chest is weighing me down so that my shoulders, reflected in the kitchen window, are slumped forward. That's my heavy heart, weighing me down, I think.

So on Tuesday I go after all to the writing group, and Jocelyn at least is pleased to see me. 'I thought you said you weren't coming.'

'I did. But I'm here. My daughter couldn't make it after all.'

'I'm glad you've come.' Jocelyn doesn't have any children; if Jean was here, she'd sympathise with me, but again she's stayed away, along with Julia.

Times they are a-changing

Ted Doughty liked having children. He was still in the army when the eldest was born, and Kath sent him little black and white snaps of her sitting in her pram in the garden, squinting into the sun.

He kept them in his wallet, with the picture of his mother. When Theresa was born, he had been demobbed. He cycled to work every day, and back home to a house that for all that the babies cried and squabbled, had in it the deep peacefulness of family that he had wanted. Kay was born eleven months after Theresa.

Ted was a nice dad. If he was digging the garden, he would stop and gently remove from Kay's hand the worm that she was raising to her lips. On summer evenings, he let them play in the water as he hosed his roses. On winter evenings, he played Snakes and Ladders with them. On Sundays, he dried them in front of the fire after their bath, and cut their finger and toenails for them, with great care and calmness. When he smacked them, for quarrelling, or snatching, or answering back, he did it slowly as if reluctant to hurt them, or else half-heartedly because he thought they were funny but had to stop himself laughing at them. They feared their mother's smacks much more. When Kay was seven, Kath and Ted had another daughter,

Valerie, and then lastly, a boy. The three older girls no longer wanted their dad to cut their toenails and make pipe-cleaner animals for them; they looked on indulgently as he played with Val and Tony. They knew they had been replaced and they hardly cared at all.

By the time they were teenagers, as the 50s turned into the 60s, Ted wondered how he had ever cut up their toast into soldiers, or peered into hedges with them to see the spiders in their webs, or held their skinny bodies upside down to help them do cartwheels on the grass. For several years now, they had baffled him and he had withdrawn from the struggle.

Kath continued to battle, making scenes about the height of their heels, the height of their hair, the height of their folly. The three girls argued and fought among themselves, about each other's clothes and possessions, about friends, about boys, about whether Elvis Presley was better-looking than Bobby Vee – (Rita said he was, Theresa said he wasn't, Kay said she wouldn't push either of them out of bed. Kath hit her round the ear and offered to wash her mouth out with soap. Ted lifted his Evening Standard so they wouldn't see him smile.)

Now, on this sunny May Saturday morning, as Ted was thinking he would thin out his carrots, he found himself being hauled back from the shed to take part in a new argument.

'Give me a reason,' Kay was saying. 'Go on, give me a reason.'

'You're too young,' said Kath.

'Too young for what? Too young for what? Go on, tell me. Give me a reason.'

Rita and Theresa were there in the kitchen, ready to join in, but uncertain which side to join.

'Tell her, Ted,' said Kath. 'She wants to go on holiday with Malcolm.'

The words hardly communicated anything to Ted. How was it possible to go on holiday without your own family?

'She wants what?'

'See. You're not going. You're too young.'

'What do you think I'm going to *do*?'

Rita and Theresa looked at each other. What would Kay say next?

'Your father's told you. You're not going. I don't know what his parents are thinking of.'

Kay began to cry. She knelt on the floor beside Ted's chair and leaned her face on his arm. 'Dad, it's not like that. Just, Malcolm's mum and dad are really nice, and they've got a caravan near Clacton and they said I can go with them, and help look after his little sisters.'

Ted realised that he had seen Malcolm a few times, a fair, and pleasant enough youth. Malcolm always seemed to be accompanied by at least two of Ted's daughters, and often, a number of their friends as well.

'Where do they live?' It was all he could think of to say.

'What does it matter? *'Where do they live?''* Kath was detecting a weakening in the parental position.

'They live up Willow Road. I've been to their house.'

'So have I,' said Theresa, but quietly, so nobody heard.

So have I, thought Rita, but she didn't say it.

'She's too young to *have* a boyfriend,' said Kath. 'Never mind –' She could not finish the sentence.

'Mum, he's not my boyfriend –' Rita and Theresa looked about to say something but didn't. '– he's just a friend. Honestly mum, lots of people go on holiday with their friends. Mum, why can't I go? Give me a reason.'

'I told you. You're too young. You've only just left school.'

'Too young for what?'

'That's enough,' Kath shouted. 'Another word from you, and you'll feel the flat of my hand. That's it. I don't want to hear of it again.'

In the next few days, they heard of it again and again.

'She's stupid,' said Rita to Theresa in the back bedroom that Rita shared with Kay. 'How can she think mum would let her?'

'Do you think she would – you know?' said

Theresa.

'Do you?'

'Yes.'

'Has she said?'

'She's crazy about Malcolm. She told me she wants to get engaged.'

'Silly little cow.'

'Reet?'

'What?'

'What if – would mum and dad let her go if one of us went too? We could keep an eye on her.'

'Why should they?'

'It would keep her quiet. I think dad's getting fed up of it.'

'If it was up to dad, she'd go. He always gives in where Kay's concerned.'

'So do you.'

'So do you. Ask him then. Or do you want me to ask him?'

'Do you want to go?'

'No I don't,' said Rita firmly. 'Babysitting isn't my idea of a holiday. Me and Pat are going to Torquay.'

'On your own?'

'With her mum.'

'Has mum said you can?'

'Haven't asked yet. But if she lets Kay go, she can't stop me, can she?'

Theresa hadn't been thinking politically. She

knew only that she could not – and she could feel it was going to happen – could not let Kay be on her own with Malcolm for a whole week. Rita understood this.

'So you'd go with Kay and play gooseberry?'

'I don't mind.'

'Are you sure? Because you like him too. Can you stand watching Kay snogging with him all hours of the day?'

'She might not.'

Rita laughed. 'I'll see what I can do.'

So Kay, with Theresa as chaperone, went with Malcolm and his parents, and his two little sisters, to the caravan near Clacton.

When I read the story, the third week back, there is a bored flat silence as I finish. They didn't like it. I know because none of them is waiting to say something, nobody is trying to catch Jerry's eye to put in their two pennorth; nobody is trying to catch my eye to smile or nod.

I'm going to say something. I can feel it gathering, and I jump in, just ahead of Jerry.

'I'm not very happy with it,' I say, deviously. 'Can you help me see how to improve it?'

No, nobody can. Jerry says, 'It doesn't have enough shape to be a short story, Pat. Sometimes I think you might be writing a novel.'

'If I was,' I say slowly, 'would it be any good?'

Judy's face is saying No, but Jocelyn says, out of loyalty only, I'm sure: 'Well, I'd read it.'

Joan says, 'Any novel is a big achievement, dear, even if it's not good enough to publish.'

Jeff says, 'You might as well go for it. You never know what could happen,' and he sighs dramatically.

Jerry says, 'On balance, if you ask my opinion, and it's obviously only my opinion, I would say, have a go, it will do you no harm – all that practice – and you'll learn something –'

'She'll learn that it's not as easy as it seems,' says Jeff, and that's the end of the advice. Jean and Julia aren't there – missed last week as well, and there is no word of them. I miss Julia and worry about how she is, and I decide not to bother with going to the pub. Judy and Jocelyn go anyway and I wish I could change my mind,

149

but it's too late.

The rain has stopped as I walk home, avoiding the black bags of rubbish outside the shops, and the gutters which cars will drive through on purpose to splash me. When I reach home I notice that there is no music coming through the front door, but I assume that he's on the phone, or changing the disc.

The curtains are closed, and I can't see any lights on, but I see there is a pane missing from the front door and the space is covered with a board. I still don't feel any alarm, but sticking out from the letterbox is a piece of paper torn from a diary which reads, 'Don't worry, all OK, go to no. 46 for info.'

This is not in Don's writing, or in any that I recognise, and I am baffled. 46 is next door, and although the bloke has lived there for ages, sometimes with one woman, sometimes with another, and we speak as much as a good morning, I don't even know his name. It's inconceivable that Don should be there. So I put my key in the lock, but find it isn't locked. This is insane, that at 9.45 in the evening in North London, anyone, in or out, would leave their front door unlocked.

I'm not scared of much. People with knives, people out of their heads, dogs, rats, fleas, blood, faeces, I've been sent to houses containing some or all of those. But those were other people's houses, this is mine.

My house has been violated, is completely dark, unlocked, and Don has gone. Have we been burgled? Where's Don? Who wrote the note? Is this something to do with Matthew? (Why I thought that I have no idea.)

Should I go next door? Is it a trap? I pull the door shut again without looking in. But where is Don? I imagine him bound and gagged, or bleeding and dead and I try to look through the letterbox, but everything is dark inside.

But I'm saved from the decision because Mr Nextdoor appears on his doorstep and calls me across to the fence.

'I've been looking out for you,' he says. He's about my age, with a face that doesn't know how to smile, but he seems concerned, and ready, in a suspicious sort of way, to help. 'The lady says to tell you that your husband will be at Casualty but not to worry. You can get her on her mobile, she says.' He hands me another piece of the same diary paper with a number on it, but no name.

'Which lady?'

He shrugs. 'I'm just going in me front door and she calls me, and she's sounding in a bit of a state so I go over to help and your husband, he's fell off something I think and he can't get up to open the door, so we put the glass through, and she's already called the ambulance, and that's about all I know really.'

'Is he all right?'

He shrugs again. I'm obviously asking questions that are beyond him. 'He's conscious, cos he says to me, thanks mate. Think he might have knocked a tooth out, bit of blood you know. I don't know what else. Anyway, I've boarded up your window, had a bit of board out the back, it'll be all right till the morning, and I've took the broken glass away but watch it, there might still be some about you know. Mind how you go in.' He turns to go back into his house and is almost shutting the door before I remember to call to him, 'Which hospital?' and then, 'Thank you.'

When I get there, in a taxi because I know from experience that you can't park a car at these places, and I have got some wits left about me, I ask for Don at the desk. The young woman looks through her lists.

'He's gone down to the plaster room. Your best bet is to wait here. I'll let you know when they bring him back.'

'Can you tell me, did he come in on his own? I mean, was anyone with him?' She doesn't know. I go outside and ring the number on the piece of paper, but the Vodaphone I have dialled has been switched off.

Eventually, after the plaster room, after the emergency dentist, after waiting for the painkillers and the appointments, at two in the morning, I get home, leaving Don under observation on the ward in case he's concussed himself. I'm glad now that I didn't open the door before. The sideboard in the hall – used to be Auntie Peggy's – is listing sideways, there's blood on the carpet, and glass and shards from broken ornaments as well.

Tomorrow, I'm thinking, let me just get to bed and tomorrow we can get down to all the practicalities. Ever since I knew that Don was not going to die I've been making a list in my head. Phone his work. Phone Katie, Zoe, Kez and Matthew. Phone the mysterious number.

Call glazier. Clean up hall. Set Don up in comfort with a way of summoning me from anywhere else in the house. Get in stock of magazines and sudokus for him. Also drinking straws. Special diet. Make dentist's appointment. And even while the list is arranging itself in my head, under the fluorescent lights of the waiting room, I'm also remembering that we did go to Torquay, Rita and I, with my mum and a woman from mum's work, whose name I forget, but who remains in my memory as person who had three ice-creams a day, every day, while we were there, as if it was a duty.

Our excitement, mine and Rita's, as the holiday approached, well I couldn't begin to explain it to one of today's seventeen-year-olds. It was a feeling that this was the first time we'd been grown up, that there were unknown delights in store for us, that Torquay was the most exotic destination ('They call it the Riviera, you know.')

Mum and I had been on holiday before, usually to Clacton; this year was arranged under the influence of this new friend, and was seen as a rare adventure. Rita I don't think had ever stayed away from home; they never went on holiday, and if you asked her about a holiday, she would say something about 'days out' – but I never heard of any specific day out. Really, when you think about it, she had quite a deprived childhood, being the eldest of five. Her dad worked in a factory and wasn't even a charge-hand, and her mum never got a job to help out, even when Tony started school.

I get into bed, never more thankful that I haven't got to get up early, but of course, I can't sleep. I know now that Don fell off the hall sideboard while he was changing the light bulb, but I don't understand it. My mind is circling round the question of whether I should take the car to pick him up or a taxi, should I get some shopping before I go, or will it be all right to leave him on his own for half an hour in the afternoon?

Stupid questions which I can solve easily, but which persist in returning over and over again. I will think about something else.

Torquay, 1963. Rita and I sitting on beaches, strolling round shops, meeting boys, going to dances. It was one week, but we must have packed a lot in because just the memories would take me more than a week to get through. People's heads turning to look at Rita in the street. Music in the fun fair, songs from last year or the year before, Brenda Lee and Billy Fury, and young men spinning us on the Waltzer. The sun going down over the sea, me saying 'Can you imagine what it would be like to live here?' and Rita replying, 'Or somewhere even better?'

One day – on quite a few occasions actually – we talked about Malcolm.

'Oh I know, Pat, I've said all those things about him but I do like him, really. I think,' she said, 'that you could say I'm in love with him.'

'But do you love him?' This was a distinction we were grappling with.

'I don't know. How do you know?'

'Would you marry him?'

'Not on your life. That's the trouble, he likes all the girls and they all like him.'

'But he fancies you.'

'When I'm there with him. Have you seen him with other girls, with those cows down on Cosmetics, and the two in the tea room? And I bet he chats up the hairdressers when he goes up there with their boxes of shampoo. Come on Pat, you've seen how he lets Kay think he's her boyfriend.'

'Well she says – I mean, she has gone on holiday with him.'

'You see. And she won't fight him off, will she?'

'But Theresa's there too. They can't do much in front of her.'

'No I know. But that's not the point is it. The point is that you couldn't trust Malcolm Johnson as far as you could throw him. If you think I'm going to put myself through that, now or ever, you've got another think coming, Pat Plant.'

When I look at the hall the next day, I realise that the reason the sideboard is listing to one side is that the floorboards have disintegrated underneath it. Don is home – unconcussed – and in bed, with a CD player, dosed up to the eyeballs with Co-codamol, but even if I could call him down to look at this, I don't know if I would. I know what I'm looking at and it's called woodworm. It's going to cost money.

I search through the garage for a bit of something to slide under the sideboard to get it looking horizontal while I think about this. When I've swept up the glass, and taken the bloody rug away and replaced it with another one, and tidied away the broken ornaments into a cupboard – I think they're beyond repair but I'd be sad to see the back of Auntie Peg's whistling boy – it looks unremarkable again.

I phone the girls, whose mobiles are all turned off, but I leave the same message on each. Matthew's will not even go to voicemail, but that's nothing unusual. As the day goes on, the girls call me back one by one, and I tell them the story, leaving out the awful bits about fear and pain, both mine and Don's.

'Well, one broken wrist – that's the left one, and one broken collar bone – that's the right one, and really bruised ribs and a bumped head, but they say he wasn't concussed – no I don't know how they can tell – and he's loosened some teeth but they think they'll be able to save them. He's got this sort of gumshield in and he's just on soup and tea through a straw. I'll get him to ring you later, when he wakes up.'

Each of them blames me, or so it seems.

'What was he doing standing up there when there was no one else in the house?'

'Mum, I've always told you your house is a death-trap.'

'Where were you?'

And I counter with: 'Have you heard from Matt? I can't get through to him.'

'He was OK on Saturday,' says Zoe. 'He texted me to say he was on a National Express bus.'

'Going where?'

'Didn't say.'

'Didn't you ask?'

'All right. Wouldn't say.'

I also ask each of them if they recognise the mysterious number, but they don't, and so I ring it once more and this time get voicemail: 'Hi, it's Val. Leave your number and I'll ring you later.'

Val. What, Rita's Val? My Val? I ring it again to check out the voice and I believe it is. What was she doing here? Briefly, I consider the possibility that she and Don were having some sort of affair but it's too ridiculous to go any further with the thought.

The day goes quicker than I thought possible, with much running up and down stairs. I have to feed Don, change the CDs, flush the toilet – actually I have to hold his willy for him, and it's a long time since I've done that; we don't look at each other – hold the glass to his lips when he takes the painkillers, adjust the duvet and the pillows, hold the phone to his ear. When he starts to feel a bit better and wants to get up, I shall have to open doors, turn on lights, put his clothes on for him, turn pages, and probably write the numbers in his sudokus for him. At the moment, I'm all concern and solicitousness but I know it won't last, I was never cut out to be a nurse.

In the night I am woken from sleep in the spare bed by Don calling me.

'I'm cold,' he says.

'I'll get you a blanket.'

'No, rub my feet.' Don always liked his feet rubbed. When we were courting, he used to sit with his feet on my lap so that I could massage them, and I did, because I loved him, even when his socks were smelly. Now I sit on the edge of the bed and take a foot between my two hands; he's right, they are very cold. I rub, vigorously at first, but slow down when I get tired.

'Give me the other foot.' But it's hard on the back, sitting on the bed in a rather twisted position. 'I'll go and get you a hot water bottle.' Because I know we've got one, downstairs in a cupboard, along with a pile of cushion covers and rubber undersheets and pillow protectors and a bag of clothes from when the children were little that I have never parted with.

Don might say they are white elephants, it's the sort of phrase his mother would have used, but saying that only proves to me that he doesn't understand. I know there's too much stuff in the world, in our house, in the shops, in lofts and cellars – where they have cellars. What wouldn't I give for a cellar? And all over England, in those places you get now, where you can store your stuff in boxes, and what? And never see it.

'You would forget you've got it,' I've said to Don and to the children.

And Kez says, 'Mum if you forget about it then you can't really want it, can you?' But she's wrong, the feeling of wanting it grows by having it there.

'Minimalism,' says Zoe, 'is what you want nowadays.

You'd be a different person if you didn't live in this junk shop.' She always wants me to be a different person, and she's right, I would be.

There are the sideboards: mine, my mother's, her mother's and Peggy's, and when I see them, even when I'm squeezing past them with the hoover or the shopping or a tray of cups, I get the feeling and even the smell of their old houses and their old owners.

My nan's sideboard must have been bought quite late in her life; it's a cheap, nasty thing with flaking varnish and hard art deco corners which have bruised my hips many a time, and it brings her back to me, in her black coat down to her ankles – mourning for all those men – and her black hat of matted felt and her pearl earbobs. I've got those too, in a drawer, in a box lined with maroon velvet, and if I didn't have them, I might forget that she used the word "earbobs" to name them.

Peggy's sideboard, a plain and solid Utility item, is in the hall because it's the narrowest of the four. I use it, luckily as it happened, for unbreakable things, table-cloths, lace – and I mean lace – doilies, runners – people don't know what runners are these days, even I don't use them – serviettes; all kinds of embroidered bits and pieces. Who would want them if I didn't keep them? But on the top of the sideboard, apart from the phone and the phone books, it's all Peg's stuff. She was a woman for ornaments. Figures mostly, a few animals too, and then vases, glass bowls, candlesticks, brass birds and shoes and bells.

Most of them survived the accident but the glass is

shattered of course, and the whistling boy – oh I did love him – I think he might be past repairing. I just love his sweet face and his neat pursed lips and his bare legs and feet, and I took him from Peg's house when she died – when I was only eighteen – and had him in my bedroom. I could cry now, thinking about him without his head and with a nasty looking crack from shoulder to base.

He would never have changed if Don hadn't been so clumsy, whatever else might change. Other boys might grow up and go away and turn into a strangers; he would have stayed the same. Well, I've kept the pieces and put them in the drawer where I keep spare cutlery that we never use, but he's only a cheap pot figure. No one will put him right, he'll just crumble into dust.

The whistling boy, and Peg's sideboard and the orange horse, all gone the way of all things. And poor Don up in bed with his bruises, and it's an hour and a half since I went up to change the CD, and no one wants that many repeats of Pink Floyd, not even him. Poor Don, and poor Peg dying on that train station. How will I remember her without her whistling boy in the hall seeing all my comings and goings?

Val turns up at the house at five-thirty, apologetic for not waiting at the hospital (cat had to be let out, or in, or something) and for not ringing (tried but it was engaged).

She visits Don in his room, offering daffodils and Terry's All Gold, and then comes downstairs to find me in the kitchen, pureeing. She stops at the door, there being no room for her to come any further, and I put the kettle on.

'What time was it then, when you called? I should have told you I go out on a Tuesday.'

'About seven. I felt awful, Pat, I thought I'd done it by ringing the bell, and making him jump, you know, but he says not. He says, just a coincidence, it was the sideboard that gave way.'

'I know. Don't tell him, he doesn't know yet, but the floor's got woodworm. But I'm so glad someone was here. He could have been lying there for hours.'

'Well he was for a bit until that nice man –' (Nice man?) '– came and helped. I never even found out his name.'

'No, neither did I.'

We go round and round the events of the night before, putting things in order and tying them up and decorating them with inconsequential bits and pieces, and Val joins me in some cheese on toast before I go to give Don his soup, and she goes, promising to call again next week.

The next day, in the evening, Katie arrives. Not with Alfie, which is a big disappointment to me.

'How could I, mum? When the house is all upside down and Dad's out of action?'

'But we would love to see him.'

'Come and see us when Dad's better. What would he do here? He'd be impossible.'

'But can Jay look after him?'

'They'll be fine.'

Katie and I get along well, now that we don't live together, but she still feels, like the others, that she has to give me advice on how to live my life.

'Honestly mum, there's no way you can keep the house clean like this. You need more space. You've got three housefuls in here.'

'Yes, but two of them are only little housefuls.'

'Nan had more than she needed in hers. Do you want to be like her?'

'Because she had Peggy's things. She didn't feel she could throw them out.'

'OK, but what's stopping you? How long has Peggy been dead?'

'I don't know.'

'You do, mum. What year was it?'

'Um, 1966, or maybe 65. Just before Christmas.'

'And Nan kept all this hideous stuff. Why?'

'Some of it was her mother's.'

'Mum it's junk. Junk with woodworm. Get rid of it, before your house falls down.'

Zoe arrives on Friday. She's keen on insurance.

'How much is your contents cover?'

'Zoe, no one is going to steal it, even if they could lift it.'

'If you had a fire?'

'Zo,' says Katie. 'A fire would be a blessing. This stuff is worth nothing.'

'Most of it,' agrees Zoe. 'But some of the clocks, maybe. You should go through it, inventory it, get some of it valued. You never know.'

Other times she tells me off for not buying AVCs, for having an ISA with a low rate of interest, for not knowing how much Don's pension will be, for not making our money work for us. She wants to know what I have done with my retirement lump sum, which is a hard one to answer, given that I haven't really retired.

She takes time off to point out that we should eat more fruit and vegetables, and makes Don drink smoothies. She always buys organic.

'You should, you know,' she says (this is to Katie, not me), 'you don't know what you might be feeding your children. There are pesticides and herbicides and you never know what they might be doing to their little brains.'

Katie thinks she's ridiculous.

'Do you know Zo, even if I could afford it, I wouldn't. My kids are OK as they are. I don't want to turn them into health freaks. I haven't got time in my life to worry about what we're eating.'

'This is from you who wastes time writing to prisoners.'

'What do you mean – "wastes"?'

'Well where does it get you? Where does it get them, even? You could be spending that time with Alfie.'

'Don't be stupid. Like you spend every spare minute with Grace.'

'I do.'

'How come you go to work then? Just so you can have your new car and your new dishwasher and all the rest?'

'So you don't work?'

'You know I do, and you know I have to, and that is all you know about me, Zo. You know nothing about what my life is like, so don't you tell me – '

I go upstairs and sit with Don and listen to Bridge over Troubled Water.

Kezia comes on Saturday, full of remorse for not being here, because it wouldn't have happened if she had been, but without giving an explanation of why she wasn't.

The three of them settle back into old patterns: they talk together as if they see each other every week and they take up predictable positions, predictable and oppositional. Kez joins in with Katie, citing the appalling feng shui that we have created, and agrees with Zoe about our diet. Her own angle is my thwarted energy.

'Because what do you do with your time?'

'I do lots.'

'Like what?'

'Look after your father.'

'No. I don't mean right now. The rest of the time.'

'I just do whatever I like.'

'Which is?'

I begin to lie. 'I see people.'

'Who?'

'I go places. I look after the house.'

'No you don't,' says Katie, 'There's inches of dust under those sideboards.'

'I worry about all of you.'

'Why?'

'No – stop,' says Zoe. 'Who are these people you see?'

'People, friends.'

'Like, people you used to work with?'

They don't know it but I know that's not very likely; none of them would want to know me. 'Like Kay and Val.'

'Oh yeah?'

'And Jocelyn and Judy.'

'Who are they?'

'Just people I know. You don't know them.'

'Is this,' says Zoe suspiciously, 'that writing class?'

'Yes.'

'That one you told Matt you don't go to?'

'My god Zoe, will you lot stop ganging up on me.'

'That's great,' says Kezia. 'I said you should do something creative, but I never thought of writing. I thought perhaps embroidery would suit you, or tapestry. Are you going to show us?'

'No.'

'What are you doing, Zo?'

'Texting Matthew.'

The thing is – about things, I mean – that in the old days, when my mum was a child, say, people didn't have much stuff. Mum used to tell me about the family next door to her where they had nine children and only two beds.

'Ginger,' she used to say. 'Every one of 'em was ginger, but they didn't have two sticks of furniture to make a fire with.'

Posh people had houses that they owned, and when someone died, I suppose they divided up the Sheraton and the Chippendale between them and put it in those houses. Maybe threw a bit of the inferior stuff up into the attic for the maids, I don't know. But ordinary people, who rented, and got turned out or flitted, they couldn't pay for Pickfords to come and deal with it, it was pile it on a cart and take it to the next place, so just as well there wasn't much of it. No point having a sideboard when there was nothing to put in it.

Later though, I suppose, after the war, when things settled down again and people slowly began to have a little more money, houses started to get more comfortable. Carpets, wallpaper. My nan bought a television for the coronation; a few years later, a fridge.

Even Rita's family, by the time she left school, had a telly and a twin tub, and Ted had given up his pushbike for a moped. When Rita moved in with her Aunt Ginny, they bought her a new bed on the HP and put up pink curtains in her bedroom, and she managed to get away with the family record player, as Malcolm was going to bring his with him when he moved in with Kay.

We used to sit there on occasions, in Rita's little room, listening to singles, and it was much quieter and more comfortable than when she used to share with Kay at her mother's house; no Kay bursting in and singing along or demanding to hear the B side; no Tony whining round wanting us to play with him.

Think for yourself

The kitchen was as bleak and untidy as ever, but people had cleared out their cupboards and the bins were overflowing with boxes of cornflakes that were not worth anybody's effort to carry home to Amersham or Mansfield or Wolverhampton.

Hazel was looking out of the big window.

'Look at that.'

Rita looked down and saw that someone had parked a green Mercedes, shiny as a beetle, on the forecourt.

'Whose is it?'

'That boy, Merlin. His parents.'

Rita knew him, a tall, good-looking, puzzled, dutiful boy. Someone from one of the flats had dropped an egg on to the roof of the car, whether as a protest against the bourgeoisie, or because Merlin was always urging his flatmates to be more considerate and tidy in their habits, could not be ascertained.

'So you're not coming back?' said Hazel.

'No, I'm not.'

'Will you miss us?'

'Oh yes,' said Rita, without enough sincerity to fool even Hazel. She found the girls petty and childish. As soon as she had arrived there, she had known that she was too old for it; she was too old for them. The years at evening classes doggedly acquiring A-Levels had made her too serious; the clothes she had acquired while earning a wage made them think she was superior. There was no group that she fitted into. The folkies, the rich kids, the posers, the potheads. The revolutionaries, who sat on the floor and plotted.

When she heard them talking about the workers, Rita thought of her dad, peacefully watching *Wagon Train* and rolling his cigarettes and putting each one in a Golden Virginia tin for the next day.

She would not miss her study bedroom with its cold white walls, or eating egg and chips in the cafeteria, or the chill concrete of the unfinished buildings, or the disruptions caused by the protesters, or the squalid bar, or the windy green spaces that surrounded the campus, or the ducks and lakes.

She would only miss the huge computer, and the feel of a stack of punch cards in her hand and the peculiar joy of learning difficult things, and the pleasure of being better at it all than the earnest boys she was learning with.

Rita arrived at University full of hope and self-importance. Knowing that she would be older than the other students, she imagined herself being the centre of things. She thought of the number of lecturers – or post-grads at a push – who would take her out in their sports cars.

She had applied nice and early and was allocated a study bedroom on the fifth floor of a dark tower block. It had striped pink curtains at its tall narrow windows and a matching bedspread on its narrow bed. It was bigger and more modern than the bedroom Rita had at her Aunt Ginny's and several times nicer than the one she'd shared with Kay at home.

The other girls in the flat were all just out of school. They congregated in the kitchen, comparing A-Level grades. Before Rita's eyes, they began to pair up into best friends, and one wouldn't venture onto the campus without the other one. They all spent a lot of time in the queue for the payphone on the ground floor. They wore corduroy Levis and unsubtle make-up. Next thing, the swirly-patterned mini-dresses were being shaken out of their suitcases in preparation for the Freshers' dance.

Rita bought a ticket, but never in fact went through the door, observing that there were no men over the age of nineteen in the queue and that the whole thing was more youth club than night club.

So she spent a miserable evening in the draughty lobby by the payphone – now with no queue – trying to phone people she knew. She tried various friends, of both sexes, but no one was in, unless Pat was, but she couldn't ring her as Pat's mother hadn't yet been talked into having a phone.

Once Freshers' week was over, Rita's life improved a bit. She made the acquaintance of the computer, humming with numbers in its air-conditioned, double-locked room. She met the punch-card operators, who were young women more like herself, and she briefly imagined that one day she could manage an office like this, before she reminded herself that she was aiming higher.

There was a period of about two weeks when she was dizzy from the lectures, from new knowledge, from the number of questions she had about the computer and what it could do and what it would do next.

She had a trip to London with Howard (not his real name) and in that crowded flat with flowers in the bathroom, saw another future for herself, with people more beautiful than Howard with his struggling beard, more successful than her tutor with his pigeon toes and nervous eyes, whom she had already caught out making mistakes in his algorithms.

She stuck it out though, through the first term, as the winds grew harsher and colder across the marshes and whipped between the tower blocks. Her friend and the friend's boyfriend came up for a weekend and they went to the Saturday disco, and her friend's underwear was shown up for all to see by the ultra-violet light at the entrance. The boyfriend was bemused – shaken even – by the anarchy of the place, and expressed doubts that the DJ would survive – electrically speaking – the amateur setting up of his equipment.

Then it was Christmas, and there was a brief interlude of going home and trying to make people (Aunt Ginny, Uncle Bernie, Mum and Dad. Malcolm) understand even a hundredth part of what she was doing. But also of being able to have baths, and proper food, and a house where there were no fire doors banging through the night, and where dishes were washed up and put away.

Going back to her lonely study-bedroom was something she thought about with dread, and when she got there and the rain drummed on the windows and she had no friends, it was even worse than she expected. Suddenly she began to wear old jeans and let her hair fall straight, tucked behind her ears; she no longer carried a handbag. She was making less of an effort and beginning to blend in, against her will almost, but she still had no friends.

As the evenings began to get a little lighter and the winds a little softer, Rita became aware – slightly – that some of the students were behaving in a louder and more animated way. There was some purpose in the air. People accosted her to ask if she was going to the meeting. She found her path to the computer suite barred and all the punch-card operators standing in the corridor smoking and chatting.

'Come on,' said her tutor. 'We might as well go.' So she and several others made their way to the big lecture theatre, where one of the many meetings was in progress, this one seeming to be about whether to boycott exams. Young people Rita had never seen before jumped to their feet, shouting 'point of order'.

The talk was of resolutions and amendments. They were busy being angry with great enjoyment and seriousness.

Rita was baffled. She had no opinions, except that they seemed to be wasting her time. Her experience of the previous weeks – of hermit-like study and miserable self-sufficiency – was more attractive than this.

What was wrong with the world, that they should get so angry, and if they wanted to change something, why go for a few exams, which would not hurt anyone if they were taken, and not benefit anyone if they were not? She couldn't even leave the room, she felt, squashed as she was between her tutor and an unknown young man with a pile of chemistry text books.

There was an interruption. A person detached himself from a group which seemed to feel itself central to the proceedings, judging from the amount of noise that came from them.

He came down the steps towards the doors, shouting.

'This is all piss,' he shouted. 'This is fucking nothing. I'm going to Paris.' And he shouldered his rucksack (ready-packed, Rita noted, so this wasn't a totally spontaneous gesture) and made as dramatic an exit as he could, to some scattered applause.

If he can I can, thought Rita. Not Paris, obviously, but I can leave.

She stood up and edged past the chemist, and left the hall, as unobtrusively as she could, and went to the department office and told them she was leaving at the end of term.

She told me all this, or some of it at least, on my hen night.

Hen nights weren't what they are now. It was the evening before the wedding. Don was out with his brother and some others, but as he didn't really have friends, I wasn't expecting that he'd get into any trouble.

Rita and I, and Kay and a couple of others – Merle from school and a girl from my office – had a Chinese meal and a bottle of wine and then came back to my house to look at the dress. The others had all gone by ten o'clock, and then Rita and I sat on my bed and talked as if it was the old days.

It was that meeting – or glimpse – of Paul that made her give up uni. It was so easy to meet famous people, she said. You just had to be where they were, and she turned her head away from education – which had been till then her road to bettering herself – and towards some sort of idea of celebrity.

But Rita and University were never going to work out. How many reasons do you need? She was twenty-one nearly, when she started, she'd supported herself – financially and academically and emotionally through her A-levels, which she'd done at night school, in secret.

I never knew until Zoe did hers, requiring round the clock support, reassurance, counselling and coffee, the magnitude of what Rita had managed to do. Anyway, she got her A-levels, she opted to do computer science, which no one had ever heard of or knew anything about. It was going to be, she said, a big thing.

There was only one other girl on her course, who played in goal in the hockey team and went home to Grimsby at weekends. The rest were boys, and they were – just boys. Rita – older, beautiful, clever – must have frightened them witless. So no one ever spoke to her.

The lecturers, she told me, treated her as if she had strayed in from the office and should not worry her pretty little head about all this, until she showed them what she could do, and then they retreated into being hardly more socially able than the eighteen year olds. Only lecturers from other departments – sociology mostly – took an interest, but she found them earnest and obsessed with politics.

'Married Marxists,' she said to me, though neither of us knew what a Marxist was.

So Howard, or whatever his name really was, because he had the nerve to approach her, was the best she could do.

She might have been different from me in some ways, she might have had a vision of some kind of independence, but after all she came from the same place I did, and if you were twenty-one and not courting strong, then there was something wrong with you. For the first time, I was doing something Rita hadn't managed to do.

Nobody lived with their parents when they got married any more – I think Kay and Malcolm were the last people I knew who tried it, and it didn't last long, whichever family they tried.

Don and I were moving to what we called a flat, but what other people would call a bedsit, on the Hertford Road, above a hardware shop. But it was unfurnished, so we could take the furniture that I'd saved up for, and because the landlord knew Don's mum and dad, it was quite cheap, so that we knew we'd soon have enough for a deposit on a house.

Buying a house was amazing stuff in those days. Most of our parents had never done it and it was aspirational beyond anything they had ever considered. My mum was pleased to be getting rid of me and my furniture (one sideboard, Ercol, one folding Formica kitchen table in a colour called Tango, and a quantity of towels, plates, sheets, mugs and cleaning implements, which I stored inside the sideboard thinking aspiration- ally of the day when it would house a proper dinner service and some Dartford crystal.)

The thing was that when my aunt Peggy died, a lot of her stuff was taken on by my nan, but nan was getting a bit wobbly on her legs and whenever she bumped into bits of furniture, she was inclined to threaten to get rid of it, and mum would say, 'You do that, mum, but wait until Pat leaves home and I'll take it off your hands.'

Mum loved a bargain, and a free chair or occasional table was even better than a bargain. So with me out of the way, she would have room to fit it all in.

Don and I were together for more than three years before we got married. I'd had quite a few boyfriends before, I never knew why because I never claimed to be pretty, but maybe it was because I wasn't shy. Don was shy. Still is.

I was three months off my twenty-second birthday when I got married, which was considered old. A year earlier, we had got engaged and decided it was time to stop being virgins – everybody thinks now that the sixties were full of free love, easy sex, zipless fucks, all those things, but although we heard about it, it was quite another thing to do it. People – our sort of people – who did, ended up getting pregnant. Kay and Theresa and Linda Dickinson were far from being the only ones. The problem pages at the back of the women's magazines were still advising girls against "anticipating the wedding", and warning that heavy petting before marriage could lead to sexual problems afterwards – well I don't know what those problems could have been, because we certainly didn't have them.

But it was only six months before the wedding that I went to my GP and lied about the date of the wedding and got a prescription for the new contraceptive pill. They were horrible, they made you feel sick and headachy every afternoon, and I put on weight round my hips, which were big enough already, but it was worth it for the freedom from the awful fear every month – would I be pregnant? Was I just late or was this it? Did I feel sick or was it just the office cream buns?

In those last months of our engagement, we finally got down to it – proper sex I mean, seeing no point in waiting any longer. We used to talk about it then, describing it to each other, having it all over again, so to speak.

Our wedding was on the same scale as the hen night. I didn't have much family, and Don didn't have any friends, so although it was in the church – the same one where Rita and I used to go to the youth club – we had it in a little side room so that we weren't rattling around like peas in a drum. There was my mum (in a blue suit) and my nan (in a ghastly dress with coffee-coloured lace), both in hats.

There was Don's mum (pale green dress and jacket), and his dad, who was just as shy as Don and never looked anyone in the eye. His brother and sister were there, and an aunt and uncle and one of the cousins.

In the evening, Kay and Malcolm looked in, and Malcolm gave me a kiss and told me I looked beautiful, which I didn't believe for a second, but it was nice of him to say it.

Rita came, with a man I never saw before or after, very tall, rather posh, with nice manners, but apparently bewildered. Rita told me later that he was the only person she knew who owned a suit, so she had invited him to be her boyfriend for the day.

We went to Torquay for our honeymoon, possibly to the hotel that Fawlty Towers was based on, but we didn't know enough to know that it was bad.

We felt grown up – we could have sex when and where we pleased, instead of waiting for my mum to go out, (which, to be fair to her, she had done more and more often). We could look forward and plan for the rest of our lives: a house first, and then two children, a boy and a girl for preference.

We sat on the sand and watched sailing boats in the bay and I said that Darren was a nice name for a boy.

'A bit modern,' said Don, and I thought of Rita's story of how her grandmother had chosen her name, but then he said, 'But, you know, we are modern. We're not going to be like my parents. We don't want to grow apart, do we? We'll always be like this, won't we?'

'Yes,' I said.

Another girl

Malcolm's parents, Ruby and Johnny Johnson, were preoccupied with their younger children. By day, they went on the stony beach next to the caravan, or more often into Clacton for the amusements, or to Walton-on-the-Naze for a good stretch of sand. Malcolm, since he no longer played in the sand, was difficult to cater for on holiday, and they were glad that he'd brought his friends along. His friends, being girls, had the advantage that they could babysit in the evenings while Ruby and Jack went to the clubhouse. So most of the time, Malcolm, Theresa, and Kay, were left to themselves.

Theresa knew Malcolm liked her. On the way, in the train, he had rubbed her foot with his under the table, even while he was holding Kay's hand.

In the caravan, if Theresa was making a sandwich in the kitchen, he would be sure to go past, pressing himself against her as he did, and then go back again. Whenever Kay wasn't looking, his hands moved towards Theresa, and she kept quite still, so as not to draw her sister's attention, and both of them kept their eyes on Kay while he brushed or fondled whichever bit of her was in reach. So far, he had never kissed her, but she knew that he would as soon as the opportunity was there.

Nothing was said.

Malcolm and Kay kissed a lot. Even when his parents were there, she would kiss him, a proper arms-round, full-mouthed kiss.

When there was only Theresa and the children around, she would put her tongue in his mouth and her hands up his shirt, and roll her eyes at Theresa to tell her to take the children out to the swings.

Theresa lifted little Lynne and little Karen on and off playground equipment, and her body was hot and buffeted with knowing what Kay and Malcolm were doing back in the caravan.

Tears came into her eyes as the evening darkened, and she stood at the back of the swings and pushed them alternately, and thought of Kay's plump little body pressed against Malcolm's skinny one and the days seemed endless until they could go home. She hoped – she sometimes believed – that Malcolm would get tired of Kay, and that once they were home he would chuck her and belong to Theresa instead.

At last, the gas light would go on in the caravan, and Malcolm would come out to the swings to fetch them back in, and as Theresa went up the steps, he would stand behind her and run his hand over her bum and down the inside of her leg.

It seemed to her – and she was not an imaginative girl – that it was quite likely she would die before she got home.

On Tuesday afternoon, Malcolm said, 'We need some bread and some things from the shop.'

Theresa was reading a magazine. She knew she would end up going to the shop but she wasn't going to offer and make things easy for them.

Malcolm said, 'Your turn to go, Kay.'

Kay was leaning against him with her head on his shoulder and she rolled down so that her head was in his lap, looking up at him.

'Theresa will go,' she said.

'I went this morning,' said Theresa.

'Go on, Kay,' said Malcolm. 'It's your turn.'

'You come with me then.'

'I'm tired.'

'You come then, Trees.'

'Don't be awkward, Kay,' said Malcolm. 'Theresa will make a cup of tea while you're gone. Get some ice creams as well.'

As soon as Kay was out, into the fine warm drizzle that was falling, Malcolm said, 'Quick.'

Theresa remained where she was, until he pulled her by the hand into the end compartment that she and Kay and the two little children slept in.

Then he kissed her on the mouth, and the

feeling that she had now got what she wanted was quickly followed by the feeling that she wanted something more.

Theresa did not intend to go all the way. She knew that Kay would, maybe already had, but she and Rita had had serious talks. They knew what happened – you got pregnant, boys didn't respect you, your parents turned you out, you had to have a registry office wedding.

Theresa didn't want to get married at the registry office, in a suit, and have no reception and no honeymoon. She wanted a three-tier cake and bridesmaids in pale blue, carrying pink rosebuds. She was also scared of what her parents would feel and do and say. ('You make sure you come back the same as you go', their mother had said when they'd left the house last Saturday morning.)

Rita and Theresa had solemnly agreed that, if the diamond ring was on the finger and the date was set, and not too far away, then they *might* go all the way, but that Kay was common and a scrubber and would end up having to get married. They had seen it happen to other girls often enough. What Theresa hadn't known, and what Rita hadn't known either, or surely she would have mentioned it, was how much she would *want* to do this thing that she believed she did not want to do.

So when Malcolm slid his hand up her skirt

and into her panties ("Downstairs inside" as they called it), she protested with a very small noise which might have meant something else. As he pulled her panties off she squirmed in a way that could have told him she was trying to get away but instead seemed to encourage him, and as he slipped inside her and she gasped, maybe he understood it as a sound of pleasure, not of outrage.

When Kay came back with the bread and ice creams, Malcolm was lounging once again in the sitting area and Theresa, still trembling slightly, was filling the kettle to make tea.

For the rest of the week, Kay and Theresa shared Malcolm's attention, with the difference that, although Theresa knew what he was doing with Kay and when, Kay was unaware that the times she took her turn with the shopping, or visits to the swings, were times that Theresa took her turn with Malcolm.

Kay wanted to stay in the caravan for ever. Theresa was only waiting to get home again so that Malcolm could chuck Kay – because obviously he couldn't cause a scene while they were on holiday – and become her proper boyfriend.

Malcolm was not thinking at all.

This is the story that I would be reading out this evening if I wasn't driving north this morning. Or not reading out, because as soon as I finished it – and I didn't know until I was writing it what it would say – I knew I couldn't face them again if I did.

Not one person in the whole of last term contributed anything with the slightest mention of sex, except, I remember with shame, me with my story of Rita, Tim and Si. The group were not at all positive after that one and I can imagine the horror and embarrassment that will ensue if they have to hear about Malcolm having it away with two sisters; only Judy would cope with it, I think, but John and Jim would never look me in the eye again.

On Saturday, Don comes downstairs and sits, as the centre of attention, in his usual chair. The girls fuss round him, bringing a footstool, and tea and biscuits, asking how he's feeling, is he tired, is the music too loud? After an hour or so, they have reverted to normal, teasing him about his ancient musical taste and singing 'When I'm sixty four' to him, the electrician's song. Ironic, at the moment, given that the lights in the hall are still out.

When we first heard this song, it was funny. It was Paul being cute about old people. We didn't think it would ever be us. I didn't ever foresee then that I would have three grown up women as daughters who would be, in a rare moment of fun and togetherness, jigging round their father and digging each other in the ribs like children.

Even when they stop singing, they carry on laughing at Don and try to think of songs about electricity. Jumping Jack Flash, they say, Electric Dreams. But Don and I know, though we don't look at each other, that his favourite song is just that: Electricity, by Joni Mitchell, and that the kids would never think of that, Joni Mitchell being a sort of joke among them.

On Sunday, Katie and Zoe have to leave to get back to their jobs and families. The house is relieved and lightened without them, I'm sad to find, in spite of the occasional jollity. Kezia assures us she can stay as long as we need her.

I find her turning out a sideboard, not the one in the hall, currently propped up on a bit of an old door from the shed, but the one we've had since we got married, the one I was very proud of, Ercol, that I saved up for and kept in my bedroom until I moved out, just before the wedding.

She's a tall young woman, Kez, rounded, with hips that she inherited from me, but somebody else's breasts. Kneeling on the floor, surrounded by piles of goods like a jumble sale, with her hair tied up in a scarf, she looks, except for being white, like an African market trader.

'What is all this stuff, mum?'

It looks unfamiliar to me, in piles on the floor.

'OK, look. This pile's table mats. How many do you need?'

'Um.'

'You don't use any, ever. And they're hideous. Look, still in the box, never opened. How long have you had these?'

'My mum gave them to me.'

'You mean someone gave them to her and she off-loaded them on you. They're not sacred. They have pictures of Eastbourne on them.'

'Well, they could go.'

This does not stop her, only gives her encouragement. 'This pile is all milk jugs and sugar bowls, and what's this?'

'It's a cake stand. Look, it screws together so you've got two layers.'

'It needs to go. You don't even make cakes.'

'I could.'

'You shouldn't. You're putting on more weight already, since you've stopped working. Now, this lot is tablecloths and stuff.'

Someone knocks at the front door. There is a policeman there.

'Mrs Childs? Can I come in?'

Just as you would expect, my brain runs like a fruit machine through the people I love, and comes to rest at Matthew, just before he says, 'Are you the mother of Matthew Childs?'

We are sitting by now, all of us, at the dining table, him with his notebook open.

'What's he done?' says Don.

'Well nothing wrong, as far as we know. The station's been contacted by South Yorkshire Police and they've asked us to contact yourselves with a view to establish the identity of –'

'He's dead,' says someone, and everyone looks at me.

The policeman looks distressed. 'I'm sorry, ma'am, I've gone and misled you. He's not dead, don't worry about that. No no, I'd have had a WPC with me if it was that bad. Thing is, there's a young man in a hospital in Sheffield. No bones broken, but he's had a bit of a knock on the head and apparently he's not making sense all the time.'

Trust Matt to be a nuisance, I think to myself. Why do I think these things?

'Now, I have to ask you, when did you last see your son?'

'About, I don't know, three weeks ago.' Don and I look at each other, unable to work it out, time has got so peculiar lately.

'This side of Christmas?'

'Yes,' I say.

'No,' says Don.

Kezia looks at us reproachfully.

'Have you spoken to him lately?'

'I've been trying to,' I say. 'I've been phoning him since last Wednesday, to tell him his dad's had an accident.'

'So I see.'

'But his phone's been switched off.'

'He had a phone then? Probably stolen.'

'No it wasn't,' I say. 'He's had it ages. We bought it for him.'

'No no,' he says again. 'What I mean is, the assailant probably stole it from him.'

'What assailant?'

Poor man, his nice face furrows with effort because there is no way to get this in the right order.

'Tell you what,' says Kezia. 'Mum, you go and find a photo of Matt. I'll make a cup of tea. Then we can start again.' She smiles at the policeman.

And I think, while I'm rummaging through a drawer in the front room sideboard, that we must have done something right, because look at Kezia, what a nice person she is, and sensible with it. Mostly, except for the feng shui.

We establish from a description that the young man in the Northern General Hospital is probably Matthew. We learn that he was attacked, or got into a fight, in the early hours of last Thursday, was taken to hospital unconscious, unaccompanied, and without any identification, but has come round, given his name and an address in Tottenham that we don't recognise, but wouldn't – or couldn't – say where he was staying in Sheffield.

We are shaken. Don is white under his bruises. The policeman leaves us with the number of the police station in Sheffield, and the number of the ward. The news has sunk in, so there is no possibility of a mistake. If we found out now that it was a different boy in that bed, we would be puzzled and disoriented. We know it's Matt.

'What shall we do?'

'I'll go and see him,' says Kezia.

Gratitude fills me. 'Can you?'

'But,' says Don.

We have sorted out money for petrol, provisions for the journey, check the route, decide that she won't set off till morning, and then, when she's gone to her room, a strange feeling steals into me, that I find difficult to identify. Envy, disappointment, the feeling that someone has done something wrong. I look at Don listening to Tubular Bells (he's played everything else by now), and he says:

'Better if you went.'

'Do you think so?'

'Well I'd go, but –'

'I'd like to go. Do you think I should?'

'Bloke wakes up in hospital, been beaten up. Does he want his sister or his mum?'

'I haven't been very nice to him.'

'You're still his mum. You go. Kez can stay and look after me.'

So I'm driving north. Our car, kept most of the time in a lock-up garage in the next street, has, as you'd guess, a fine CD player that is probably worth more than the car, but after days of Don being at home and a complete run through of every CD he owns, I have switched off all sound. I have the drumming of the wheels and the swish and thud of the windscreen wipers, and thoughts.

After Don had taken his painkillers and gone off to

bed, Kezia and I talked long into the night, and I would have stayed awake longer if I hadn't had this journey in front of me. Where did it go wrong, I wondered?

'Don't you know, mum?'

'He was a lovely little boy. Then, even before he was a teenager, he just changed. We lost him. And it's just gone on getting worse and worse. I worry about him turning out like Tony.'

'Mum, you have to get off comparing us to that family. We're different.'

'In some ways. But I remember Tony and how he hated everyone after his dad died, and that was the start of it, and Matt seems to hate me, not Dad so much, but me, and Katie.'

'Mum, think about it. Think about what went wrong for him. It's obvious.'

'Not to me it isn't.'

'OK, how old was I when Matt was born?'

'Ten.'

'And Katie?'

'Fifteen.'

'And what happened next?'

'Katie went and got pregnant and had Jay.'

'Yes and moved in here with him and we were all crowded in together and it was like there was a dad – I mean our Dad – and four mums and two little boys. Wasn't it? We all loved Matt and we all loved Jay. Didn't we?'

It's not how I would have put it, but she wasn't wrong. We did all do our best to cherish and deal with and entertain and talk to and have fun with the two little boys, the fair one and the dark one, only six months between them.

But I remembered the arguments I had with Katie over who should do what, the rows that used to spring up like gusts of wind between Katie and Zoe, when Zoe would throw it over her shoulder as she stalked out of the room that Katie was a slag and she was never going to be like her.

I remembered the juggling of babysitting arrangements when I went back to work, and I went back because I thought it would be easy, with having so many women in the house, but I didn't reckon on the complexity of everyone's separate routines, and we used to spend hours working out if Zoe came out of school promptly on time, would she have time to get to the nursery early to collect Jay and take him to meet Katie at the doctor's? And Matt didn't have an appointment, so could Kez pick him up from nursery at the normal time and bring him home? And then I would spend the day, most days, worrying about whether one of them would forget who was doing what.

'Yes I remember all that,' I said.

'And then Katie left home.'

Oh yes, that time. 'Everyone left.'

Zoe had stayed at home while she was at university, as she went to Bedford College, and as she was never the type to want to have a wild time, it suited her to save on rent money. But when she was twenty-two, she found a job in Birmingham and moved out. I thought it would make life easier, but somehow, I took her place in the Arguments with Katie Department, and that was made worse by Katie's new bloke.

I didn't like him. Jay's father had been OK; we liked him well enough, but they were just kids, and naturally he couldn't stay the course; but he paid up when he could, and occasionally took Jay to see his family. But this new one – I don't even remember now what I found so horrible about him – yes I do, it was his show-offy, look at my new car, I've got more money than you attitude, and his ugly face, and the way he put Katie down, while expecting her to go to his flat and clean and cook for him.

I used to tell her that he was lying to her about never being married before; he had all the signs of someone who was trying to replace a wife; a wife who had finally seen the light and left him, and now he couldn't look after himself and he thought if he was just slightly nice to poor plain clumsy Katie, still living with her parents at twenty five, then she would replace the down-trodden wife who had just binned him.

He was nasty to Jay as well. But poor Katie, she hadn't had a boyfriend for years and she didn't want to listen to me. I was terrified that she'd go and have another baby – she did love babies – and we'd be stuck forever with this ghastly Richard in our lives. So we argued.

'We did argue a lot,' I admit.

'Mum, I know why you got on at her. He was awful, that man, but she couldn't see it.'

'I think she shut her eyes to it, she didn't want to see it. You can't blame her.'

'But it was horrible living here with that going on.'

So that was why Kezia left. She just sort of drifted away, staying with different friends, wandering round the country doing casual work, and then coming back home for a spell – to see if things had changed, I suppose.

But they hadn't, and at last, when Jay was ten, and Matthew was eleven, Katie packed up and moved to Bristol.

'Why did she go so far? She could have found somewhere nearer. It's not as if Bristol is particularly cheap.'

'She got that job,' said Kez.

'I know. It was awful. I missed them so much. So did your dad.'

'Well, how do you think Matt felt?'

Oh. Yes. So that left a tiny family, a little limb cut off from a whole body, me, Don and an adolescent boy. It was new to us. We'd never done a teenage boy before.

We didn't have the energy, I think, or the tolerance, or the interest in what he was interested in. We didn't make enough effort. We were tired, and working hard, and worrying about the ones who had gone, and Matt was a sensitive, prickly type, quick to realise when he was just being humoured, upset when he was ignored (and he was, often), not above provoking arguments just to make his presence noticed, and different, different from the girls, different from Jay, different from me and Don.

Arguments about his friends, his clothes and as time went on, his lifestyle. About loudness, lateness, lack of schoolwork; about eating, sleeping (too much, too little, wrong places). Arguments about money, piercings, drugs and drinking, the future and the past. They could go on for days, as neither Matt nor I could give up while there was still a chance of winning. They could be loud, shouty hurricanes through the house, or largely silent, with only meaningful remarks and hurtful exclusions to show that we were at odds, or any combination.

We both had A* GCSE in arguing. And Don had an A* in turning up his music and pretending it was nothing to do with him. And then there's a policeman at the door and you wish it could all have been different.

Matthew is in a bed in a ward in a hospital the size of a large village. He doesn't see me approaching the bed and I don't know what to do – big smiles and hugs? Quiet concern? So I stand there uncertainly until he looks round slowly, and then I smile – I think – and say: 'Hello love.'

It's more than five days since the incident, as I suppose we have to call it, and I dare say he looked worse at one time than he does now, but his bruises are pretty impressive even now. He and Don could hold a colourful face competition.

Tears run slowly out of his eyes, which I never thought I would see, and I sit down on the bed (forbidden by the rules) and take hold of his hand. So clean, his hand, I haven't seen it so clean since he was a tiny child.

Of course, hospitals throw you out at eight o'clock. Kezia has texted me the name of a guest house and I make my way there, stopping at a Pizza Hut on the way. Sheffield – or this end of it – has an abundance of fast food, but not much else. Still.

By the time I'm in my room – and I'm so far on the edge of the city I'm practically in Barnsley – it's not much past nine, and I'm wondering how I can pass the time, not tonight, because I'm ready to sleep, but the other evenings, and mornings, until I can take Matt home.

Maybe baby

Theresa's mother, quaintly, and Theresa copied her, called it "flowers".

Rita, and Kay, copying Rita, called it "the curse". Usually they all came on more or less at the same time, within a day or two, and they all used the same big brown paper packet of sanitary towels that lived in the airing cupboard, on the top shelf, where Val and Tony couldn't reach them, and where it was presumed their dad never looked.

In winter, the airing cupboard was the warmest place in the house, heated by the water tank which was heated by the back boiler and smelling strongly of clean, faintly scorched sheets.

Now, in summer, the smell of ironing was still there, but the cupboard was cool and dark. The first week in July Theresa went to it two, three times a day, took out a towel and hid it in the chest of drawers in her room, underneath Valerie's winter jumpers. She counted how many there were left, and calculated, though she couldn't be absolutely sure, that maybe there were more than there should be.

Theresa was watching herself, and just as carefully, she was watching Kay. Just because you were late didn't mean you were pregnant; the doctor's pages in the magazines always told you to wait till you'd missed twice before going to see the doctor – not that Theresa was planning on doing that, however many she missed. Just because you were late, it didn't mean...

And if Kay was late as well, maybe that was a good sign. Maybe it meant that it was normal. But if mum asked, if she noticed and asked, what would they say? And Theresa realised that she might notice that there weren't enough brown paper bags in the bin in the bathroom that mum emptied (and dad was presumed not to notice the existence of), so she took some of the towels out from under Val's jumpers and put them in the bags that mum saved from the greengrocer and put them one at a time in the bin. She knew Kay would not be bothered with such a performance. If anyone gave the game away, it would be Kay.

Lying in bed one morning, before mum called her to get up, before mum and dad were even awake, Theresa heard the door of Rita and Kay's room open, heard someone – Kay, she thought, going downstairs. Theresa slid out of bed and to the top of the stairs, heard the key of the back door being turned, carefully. A half-thought came into her mind, that Kay was going to run away, with Malcolm.

When she reached the back door it was standing open and Kay was nowhere. Well, yes, she was somewhere, for the sound of retching came from the outside toilet.

Theresa stood in her bare feet on the concrete path, noticing, maybe for the first time in her life, the cool sunshiny stillness of the early morning air, and wondering why she herself wasn't sick. When she heard the toilet chain being pulled, she nipped back in through the open door and back upstairs to bed. Kay must have stayed downstairs.

What did it mean, if Kay was sick and she wasn't? There was no one to ask.

Theresa almost wondered how she lived through the days, or whether she was really alive, the times seemed so strange. Sometimes it seemed impossible that she could be pregnant, and then she wished she was and was jealous of Kay, and sometimes it seemed certain that she was – her breasts were hard like potatoes and sore like toothache – and then she felt full of panic and despair and wished to tell Malcolm and run away with him to Scotland and get married.

She should have told Malcolm straight away, as soon as she suspected and never mind if she was mistaken. She should have told her dad and made him tell Malcolm that he had to marry her.

But since they came back from that holiday, Malcolm had hardly spoken to her – but then he never really had – or looked in her direction. He sometimes came to see Kay, not as often as she wanted, but once or twice a week, and when he came, he was affectionate and boyfriendly to her.

He flirted with Rita too, and Rita let him, because she had a new boyfriend and it was fun to show off in front of him, and make Leslie glower.

The days passed. Rita went every morning on the bus to Town, where she worked in Pearsons, in the office. Kay and Theresa went on the bus in the opposite direction, Kay to the pen factory, Theresa to the big hot dusty machine room where she struggled with pieces of cloth that would not, would *not*, make themselves in to next winter's coats, and a sharp woman who had been at school with her mum came to her machine and tore out her seams and made her do it again.

Sometimes, Kay got on Theresa's bus after work, and they got off at the park and walked home together. Theresa looked sideways at her sister, observing the dulling of her brown hair, a hardly perceptible thickening of her jaw, and wondered if she had changed too. She couldn't ask, and Kay wasn't bothered to look. She had no reason to suspect.

'I wish we were on the phone,' she said. 'If we were on the phone, I could phone Malcolm and ask him to come round. When I get married, I want to be on the phone.'

'You can always get Rita to ask him to come round,' said Theresa.

'I think she forgets,' said Kay. 'Or else she doesn't want him to come. She doesn't like to see her Leslie next to Malcolm because it makes him look so ugly. Which do you like best, Malcolm or Leslie?'

'I don't know,' said Theresa. Somehow, she couldn't pull up a picture in her mind of either of them. She was confused about how to hide her feelings from Kay: which was it best to say?

'You like Alan, don't you?' said Kay, teasing.

'I do not.' Here at least, Theresa was sure.

'You talk to him.'

'I don't like him though. Not like that.'

'He likes you.'

'How do you know?'

'I've seen him looking at you. He'd ask you out.'

'No, thank you.' Theresa felt as if she was behind a huge painted sheet, that smiled, and said words and even walked along and felt the hot, spent, late afternoon air, while behind it she was thinking only one thing. And Kay didn't notice that she was talking to a formless billowing thing, she carried on as she always did, pulling out ideas for moves in the boy-girl game.

'Rita might get married to Leslie.'

'She's only been with him a week.'

'And I can marry Malcolm, and you can marry Alan.'

'Get lost.'

It could not be real, it could not be true. This afternoon, the knowledge was big and scary and inescapable: they both needed to get married and they could not both marry Malcolm.

Then Malcolm stopped coming to the house. It was late August. Kay and Theresa had missed two periods apiece and Malcolm had stopped coming to the house. Since last Thursday, he had not been seen, and now it was Friday.

Rita shrugged when asked if she had seen him at work. Kay gave her messages for him daily, growing more urgent, demanding for him to come.

'I know what will fetch him,' she said, as they walked home.

Theresa's Pat was with them.

'If he's gone off you, you can't do nothing about it,' she said, glumly.

'I bet I can,' said Kay.

As soon as they got home, Theresa and Pat went upstairs.

'I'm not coming out tonight,' said Theresa.

'I thought you were.'

'I can't.'

'Why not?'

'I've changed my mind.'

'Why?'

Theresa could not think of answers. Her mind had only room for her own plan.

'Just have, that's all.'

'But I can't go without you.'

'See if Kay wants to go.'

Pat trudged downstairs and didn't come back.

Theresa washed herself. There wasn't time to wash her hair, which was so thick it took four hours to dry, but she put on new make-up, and changed her clothes. Her best summer dress, would not fit, not because of her belly, which did not seem to have grown (and was that right? did that mean she wasn't –?) but because of her breasts.

She tried it, but she could feel it straining and she was afraid the stitches would burst. She wore her best winter dress, reluctantly, because it was red and she feared it was a bit brash in the bright sunlight, but she also remembered that she had worn it the night Malcolm came to the dance. She planned to sneak out, not to avoid her parents, but to avoid questions from Kay, who must still be downstairs, probably watching television with Val and Tony. Her mum was setting out the knives and forks as she went into the kitchen.

'Got a date?' she said, noticing the brushed hair and the nice dress.

'Sort of. Mum, I don't want any tea. I've got to get to the Regal to meet someone.'

'Mind how you go then,' said her mum, as she always did. Theresa stood beside her, watching her hands lay the places and smooth the cloth.

Six right-handed places and one left-handed for their dad. 'You'll have too many,' she said, for something to say.

'One for Roger the Lodger then,' said mum, and laughed.

Theresa, often bewildered and not always happy in her family, knew that she was not her parents' favourite. She was never as clever as Rita, nor as lively and demanding as Kay. She got through life by trying to be quiet and good, but her family seemed to feel she was secretive and awkward. The other girls bossed her about, and most of the time she went along with whatever they wanted. On the occasions when she didn't want to go along with them, she had no ways of explaining, and instead would just hide out of the way until the situation had passed. Other people thought this was underhand and sometimes told her that they didn't trust her.

Now she felt suddenly the fragility of her home and her place in it. She leaned sideways, cautiously, and kissed her mum on the cheek.

'What was that for? You must be after something, my lady.' She pushed Theresa out of the way, but not as roughly as she might have done.

Instead of taking the bus to the Regal, Theresa took the bus to where Malcolm lived. He had just got home from work and he was sitting in the kitchen with his dad, eating smoked haddock with a poached egg on top. The two little girls ran in from the garden and the littlest one hugged Theresa's legs while Karen watched from the doorway.

'Come and sit down, then,' said Malcolm's dad. 'There's a cup of tea in the pot.'

'No, thank you. All right then.'

'All done up tonight aren't you? Is he taking you somewhere nice?'

Malcolm ducked his head and dipped a piece of bread and butter into his egg yolk.

'I don't know. I just came...'

Theresa hadn't reckoned on dealing with other people besides Malcolm; in her rehearsals it had been just her and him.

Soon however, his dad finished his tea and stood up.

'You're doing the washing up, son,' he said. 'I'm off to see what your mother's up to.' And he went into the front room where Ruby was watching television with the curtains closed.

'Shall I wash up for you?' asked Theresa, but Malcolm piled the dishes in the sink. 'I'll do them later,' he said. 'Mum won't mind.'

They sat for a little while, Theresa looking sideways at Malcolm, Malcolm looking at the table and sideways at the clock. 'Tell you what,' he said. 'Let's go for a walk round the block.'

Children did not play in the street round here,

but Theresa could hear their voices calling from gardens behind houses as she and Malcolm walked between the dusty grass verge and the clipped privet hedges.

'Did Kay send you round?'

'No, I...' She could not say it.

'Because I don't want Kay telling me when I've got to go and see her. We're not engaged, are we?'

'No.'

'I know she's your sister,' he said. 'But you and her, you're different from each other, aren't you? You're too quiet and she's too noisy.'

Which one do you like best? Theresa wanted to say, but instead she said:

'What about Rita?'

'Oh Rita. She thinks she's too good for me.'

'Do you like her, then?'

'She's all right,' he said carefully. 'Tell you what. She is too good for that Leslie she's going out with. I don't know what she sees in him.'

'I think, I think he spends money on her.'

'My dad's always told me,' said Malcolm, 'that what women want is someone to make 'em laugh. He says that's been the secret of his success.'

'What success?'

'Oh,' said Malcolm airily. 'He's one for the ladies. Not that he's done anything. I mean, he's faithful to my mum.' He blushed, but Theresa didn't see. She was looking down at her feet, in their tight black shoes with the little strap across, putting themselves, it seemed, because she wasn't doing it. Her feet were walking and she was somewhere else, her feet were carrying her red dress and her handbag and her head and body and legs and arms along the pavement, but she wasn't there at all.

They'd gone, as he'd said, round the block, and were back at his gate.

'Well,' he said. 'I've got to be getting ready.'

'Shall I help you?'

'What?'

'I mean with the washing up.' She blushed, confused about what he might have thought she meant.

'No, Mum'll do that. I'm going out.'

'Oh.'

'I'll be seeing you. Drop in again if you're round this way.'

'All right.'

It was two days later that Kay told.

I wrote that early in the morning, sitting up in the plump bed of the B & B, too early to get up and have breakfast, too early even to be properly light. I thought I must be worrying about Matt and Don, but when I tried to work out which was the most in need of my worry, it turned out neither of them, but I still couldn't get back to sleep.

And even as I was writing, I was thinking, well I don't think I'll be reading this one out either, and at the same time, what is the point of going there if they can't help? And then, while I'm in the shower: help with what?

On my way to the hospital, I buy an A to Z of Sheffield, and a new mobile phone for Matt, and though it's not an expensive one, he's pleased with it and straightaway starts texting people, beginning with, I'm touched to see, his dad and his sisters.

I feel better about leaving him today. He's looking more composed, more himself, though he still fills up with tears easily, just looking round, or when I reach out – gingerly, this – and pat his hand; so at eight o'clock I make my way, full of curiosity, to where Les and Theresa live.

Theresa and Leslie live, fortuitously it seems to me, more or less on the route from the hospital to the guest house. When I ring, having got the number from Val, it's Les who answers, and he sounds surly, or maybe I mean that I can still recognise his voice. I haven't seen him since his mother's funeral.

Theresa I've seen, at her mother's and at Malcolm's funerals, bewildered and shut off behind her ruined prettiness, but never Les, in more than thirty years. But he says the right things.

'You can come round. There's only me here, evenings.' His voice has flattened and softened with the years of living away from London.

It's nothing to write home about, as they say. It's a little red brick house among a thousand others, in a scruffy street where it's clear that not many people bought their council houses, judging from the lack of fancy porches and fences. Something has been done to upgrade the properties, it would seem, by the Council – they all have new garden walls and new windows, but most of the front gardens, including the one I'm approaching, have been left to get on with it, just a square of unmown grass and an overgrown privet hedge. A small white van is parked outside, with 'L. Plant, Carpet Fitter' stencilled on the side. Self-employed, then.

I'd known him all my life because his mum was my dad's Aunt Peggy. He didn't have a dad, like I didn't, and though he put it about that his dad had been killed in the war before he was born, and he may have been, I knew, being family, that he'd never married Auntie Peg.

It wasn't a secret, nor was it anything we ever had conversations about. It was just something we knew. Auntie Peg was all right, older than most people's mums, so that people who didn't know them used to think she was his nan, and she was a bit sharp, or blunt, I'm not sure which, and I don't see how one person can be both, but she was.

Thinking of Les when he was a little boy, I remember him as being a merry, cheerful soul. Aunt Peggy too – well, she remained cheerful, or stoical at least until she died. They got on well together, although she was a much older mum than is normal, not my aunt in fact, but my nan's much younger sister – therefore my great aunt.

They did a lot together, Leslie and his mum, went shopping, and for walks in the park to sail his boat, and they would get on a Green Line bus and go and have a picnic in the country, and every week, they went to the pictures together and whenever you saw them, they were chatting and laughing.

But he changed, just as, come to think of it, Matthew did, I remember one time when he was about fifteen, Peggy came to our house in a great upset, not crying but pale and flustered, and said that he'd pushed her aside when she said he wasn't to go out: shoved her to one side up against the coat stand by the front door so that she lost her balance and knocked it sideways, and then he swore and went out without waiting to see if she was all right, just left her there standing in a little heap of coats and scarves and string bags.

We had a good idea, mum and me, about what was getting to Les. Nan had told mum, and mum had told me – she told me all sorts – that Les had asked who his dad was.

'Well,' said mum. 'She couldn't tell him, for the simple reason that no one knows.'

'Peggy must know,' I said.

'Well –' and mum made the face she made – a sort of screwing up of lips and eyes, making believe she was considering whether to tell me something or whether I might be too young, but she and I both knew she would tell me. 'There was a war on of course. Things were different. We had Doodlebugs and I don't know what else.' Well I knew that – it was a big story in the family that Leslie was born on VJ Day, so I waited for more explanation.

'She wasn't getting enough to eat, for one thing. That's what did it.'

'I thought everyone got their rations.'

'Oh yes, but Peg was so busy, rushing about, working, doing overtime, firewatching, going out, she never came home to eat lots of evenings. Well you couldn't just buy a sandwich like you do now. I know she's not now, but she used to be thin, skinny as anything and always on the go. She wasn't no spring chicken but the men liked her – she had plenty of boyfriends.'

'So, Les?'

Mum looked at her nails, or maybe at her wedding ring which she never stopped wearing. 'You be careful now, what you go saying. I don't know what Peg has told him, but if you ask me, Peg don't know any better than I do who his father was.'

'So was she –?' I wanted to say "a prostitute", but it seemed too rude, '– on the game?'

'Will you watch your mouth?' said my mother.

I was what? fourteen? and I must have surprised her. 'It wasn't like that. She was just friendly, and if she got

211

some stockings or some fags, why not? She was never a bad girl. Not,' she added, 'that I really knew her that well in those days.'

When his mother died, Les came down from Sheffield on a coach and stood in the cemetery in the freezing cold and wouldn't allow anyone to speak to him.

Everyone tried: his Auntie Glad, who was my nan, my mum, all the neighbours and the various people you've never seen before but who appear at funerals to be discussed afterwards by those more entitled. ('Didn't think she was looking well, did you?' 'Well what can you expect?') Anyway, Les kept his eyes on the ground and his shoulders up round his ears, as if he was being beaten with a stick.

'You go and talk to him,' said mum to me, so I tried.

'Hello Les. How are things?' He shrugged. I didn't dare ask about Theresa, or the baby, or say anything about his mother, and what did that leave?

I couldn't ask him what he thought of Spurs' form, or if he ever got to go to a football match these days. I couldn't tell him I was going out with his old friend (though that would have been overstating their relationship a bit.) So I walked away like everyone else had done, thinking: well I did my best, can't do any more than that.

It's not Les who opens the door. It's a young woman, younger than Kezia, older than Matthew; a good-looking girl, maybe with something of Rita about her, though she's taller, and her face is somehow heavier. Glossy, is what she is, her face soft and brown, her hair shining and straight, her eyebrows perfectly pencilled in, nails red and immaculate.

She smiles a professional sort of smile and the way she says 'Come through', assures me that she works dealing with the public – a receptionist, hairdresser, something like that.

Les is sitting at the kitchen table and I would never have known him. He's over sixty, it's true, but there are people who remain themselves, or retain the appearance of being themselves, and he hasn't.

And it's not that he's gone bald or put on weight; he has a full head of hair, rather greasy-looking, and as for weight, I should think he's lost most of what little he ever had. Wizened is what he is, like something dried. I can smell what he's just had for his tea, a fried chop.

'Well, you've not changed much,' he says, and I don't think he's offering me a compliment.

'Lovely to see you,' is what I say in the end, thinking, this is awful, how can I get away, how soon can I go?

'I'm Kim,' says the young woman. Of course she is.

She picks up a plate from the table and puts it into the washing up bowl, puts the sauce bottle into the fridge, switches the kettle on, and gets her coat.

'Sit down,' he says to me, and I sit at the table while he makes two cups of tea, and Kim leaves without any further conversation.

I tell him what has happened to Matthew, and he tells me that there are seriously bad parts of Sheffield where no one should go at night, and tries to find out from me where it happened so that he can judge whether it might have been the Somalis that did it or the Pakis.

'Was it London Road?' he keeps asking, but as I don't know the city any names the policeman told me have slid from my memory.

I ask him about his family, I say what an attractive young woman Kim is and ask what she does ('Beauty therapist') and whether she is married.

He scowls.

'Divorced,' he says. 'Thousands I paid out on that wedding, for less than five years' worth.'

'At least there were no children?' I'm guessing and he agrees.

'These things happen,' I say. 'People make mistakes.'

'Then people should learn to live with their mistakes,' he says, and I can see that that's what he has chosen to do. I dare not ask him about the rest of the family.

This feels like a replay of our last meeting, him sullen and uncommunicative, me helpless and clueless, which I shouldn't be now, after all these years and experiences.

When I've drunk the cup of tea, I make the excuse that I have to go and get something to eat somewhere, and leave. He sees me to the door.

'If you want to see Theresa,' he says, 'she's at home Mondays and Saturday mornings.' There is no expression on his face but I wonder now, after having seen her, if it cost him something to say that.

Come and get it

So now Theresa is sitting in the park, on the motionless roundabout, in a warm September evening, watching the light fade. She has no memory now of the park where she pushed Malcolm's little sisters on the swings, no memory even of making love, if that's what it was, with Malcolm. No past. Only a present in which she is scared to look at the future.

Kay has told, words have been shouted, tears shed, threats made.

Rita and Theresa have been called as witnesses; Val and Tony sent out to play until well past their bedtimes so as to be out of earshot.

Malcolm has been summoned, and his dad, and has promised to marry Kay as soon as she is sixteen.

Theresa has seen him, looking sheepish and oddly pleased with himself, and Kay, hanging on to his arm like a little girl onto her father.

'Do you know,' said Rita to Theresa. 'I'd sooner give my baby away to be adopted, than marry him. Wouldn't you?' Theresa could not answer, wondering whether Rita suspected, but for the first time, she thought of her baby as something real, and wondered whether she might be able to give it away. Would anyone want it?

Theresa, nowadays, does not know what to do

with herself. She still gets up in the morning, gets ready, waits for Kay to be sick, which she does now in the bathroom, sanctioned by everyone's knowledge, goes to the bus stop with her, listens to her telling the other girls that she'll be married by Christmas, comes home with her, listens to her and their mother discussing plans, prams, places to live. In the bedroom, Val talks about the baby all the time. Only Dad and Tony are uninterested, and she can't talk to them, because the only things she wants to talk about are babies and pregnancy, and what's going to happen next. Kay's baby is part of the family now. Hers is like an unmentionable disease.

Walking back through the dark streets, Theresa meets Leslie.

'Where's Rita?' she asks.

'Gone off with Pat somewhere.'

Theresa says nothing and they walk together in silence.

'I think Rita might have chucked me,' he says suddenly.

'What for?'

'How should I know?'

'Did you have a row?'

'Sort of.' He waits for Theresa to ask him more but she has used up her store of curiosity.

'I think I might not be tall enough for her,' says Leslie gloomily, and Theresa looks at him to measure his height and sees for the first time his sallow skin and lean cheeks, his rather girlish lips and his brown long-lashed eyes – lashes too good for a boy, as she has heard Rita remark.

'I think you're tall enough,' she says, not with the intention of flirting, but it cheers him up and he puts an arm round her shoulder.

'I tell you what,' he says. 'I'd be better going out with you. And I don't mean because you're shorter than me. I think you're nicer than Rita.'

Theresa is silent.

'What about it, then?' he says, pulling her towards him. 'Do you fancy going out with me?'

'I would,' says Theresa. 'Only I can't really go out with anyone. I need to get married.'

'What you on about? Married to who?'

'Oh, I can't tell you.' She realises she's said the wrong thing. 'Well, I might as well say. I'm expecting.'

'Expecting what?'

'Like Kay.'

He laughs shortly and loudly, like a door banging.

'Now that is something. Two of you up the spout. Not like Rita, then.'

'No,' agrees Theresa, though she doesn't know what he means.

'And he won't marry you.'

'No.'

'I could fight him for you, if you like.'

'No,' she says seriously. 'It wouldn't do no good.'

They sit together on a wall outside the church. Theresa likes being with him, likes the fact that she's told someone and nobody's shouting at her.

'I'd still go out with you,' he offers.

'All right,' she says, and turns her face to him, her eyes shining.

'Give us a kiss then.'

He seems to like kissing more than Malcolm had, and by the time they are lying in the long dry grass of the churchyard, Theresa is feeling moved in ways that Malcolm never moved her.

'You might as well let me,' says Leslie. 'You won't get pregnant anyway.'

Might as well, thought Theresa, and she did.

'It was your idea,' she said to him, in later months. 'I never asked you, it was you asked me.'

'I didn't know what I was saying,' he said. 'I didn't mean it.'

Too bad, thought Theresa, and it was.

I never understood why Rita found it so hard to let go of Leslie Plant. She knew Les from childhood, of course she did, but she'd only been going out with him for about three weeks when they had a bit of a row one night and the next thing she knew – and I mean the next thing – it was only about two days later, he said he was going to marry her sister.

I can't describe how furious Rita was. She knocked on my front door (now we were grown up we didn't use the back) at about ten o'clock, just as my boyfriend – not Don, his name was Norman – was leaving and we were having a bit of a snog at the back door where he'd left his bike, when I heard the front door and my mum grumbling to open it.

'Pat. It's Rita.'

'I'm offski,' said Norman, and wheeled his bike out of the yard. 'See you tomorrow.'

Now that we had a television, we used the front room in the evenings, but when I closed the back door, I turned to find Rita standing in the kitchen, looking feverish and grumpy, like someone who has run for a bus and missed it.

'I've got to talk to you. Alone,' she added dramatically, as mum came through from the front room.

'Don't mind me,' said mum. 'I'm just off up to bed. Don't sit up all night talking, you – and don't forget to bolt the door when you've finished.' She went, but put her head back round the door to add, 'You might as well stay in the kitchen, then I won't hear you when you start your giggling.'

Rita was still standing, now facing the wall.

'I don't think there's much to giggle about,' she said.

Mum opened the door again. 'And keep that back door shut or we'll have all those moths in.'

'All right, mum.'

I would have liked to open the door; though it was September, it was a stifling night. Rita was dressed in the white blouse and grey skirt that she would have worn for work; her hair was untidy. Strands of it had escaped from the hairpins, and her bouffant was lopsided.

'What's the matter?'

'Men.'

I thought fondly of Norman, cycling by now along the Hertford Road.

'Malcolm,' she said.

I'd heard about Kay and Malcolm, not from Rita as it happened, but because I'd met Kay in the paper shop, buying sweets, and she was full of it.

'I thought my mum would kill me,' she said. 'She was going to, but I knew me dad would stop her, and it's all right now. Just three and a half months from now and we can get married. He's lovely, my Malcolm.' And so on.

'I know about Kay.'

'Everybody knows about Kay. Nobody expects her to keep quiet about it, though by the time she gets married, it'll be obvious anyway. She needn't think I'm going to be there.'

'At the wedding?'

'At any wedding.'

She was clasping her hands together as if to stop them from doing something dangerous, and every now and then, her mouth twisted and quivered.

'Have you seen your Leslie lately?'

'No. Why?'

She took a breath to say something, but tears came into her eyes and she shook her head sharply. One of her tears flew into the sugar bowl. She tried again:

'Your Leslie is getting married to my sister Theresa.'

'Who says?'

'I do. He does. She does. Mum and dad say she can.'

'She doesn't know him.'

'She does now.'

'I don't get it Reet. Why all of a sudden?'

'Why do you think?'

'She's expecting? She went with Leslie and then he went with you?'

'Looks like it.'

'But we would know, Rita. We'd know if she was going out with someone. Theresa hasn't had a boyfriend in ages.'

'She's had something,' said Rita grimly.

'Is she sure? She's not just saying it because Kay is?'

'I don't know. I don't even care. Both my sisters are trollops, both of them.' She was pulling hairgrips out of her hair and bending them till they broke. Their little metal bodies were beginning to litter the table.

'I don't get it.' I truly didn't. Theresa would not have kept quiet if she'd been going with Leslie before Rita.

We all knew that she fancied Malcolm and was just waiting for Kay to let go of him. She would be unhappy that it hadn't worked out that way – devastated, we would say now, and I could see her saying she was going to marry Leslie as a way of getting her own back, and showing that she didn't care. But she couldn't be pregnant with Leslie's baby, she couldn't be.

'How far gone is she?'

'Same as Kay.'

'Then...?'

Rita pounded both fists on the table top, making the dead hairpins bounce.

'I know. She's disgusting. She's taken Malcolm off Kay, and now she's taking Leslie off me.'

'I thought you'd chucked him.'

'Yes I did.'

'Then...?'

She put her head down on the table and stayed there for some minutes, while I considered the situation. When she lifted her head again, her eyes were dry and her voice was flat.

'I know, Pat. It doesn't make sense, how I'm feeling. I just hate her, Theresa, and I know I should hate Malcolm for what he's done, but that's just him, isn't it? And she knew what he was like.'

'Well, Kay...'

'Kay was always going to get banged up by someone. She doesn't think, and me dad's spoiled her. Theresa's that stupid she can't think. All she had to do was listen to me, and do as she's told. There was no need for all this.'

'But if she loved him?'

'If I hear that word again...They're round there now, crying their eyes out and going, *But I love him*. It makes me sick.'

Rita moved out of the family home after that, and went to live with their Aunt Ginny. She gave up her job at Pearson's and went to work at the National and Provincial Bank for a while, before she gave that up too and just lived on what modelling paid. Then she went to University for that brief year, or less, and then, well, then her life seemed to take off in the directions she must have been planning all along.

Theresa and Leslie got married – I went to the wedding, which was as dismal a do as I've ever been to – and went to live up North.

Kay and Malcolm had to wait for her sixteenth birthday, and then he moved in with her and her parents, but once Debbie was born, and Kay and her mum started rowing all the time, they moved in with his parents and then into a little flat. I don't think I ever went into the house again.

Anyway, I find myself remembering poor old Theresa. I do think Rita was hard on her. Kay seemed to have done no different and she ended up with the boy she wanted and the more-or-less approval of her parents. Even though I liked Leslie, because he was my cousin and I'd known him all my life, I wouldn't have wanted to be married to him. I knew he was moody, bad-tempered; a tortured soul if you wanted to be charitable but Theresa would never have the skill to help him be nice to her, and she would be miserable.

Thinking now about Theresa, I feel even more sorry for her than I did then, and quite exasperated with Rita. She should have known even at that time that she was going to pull the long straw; she was going to end up with the good job, the good education, the nice apartment in Finchley, even the wedding with photographers from the Sunday papers.

Theresa never expected more than marriage and babies – like I didn't, I suppose – but she could have expected a nicer life than the one she ended up with.

Not that I know much about it, but just seeing her those couple of times, and hearing comments from Val, which she must have pieced together from infrequent phone conversations, has given me an impression that Theresa's marriage, and life, are basically pretty bleak.

I phone home and talk to Don. I can hear Mod music in the background.

Substitute

A cold November rain snapped against the kitchen window, which on the inside was misted with condensation from the cooker and from the washing drying, or not drying, on the overhead rack.

Theresa took the lid off the saucepan, releasing another burst of steam, and peered unhappily at the mince. It was grey, and the smell of it made her throat contract. The baby sat in his pram, banging frantically on the waterproof cover and grizzling in a despairing kind of way. Theresa reached across, knocking a knife on to the floor, and pushed his dummy into his mouth, but he tore it out angrily and threw it on the floor.

He was beginning to wind up to serious crying, when he was distracted by footsteps on the stairs and noise on the landing.

Les had met his mother at the station and brought her by bus to the flat. Theresa's dread and despair deepened further. She was afraid of her mother-in-law, as she was of any older woman who might see how inexperienced and inexpert she was, and judge her harshly. She knew that Les' mum, old, poor and lonely as she was, could yet keep her own little house warm and sweet-smelling, with cheap and wholesome meals produced on time, and clean sheets on the bed every Sunday.

She knew this because Les told her, often and loudly. She was ashamed of herself for being spoken to rudely by Les; she did not want anyone to see how he treated her. Then, she did not know what to call Mrs Plant, and was afraid of giving offence by saying the wrong thing. She did not want to see her, finally, because she was not her own mother, she was not the person who Theresa really wanted to see. Whatever else, she was never going to call her "mum".

They were in the room; Les dark and sullen, his mum for the moment polite and pleased.

'Put the kettle on,' said Les.

Theresa obeyed, and the sight of her compliance seemed to raise a spike of hostility in his mother.

'Les tells me you're expecting again,' she said. 'You didn't waste much time.'

'It takes two,' thought Theresa, but she didn't have enough spirit to say it.

Mrs Plant turned her attention to baby Mark. She approached him kindly, tickling him under the chin, and rocking the pram in a way that was supposed to soothe him. The baby chuckled and grinned, showing sore red gums and one new sharp tooth.

'He likes you,' said Theresa, not betraying her surprise.

'You don't want to bother with that,' said Les.

Mrs Plant took no notice. She unfastened Mark's harness and picked him up, and so it was that her first cup of tea under her son's roof was taken with her (nominal) grandson on her knee, grabbing at her beads and patting her cup as she lifted it to her mouth.

'You can call me Peggy,' she said to Theresa. 'Now, what are we having for our tea?'

'I was trying to make a shepherd's pie,' said Theresa, softened. 'But the mince doesn't look very nice. I've done the potatoes.'

Peggy put Mark back in his pram and looked into the saucepans. The potatoes had broken up and were looking like watery porridge; the mince had stuck together in a lump and was smelling rank and raw. Les did not look in the saucepans, but from his seat at the table he made disgusted noises and said:

'She needs lessons.'

'What have you got in your cupboard?' Without asking, Peggy opened the kitchen dresser and surveyed the pitiful stores. 'How much housekeeping does he give you?'

'She gets enough.'

Theresa looked at Les and said nothing, from a complicated mixture of loyalty and fear and embarrassment. She did not know whether she should be able to manage on what she got or not.

'Right then, Leslie. Nip down the shop for us.'

'Why should I? If she can't do the shopping properly, why should I?'

'Come on, son. I'll give you the money. It won't take you a minute.'

Peggy came and stood beside Theresa as she poked at the mince with a knife.

'Stir with a knife, stir up strife,' said Peggy firmly, and pushed her out of the way, and found a spoon, and began to take over the cooking.

The evening was transformed. Under Peggy's direction, the baby was fed and changed, gravy browning and onions bought and added to the mince, the potatoes drained and dried and mashed and the meal put on the table, eaten and washed up with goodwill and even cheerfulness. Theresa never forgot her words, and never stirred with a knife again. She understood that the equilibrium of life is delicately and dangerously balanced and has to be sustained by any means possible. She added it to other bits of information that she had from her own mother, about passing on the stairs, putting shoes on a table, bringing May blossom into the house. These things did not get her very far, but they were the best she had in the way of instructions for living.

'Where am I sleeping?'

'I've borrowed a settee from this bloke I work with. Like a studio couch kind of thing. It's out on the landing. We'll have to push the table back and squeeze it in here. You'll be warm enough anyway.'

'I'm too old to be sleeping on any settee. You can move out for a couple of nights, Les, and I'll sleep in with Theresa.'

Les sulked. Theresa felt her nervousness return.

When it came to it though, it didn't seem so bad. Peggy was much older than Theresa's mum, but her smell of talcum powder and cold cream, and her winceyette nightie reminded her of her own nana, and nights spent with her long ago, in a big feather bed, in a room that shook whenever a train passed on the line at the bottom of the garden.

'Well now, dear, have you heard from your mum?'

'No.'

'I heard your sister had a baby girl.'

Theresa was silent, the past suddenly with her again, that she had tried and tried to push down, out of range of any thought or feeling.

'And is Leslie good to you?'

Theresa stayed silent. What could she say?

'You're a quiet girl, aren't you? You need to stick up for yourself.'

Peggy gave her pillow a sound bashing and settled her hairnetted head into it. 'Don't let him push you around. He will, you know, if you let him.'

'He hates me.' Theresa said it without wanting to.

'Now what does that mean? He married you, didn't he? It's not that long ago, is it?'

'A year.'

'Oh yes, it was the day that President got shot, wasn't it? What a day to choose. Still, you weren't to know, were you?'

'No.'

'And you're pregnant again. When is it due?'

'March.'

'Only a year between them. You'll have your hands full, my girl.'

'We'll be getting a council house. We're on the list.'

'Well, that will be better.'

The old lady wheezed and began snoring, surprisingly loudly. The baby stirred and snuffled but didn't wake.

Next day, Les went to work. Theresa and Peggy, and Mark in a pushchair, went to town and looked at the shops. Peggy bought toys for Mark and nappies for the new baby.

They made their way through the crowds in the covered market, hearing the dialect of the unfamiliar town, and feeling the fellowship of their own shared accent.

'Have you seen my mum?'

'Not to speak to, dear. I've seen your Rita

now, in the bank, you know, but she wouldn't talk to me. I was with my friend – you know the one – and she said they weren't allowed to talk to customers, but if you ask me, she was very stand-offish.'

She would be, thought Theresa grimly.

'Doesn't your mum keep in touch?'

'She doesn't want anything to do with me.' Theresa's voice faltered and all of a sudden, tears – they were standing at a bus stop and she was lifting Mark out of the pushchair – and the words burst out of her.

'It's not fair. Kay got everything. Kay got Malcolm and she got to stay at home, and she did the same as me, and me dad didn't show her the door. I bet they bought her pram, and gave her money, and we've had to buy everything ourselves and Les doesn't earn as much as he earned down south, and me mum's never even sent me a birthday card or a Christmas card last year and I bet she won't let Val write to me.'

She stood at the bus stop in the cold wind, clutching the baby to her, her eyes red and her face pale.

'I miss my sisters, I really do.'

'Why don't you write them a nice letter? You could send a picture of the baby. Tell them you're expecting again.'

'Maybe I will. But Rita would probably rip it up. It's Rita's fault. She's told mum not to write to me. I know she has. She hates me.'

'Is this our bus? Come on, I'll get them. Let's get home.'

On the bus, they were separated by the press of shoppers, but walking up from the bus stop, Peggy looked slyly at Theresa.

'Was it over my Les that you and Rita fell out?'

Theresa stared.

'Don't you know?'

'Les never said. And I don't like to listen to what people say. You don't have to tell me. I was just wondering.'

'I thought everyone knew. Rita was going out with Les. That's why she's so mad at me. She thinks I took him off her. But it wasn't my idea. He asked me.'

'You don't have to tell me,' repeated Peggy, and as they arrived at the flat, the conversation ended.

That evening though, after the baby was asleep, it started up again.

'Why don't you come down for Christmas?' said Peggy to Les. 'You can stop with me. We'll make room. I'd like to see you at Christmas. There's only Edie and she can come round like she always does. Then Theresa can go and see her family. She'd like that.'

'I don't think so.'

'Go on, Les. You can come down on the train.

I've come up to see you, haven't I?'

'I mean, I don't think she'd like to see her family. Or I don't think they'd like to see her.'

'Course they would.'

Theresa was feeling like a door being banged by the wind, open, shut, open, shut.

'What do you know about it?'

'I know she misses her mum. She's only young. And her mum would want to see the baby. Stands to reason.'

Open.

'She's not going anywhere near. Let her mum come up here. I'm not stopping her. But she's not going down there.'

Shut.

'Don't be rotten. I'll pay your fares if that's what's bothering you.'

Open.

Les was leaning across the table, shouting now. 'Don't be such a stupid cow. She isn't going. We're not going where we're not welcome. Keep your stupid nose out of my business.'

Shut.

'Well, if that's how you feel. I'm only saying.'

'I don't want your "only saying". You've come up here, poking your nose in.'

'I have not poked my nose in.' Peggy was indignant now, hurt at being misunderstood. 'I've just come up here to see my only son, and my grandson.'

'The little bastard.'

'I've come up to see you, though I'm not well, and I find I'm not wanted. Nothing against you dear –' to Theresa '– I can see you're doing your best, but I think I'd better go. There'll be a train tonight, I expect.'

'No, don't go,' Theresa said.

'You'd better wait till tomorrow. It's freezing out. Anyway –' he added as if he couldn't help himself '– I don't want you telling everybody I've chucked you out.'

'I'll tell people what I like. And I'll go where and when I please, Leslie, so I'll thank you to carry my bag down them stairs.'

'Don't go,' pleaded Theresa. 'He doesn't mean it.'

'Don't you tell me what I mean.'

Peggy stamped off to the bedroom and filled her bag. She was angry, but also a little exhilarated that she was having the last word, and also looking forward to getting home, where there was a TV and her own bed. She could hear Les' voice, still raised, and an occasional fretful whine from Theresa. The baby did not stir. Used to it, obviously.

'Right then, I'm off.'

'Go on then, don't stand there.'

'She can't go on her own,' said Theresa. 'Go to the station with her at least. She don't know the way.'

'You go with her if you're so keen.'

'All right.'

They walked to the bus stop again and stood in the shelter. Theresa's bare legs made Peggy feel cold and she tried to make her go back home, but Theresa insisted on coming all the way to the station with her. 'If you can pay my fare. I haven't got no money.'

'I don't like to say this about my own son,' said Peggy when they were on the bus. 'But why don't you pack up and come back home? He doesn't deserve anyone looking after him.'

'I can't.'

'Your mum would take you in.'

'She wouldn't. They all hate me. I'm stuck with this. I'll be all right.'

Peggy had no more words. She privately made up her mind to go round and see Mrs Doughty, and intercede for Theresa. With that comforting thought, she dropped the subject.

They parted at the station, awkwardly. Peggy waddled slowly, the bag slowing her more than normal, to the ticket office, and Theresa returned to the bus stop. There was a bus there; she ran towards it, but her heel broke in a crack in the pavement and her shoe came off. The bus moved away without her. It was only then that she remembered that she didn't get a shilling for her fare from Peggy. She made to go back, but realised that Peggy would be through the barrier by now. Pulling her green woollen coat round her, and limping because of her broken shoe, she walked away from the city centre, up the long hill to what she supposed was home. As she walked, miserable and wet as she was, she seemed to find new spirit. Something changed.

'I'll show him,' she said to herself, meaning that he would never know when, or how, or how much he hurt her.

She was nearly home, carrying both her shoes in one hand (though why, when they would never be any good?) when the police car passed her. Five minutes later, she turned the corner and saw it at the door of their house. Even then she thought it must be for their downstairs neighbours; didn't even have a flash of fear about baby Mark. But it was for Les, because his mother had died on the station, while waiting for the 8.45 to King's Cross.

She had simply sat down, rather out of breath, on a seat on the platform, and died.

Les and Theresa did not blame each other. Neither of them wished the other to know that they cared at all. But they each knew it was the other's fault. Theresa knew that any hope of seeing her own mum had died with Peggy.

Shut.

I have to stay in Sheffield for five days before I can bring Matt home.

What a strange time. Having no home and no housework makes it seem like a holiday, but a weird mad holiday where nothing is as it should be.

Matt could come home a day earlier, I'm sure, but he has to wait for things: a new brain scan to make sure that he isn't likely to go back into unconsciousness, a report to his doctor (and of course he hasn't got one any more), pain killers, instructions.

But by now it hardly matters. I'm in this new dream-like life anyway. Waking up in the pale-green genteel bedroom in the dark hours of the morning, writing until I fall asleep with the pen in my hand and the light on, waking again to the alarm and going down to breakfast, and the exchange of: 'How's he going on?' 'Much better, thank you.' 'Coffee or tea?' with Penny Brayne who runs the place – a skinny scuttling woman with – from the evidence of the walls – a passion for tapestry.

The hospital is not welcoming in the mornings, so I roam around the town, or sit in cafes, texting Kez and Don with worries.

In the art gallery, I look at a postcard of a little boy – about Alfie's age, dressed in a blue and yellow clown suit, with frills. I smile to myself, thinking what my Alfie would say if he had to wear something like that, now he's at the age where if it's not football-related, then it won't do. The child on the postcard stares past me, not meeting my eyes, and I think suddenly that he must be dead by now, whoever he is, and so will all the boys one day, and all the girls too.

I turn away, and buy a card of a tram to send to Alfie, and one of a Shetland pony for Grace.

I haven't seen Leslie again, but I ring Theresa Saturday morning, knowing she won't be at work, and she invites me round. Her voice on the phone is still a London voice, after I've had a week of being surrounded by drawn out Yorkshire vowels. Beaten, is what she looks like when she opens the door, not beaten as in bruised, beaten like her sister Kay, defeated by life. But tiny; not fat like Kay, not an ounce on her, grey in her dark hair, but not much, and her face wrinkled like a paper bag screwed up and smoothed out again. She tries to smile, but there are tears in her eyes. She holds the door open wordlessly and we stand awkwardly in the hall.

'Les isn't in,' she says. 'He'll be out till gone five.'

'How are you?' I say. She doesn't answer.

As before, we sit in the kitchen. I wonder where their money goes, because it clearly doesn't get spent on the house. The coffee she gives me is cheap, and she puts three sugars in hers. 'I've given up smoking,' she says, 'so I've got to have some pleasure, haven't I?'

'I saw you last at Malcolm's funeral,' I say, and she fills up with tears again.

'How's Kay doing?'

'OK I think.' Then I think, what's the point of that? and I tell her something nearer the truth. 'I saw her just after Christmas. She's put on so much weight it's scary and Val says she doesn't go out.'

Theresa shakes her head like an old woman.

'You wouldn't think, would you?'

'I know. It's a few years now.'

'Six and nearly six months.' She hasn't stopped to calculate it, she knows to the day.

Then she asks about Tony, and I have to say that I can't tell her anything. No one knows now whether Tony is dead or alive, mad or sane, only that he refused all offers of contact from Val – who had been the closest to him – and Kay, and Rita.

As I'd said to Kezia, after his dad died, Tony seemed to want to cut himself off from everyone else. Theresa listens in silence and shrugs. Maybe it's all too long ago now for her to care.

So we talk about our children, four each. Hers are older than mine, of course, though her youngest is slightly younger than Matt. She has seven grandchildren, and brings the photos out of the drawer to show me.

Only in Angela's oldest can I see anything of the grandparents, but she has a look of the Doughtys: black hair and blue eyes, a slightly faraway stare and Les' pointed, stubborn chin.

Angie's others are tall and gangly and cheerful, snapped in running shorts or cricket clothes or swimming gear.

Mark's children are all big and fair, like him, like his wife, like Malcolm. The girl looks sullen, but she's at the age for it, the boys look bounding and cheerful and well-fed. ('Don't tell Les I've got them photos, will you?')

I wish I'd brought pictures of all mine, but all I have is the photo of Rita that I took from Kay's house, so I show her that. She sees who it is, and that's that, she closes up, ices over you might say, and gets up to put the kettle on.

When she sits down again and we have the distraction of more cups of coffee we start again, from the beginning.

'Have you lived here long?'

She calculates. 'A long time now. We were in that flat a couple of years and then when Angie was born, they give us a council house.'

'This one?'

She nods, pleased I think, and looks round in a proprietorial sort of way at the bare walls, the old orange kitchen units, the tiles behind the sink printed with the sort of vegetables she would surely never buy or cook – aubergines and pumpkins they seem to be, in nasty purplish colours.

'You keep it nice,' I say, and she looks pleased again, and so am I because it's true, everything's too old to sparkle, but clean and tidy and the floor I must say is a nice bit of thick vinyl, expertly laid.

'Do you go out to work?' I ask, knowing that she does because Les told me.

'In the pub. I do six evenings and three mornings. It's not like it used to be though, not so many people in. The way it's going, it could close, I could lose me job.'

'Would you get another one?'

'Not round here. I'm lucky to have that, but I've been there years, before Kim was born, well before, when Angie was little. They've been good to me.'

I bet. Minimum wage, covering other people's shifts, staying late, cleaning up sick, doing jobs other people should be doing. And grateful with it.

I ask about Les' business, but she clearly doesn't know much and doesn't want to talk about it.

'I saw Val last week,' I say, and I tell her the story of Don and the ladder, and then the more immediate story of Matt and his injuries. She listens intently, enjoying it, remembering it, I'm guessing, so that she can pass it on to her children, something different to say.

'You'll be waiting for the third one.'

I don't understand.

'Threes. Bad things always come in threes.'

'So they do.' I'm not superstitious but I find myself thinking, maybe the whistling boy was the third casualty, and I hope Kez hasn't found him in the drawer and thrown him away. Would she dare?

A person walks past the kitchen window, I see his shadow on the wall. 'It's Sean,' says Theresa, and her face brightens. He comes into the kitchen scuffing his nose with the back of his hand – a big young man but apparently boneless. His face is pudgy and his body undefined. I compare him to Matt, unfavourably. When he sees me, he shuffles and speaks only to his mum.

'Lend us a tenner.'

She fetches her purse, gives him the money, he goes.

'Would he have stayed, if I hadn't been here?'

'He's shy,' she says.

'He doesn't look like you.' I wish I hadn't said that, because it's clear to me that he doesn't look like Les either.

'No,' she says with a little laugh.

'How old is he?'

'Twenty one.'

'Same as my Matt. What month?'

'January.'

'Matt's November. I remember going to your mum's funeral and feeling sick as anything.'

She nods and goes to fill the kettle again. I get up though.

'Got to go. It's been great to see you again. Why don't you come down and visit? Val and Kay would love to see you.'

'They could come here.'

'Val would, if you asked her. I don't know whether Kay would feel up to it. Invite her though, see if you can cheer her up.' She looks doubtful, and I am too, doubtful as to whether Kay would come, and whether it would cheer her up if she did.

When Katie was in hospital, I was by her side nearly all the time, but of course Matt is an adult and I'm restricted to visiting times. But the experience is making me remember Katie's illness, just the smell of the hospital that catches your throat as you go in is bringing it all back to me, though I've tried for years to forget.

It happened on the day of Rita's wedding. It was a

registry office do and they close at twelve on Saturdays. Don wasn't invited, but that was all right because he could say home and look after the children. Children definitely not invited.

Well, you can imagine. Zoe was six weeks old. If I'd had something nice to wear, I wouldn't have been able to get into it and anyway would have leaked milk all over it, and I'd gone through the argument about buying something new – with Don and with myself – and I knew there were things I wanted more than a dress I'd wear once only, so in the end I wore a jacket of my mum's – actually the one she wore to my wedding five years before – though I wasn't tempted to borrow the dress that went with it. So it was an old dress I wore, and a bit too summery for April, and all the night before I was thinking: a) what does it matter, it's Rita they'll be looking at, and b) your best friend's wedding and you're too tight to buy something especially for it.

Not that it was thoughts keeping me awake. Zoe woke once as she always did, at about two, and went back to sleep after a feed. Then Katie woke, fell out of bed actually, which she'd never done before, even when she first moved into it from a cot some months earlier. Anyway, woke up, fell on the floor – or the other way round maybe – wailed and wouldn't go back to sleep, though you could see she was frantic with tiredness.

'She's hot,' said Don.

'It's just from crying,' I said. I did not want, did not at all want, an ill child. If it had been Zoe who seemed ill, would I have behaved differently? I don't want to think so but I think I would. Zoe was the new baby, she was all tiny and perfect and just new; Katie looked huge beside her, she was whiny and irritating, she was a threat to the new one, and I kept forgetting that I loved her.

Eventually she did go back to sleep, only for minutes it seemed, before Zoe woke for her morning feed, but it was a bit of a blessing because I had the opportunity to have a bath without an audience and dry my hair without a small body clamped to my leg going 'Up mummy, up.'

When she did wake, she was pale and cross and pouchy-eyed and wouldn't eat anything.

'She's coming down with something,' said Don.

She's not, she can't, I'm going out. What I said was: 'I don't think so. She's just had a bad night. A bit of fresh air will do her good.' (Don was going to take them to the park, this was the plan.) 'She can have her sleep this morning if you want, then she can sit with you while Zoe sleeps, and watch telly or something.'

I had gone to some trouble to organise this Saturday off. Expressed breast milk for the baby and made her practise drinking from a bottle, prepared meals for Don and Katie, made little piles of nappies, clothes, emergency clothes and more clothes. Explained to Katie that Daddy would be looking after her while Mummy went to Auntie Rita's wedding, told her she was a big girl to stay at home and look after Daddy and baby Zoe, all that sort of thing.

I was going, I was going out, I was going to see Rita

and see her get married. I was going to see her looking glamorous and successful and she had invited me as the only person who wasn't strictly family because I was her best friend, and even though I didn't see her much these days, I was still her best friend and she wanted me there.

Because there had been rifts between us. Rows. When she told me she wouldn't be a close friend anymore because she was going to university. When she had an abortion. When she wouldn't lend money to Don and me for an extension. We quarrelled about Malcolm, and about Les, and about Theresa. Some of these were still in the future when she married Pete, but the abortion one was still fresh in our minds.

Katie is nearly two, I am pregnant with Zoe. Our kitchen table. On it, coffee cups and a Magic Roundabout jigsaw which Rita has just bought for Katie, which is too old for her and which she can't do, and in fact won't manage to do until she is six, by which time, the pieces will be battered and bent.

'Tim,' says Rita, 'asked me to marry him.'

'What did you say?'

'I turned him down of course,' she says.

'But you've been going out with him for ages.' As soon as I say this, I'm embarrassed because it makes me sound staid and old-fashioned, as if I'd said 'walking out' or 'your young man' which is how my nan talked about me and Don.

'On and off.'

'He must think you care about him.'

'I think he knows how things stand.'

'So why ask you? Just for a laugh?'

She starts to speak, stops, starts to say something else, changes her mind. It's not like Rita.

'I won't tell anyone,' I say.

'You'd better not.' She sighs, as if I've dragged the truth out of her after hours of questioning, and says in a flat unemotional voice, 'I was pregnant. Tim thought it might be his.'

I don't know which bit of this statement to go with. '*Was* pregnant?'

'I had an abortion.'

You see, she shouldn't have told me. I've got a baby, I'm expecting another one, news like that, about anyone, is bound to unsettle me. When it's about Rita it tips me over. 'How could you do that? How could you?'

'I had to.'

'Nobody has to. I would have looked after it for you. I don't care whose it was. You can't go round killing babies. Honestly Rita, I'm disgusted. Does your mum know?'

'Well *I* had to,' she says.

'So whose was it then, if it wasn't Tim's?' I'm saying all this in the sort of hiss that you have to use when there are children present, even if they are too young to understand. Katie is looking with interest, but doesn't seem to be bothered by it.

'Mind your own business. I'm sorry I told you. I thought I'd get a bit of understanding from you, but no, obviously. Look at you, with your wedding ring and your – your –' she looks around the kitchen '– your front-loading washing machine. It's all right for you.' She says all this quite calmly, like a prepared speech, as if she doesn't care. 'You've got a small mind, Pat Plant and I don't really want anything to do with it.' Even then, she doesn't hurry about going but talks to Katie a little, turning the jigsaw pieces over for her so she can see the pictures. Katie is sitting on my knee and Rita is so close to me I can smell her hair and her skin, and I regret so much the loss of that baby, that would – though it's later when I think this – have drawn us together in a shared experience such as we haven't had since soon after we left school. Rita's hair swings across her face so I can't see her expression, and after some long moments, she kisses Katie on the cheek, straightens up, picks up her bag and goes to the door.

'And I'm not Pat Plant anymore,' I say. 'Some of us can manage to get married.' And she laughs and leaves.

We didn't see each other for a while but she sent a Christmas card and a present for Katie and I sent a card back. Just before Christmas, her father died and I sent letters and cards to her and her mum, but didn't go to the funeral.

I thought I would see her at Kay's on Boxing Day, but for the first time, she wasn't there. That's when I heard that she was getting married.

'To Tim?'

'Who's Tim?' says Val. 'Didn't she tell you? She's only marrying Pete McCartney. *You* know.'

Well I did. Marriage and fatherhood had not stopped Don's obsessive collecting of records or reading of the music papers, so I knew about Evermore, and their drummer Pete. Val was about fifteen at that time. The previous Christmases when I've seen her she was keen on playing auntie to the children, but this year, she's bored with them and wants to sit with Kay and me and Malcolm's mother and listen to us talking. It's all about Rita.

'Mum thinks it's funny,' says Kay. 'She calls them Reet 'n' Pete.' (Mrs Doughty wasn't there, Ted having died so recently.)

'Shame it's not *Paul* McCartney,' says Malcolm, and I tell them (probably not for the first time) that Rita did once meet him.

'Have you had an invite, Pat?'

I have to say no.

'It's not a big do though, is it?' This is Ruby, Malcolm's mum. I guess she's not consoling me but herself.

So when I received an invitation to the wedding, I was touched and pleased, and determined to go, no matter what.

And I did, and I spoiled it.

We were in the registry office and the registrar – a tall careworn man – was just beginning when there was a commotion outside the door, there was shouting and protesting and banging, as if someone was trying to get in and other people were trying to stop them.

The registrar looked up and seemed to be satisfied

that things were under control and made some little comment to the bride and groom, I guess about photographers, or fame, or something. But the shouting didn't stop and of course all the guests were turning round and trying to see what was going on. Then the shouting resolved into a name.

'Pat. Paaaaat,' receding as the person outside was dragged away, whoever it was.

People looked at me. For a second, I thought it was Don's voice, but that was plainly ridiculous, for not only was he at home with the children but he would not, even with a gun at his back, make a public exhibition of himself like that.

But his brother would.

Gordon was an emotional sort, and not so good at thinking through his actions before he embarked on them. Here I made a wrong decision and stayed where I was, pretending to myself that I had not recognised the voice and that it was all nothing to do with me.

So it was when we were outside and the photographers were getting busy, that the shouting started again. No one present had met Gordon before, except Rita, and that had been at my wedding, so everyone was shocked when his figure more or less threw himself in front of me and began pulling at my arm.

'You've got to come, you've got to come,' he was saying.

Do you know, I knew immediately that it was about the children; Don never entered my head. I could feel myself leaking milk as a response, and I just turned and went with him.

By the time we arrived at the hospital, I was trying to tell myself that Gordon always exaggerated and that he had probably got it all wrong.

Katie could not have had what he was calling a seizure, and if she had, she would be all right by now. Another part of my brain was telling me that the worst had happened: she was dead already, and I would want to die too but would have to stay alive to look after my baby. And then when we got there, it was somewhere in between the two.

Katie didn't die. They called it encephalitis, which seemed to be the name they gave to something in the brain that they couldn't be sure about. No one could tell us how bad it was, how long it would last, how much damage it would do.

She lay there, sedated and apparently peaceful, and I sat by her side for days, bored and anxious and desperately needing to be with my other baby.

Zoe was having an unexpected and unplanned weaning process, and spent a lot of time with Don's sister while he came to the ward, and we sat by Katie's cot together, looking at her and feeling helpless and hopeless. But she didn't die.

Sometimes, in the following weeks and months I thought to myself – I never told anyone this – that it would have been better for her if she had, but she didn't.

She came through; she opened her eyes and moved her head and closed her eyes again. This felt like a victory, and we waited for the next improvement, and we waited a long time.

Poor Katie needed months of physio before she began to be anything like herself. She could smile a wobbly and one-sided sort of smile, but her body was limp. Sitting up, controlling her hands, using her muscles, taking her own weight, swallowing – all these things, that she could do before as a normal two year old, had to be learned again.

As soon as she could hold something in her hand though, she began to take out her frustration by using it to hit anybody within reach. I was sure – I still am – that she knew what had happened to her. She knew that her skills had been taken away – on the day that I had abandoned her – and that it was my fault that she had to do all this hard and painful work, just to get back to where she started.

And Zoe too – she had been abandoned. I hardly saw her for the twenty three days Katie was in hospital, and when we were all back home again, for Zoe, it was as if she had, instead of a big sister, a giant twin as helpless as her, who had to be looked after first.

Zoe's pre-school was hospital waiting rooms and specialist playgroups; her playmates were children like Katie who couldn't walk, or couldn't see or speak, or reliably reach out and grasp a toy.

A two-year-old Zoe who could do all these things would toddle around the day centre, alternately sweetly assisting those less able, and taking advantage by snatching their toys and running off with them.

It still amazes me, and I am so grateful for it, that Katie overcame her illness. All the time, it seems to me, her intelligence was there; she just couldn't get it out. No wonder she was frustrated.

The traces of illness that remained, and remain to this day, are an awkward walk – she sort of stomps along as if her knees won't bend easily, and a very loud laugh, which I'm sure she didn't have before, which makes people jump if they don't know her.

But – what if? What if Katie hadn't been ill? Would she and Zoe have grown up friendly? Would they now be visiting each other? Would their children be the sort of cousins who know each other?

Would Katie even have felt the need to leave home when she did? Would she even have been lonely enough to have got pregnant so young? Would she have gone through with it?

What if Kezia hadn't been born – how would the two older girls have been then? Or if we hadn't had Matthew, that late baby – would Katie ever have thought of having a baby? Getting pregnant maybe, these things happen, but going through with it? What if she and Jay hadn't gone to live in Bristol? Would Matthew have grown up happy, balanced, optimistic?

Matt is allowed home at last, and we drive away down the M1 feeling – at least I do – as if we've escaped from a prisoner of war camp. He's quiet, and pale, and almost a stranger to me. It reminds me of when I was first going out with Don, and there was so much I didn't know about him, and didn't know how he would react to different things I said. And yet I knew him, Don, then, if only in the way you know someone who's had their hand inside your jumper.

'Do you want to put some music on?'

'I don't mind,' he says. 'Do you want me to?'

I feel so sorry for him, all careful and cautious as he is, and at the same time, quite cross with him. 'I'm your mum,' I want to say. 'You don't have to be so polite.' But I don't say it because I'm being careful too.

A few miles later I tell him he can smoke if he wants.

'I've given up,' he says.

This is such good, and unexpected news that I get all effusive.

'Oh well done! When? How did you do it?'

'When I was unconscious,' he says. 'It's not that hard when you're unconscious. And anyway, when I woke up, I couldn't get out of bed. So...'

And then I feel guilty for not realising on any of the previous days that he wasn't smoking.

Everybody smoked. Kath and Ted, Theresa and Kay. Malcolm. Don. Les. My mum and her mum and Auntie Peggy. Later on, Val and Tony. Only Rita and I didn't.

One time I tried. We were about thirteen and in a park with a bunch of kids.

'Go on.'

Why not, I thought. Or maybe I thought I'd look stupid if I didn't, or grown up if I did. Who knows now what I thought then? So I had a couple of drags and coughed a bit, which probably didn't look very appealing, if that's what I was hoping for, and I noticed that Rita said No in an off-hand sort of way that managed to imply that she could if she wanted, or maybe that the brand she was being offered (Number Six, probably) was inferior.

Afterwards she came round my house on purpose to tell me, very pompously, 'Don't think you can be best friends with me if you smoke.'

'Why not?' I said. I wasn't desperate to but, like I said, everybody else did.

'I don't like it,' she said. 'I have enough of it at home. Our house is just one big ashtray and Theresa's already started, you know.'

'Well my mum smokes, so I know what you mean.' Although I hadn't really noticed. It was just one of the things parents did.

'One day,' she said, 'I'll live somewhere where no one smokes and then I won't smell like a fag packet.'

This was a novel thought to me, but she always did have a keener sense of smell than a lot of people. I often thought about it, and eventually it happened: the smoke-free house, for her and for me.

For me, when Don gave up, when Katie was poorly and we gave up everything that we'd ever enjoyed, as some kind of unspoken – unthought even – bargain with fate. That was when I gave up the struggle to look halfway nice, and we never bothered decorating the house, or even tidying it very much, or buying new things, because it was all frivolous and asking for trouble.

If we hadn't, I suppose Don might have died of smoking like Malcolm did, and Ted. Funny, that. And now maybe Matthew won't die of it either.

I want to talk to Matt and tell him what Kezia and I spoke about, and tell him that I understand, or think I do, how he felt when he was a little boy and his nephew-who-was-more-like-his-brother was taken to live somewhere else. I want to say to him I'm sorry that I didn't notice, or if I did, ignored how he was feeling and didn't help him to deal with it as I should have done.

But I'm scared to say it. I don't know what the consequences might be. I don't want to remind him about it all, I don't want to make him feel worse. I don't want to remind him, now that we're getting on a bit better, what a bad mother I am.

I've been away from home for six days. Kez, I know, is still with Don, and Don is making good progress.

Katie has phoned to tell me that Alfie has fallen down the stairs and broken his wrist.

'Don't worry, mum, it's only a greenstick fracture. Six weeks and it'll be as good as new.'

'What was he doing?'

'Oh you know. Whatever boys do. He had a friend round.'

That's the third thing then, I think, satisfied.

I'm looking forward all the way home. At the end of this road is home, and Don, and my things, and I'm even in time to go to the writing class tomorrow.

No more big breakfasts – I must have put on half a stone. No more wandering around shops, wishing I could go home. No more other people's houses. My own washing machine is calling me home.

The house looks different when I stop outside. I look carefully though, while I'm opening the boot and I can't see anything to explain how it seems. In the hall though, major changes. No sideboard. No floor. We make our way over planks as Don and Kez watch us from the living room door.

Hugs, smiles and welcomes have to happen before I can look round. The kettle has to go on before I'm allowed to show that I've noticed.

The spaces, the gaps.

'Don't be upset, mum,' says Kez.

'It's all for the best, love,' says Don. He sounds scared I might go crazy.

'Where is it all?'

'Different places,' says Kez, at the same time as Don says: 'Here and there.'

'Anyway,' says Kez. 'What about Matt? How are you? How are the bruises?'

Matt's been sitting looking bewildered, much as I have, since we came in, but I think probably for him, it's more about the strangeness of being home with his family, and less about the strangeness of what his home looks like.

'OK,' he says.

Kez makes tea. We sit in armchairs, in sunshine that comes through the window, unimpeded by a tallboy that had previously stood there for years, with my nan's clocks and vases on top.

'What it was, mum,' says Kez, 'was woodworm. It wasn't just the hall floor – it was most of the furniture. The man from Rentokil said it looked as if it had been there for years – even before we got it.'

'It had to go,' says Don. He still looks nervous of me, and I realise I haven't asked him how he is, though he's looking OK, and anyway, after I've spoken to him every day for a week on the phone, I shouldn't have to ask again.

'I'll get used to it,' I say. It's the wrong moment for saying what I really feel.

I believe in father Christmas

Christmas Eve. The orange streetlights cast a different, and especially festive glow.

The houses down the street, more lit up than usual, were tense with waiting. Somewhere out of sight, a door opened and closed again.

Across the road, the door of number 10 opened, and two stout men helped a tiny old lady down the step.

Mark watched from his window as they took her, holding an arm each so that she seemed to skim the ground, to the Cortina that stood waiting. Behind them, came a small round lady, carrying bags.

They put the old lady in the front and handed her handbag in after her. They put the suitcase and the bag of parcels on the back seat.

The round lady and one of the stout men waved as the car drove away.

Mark watched them hurry, hugging them-selves against the cold, back into their house. Straightaway, the downstairs lights went off and the front bedroom light came on. He waited. Nothing happened, and then the bedroom light across the road went off too.

He could see eight houses, and now four of them were in darkness. He waited. He was cold, although he had his eiderdown round him, and his eyes wanted to close, but he continued to kneel on his bed and look out at the street.

Only number 2 had any lights on by the time the taxi stopped outside Mark's house.

He ducked down as he saw it approach, and stayed below window sill level as his mother got out and said goodnight. She didn't have to pay the man because Bill who owned the pub where she worked would pay him. Mark sat up straight, so as not to go to sleep.

As the front door opened, Mark heard the scrape of his father's chair on the kitchen floor. He imagined him stacking his pack of cards and putting them away in the corner of the dresser drawer.

The kitchen door opened with a small scrape, where it caught the edge of the lino. He heard dad's step on the stairs, and got under the covers, just in case. He didn't think dad would bring his stocking, but just in case. He held his eyelids open with his fingers.

He heard his dad peeing, and heard the clunk of the chain being pulled. Dad's steps went into his bedroom and then out again.

There was a rustling noise as he crossed the landing to Angela's room. Mark heard Angela's door being cautiously pushed open. More rustling, and then the door being carefully pulled to. Then dad went into his own room and got into bed.

It was as Mark expected. It would be his mum

who brought his stocking.

Last year, for the first time, he had known there was no Father Christmas. He had woken as his door opened, and sat up suddenly, making his mum jump.

'Caught me,' she said softly, and laughed and kissed him as she tucked him back in. 'Don't tell Angela,' she whispered.

It was rare for her to speak softly, or laugh, or kiss him. He thought that may have been the last time it happened. Maybe it only happens at Christmas. He remembers the thick intoxication of chocolate eaten under the bedclothes.

He knelt up again and pressed his forehead against the cold glass of the window. He listened to the sounds from downstairs, of cupboard doors opening and closing, of water running, of things being got out and put away.

He heard her open the door of the cupboard under the stairs – it had a fierce and sudden click – to get out the presents, to put them under the tree. Mark knew they were there. He had spent a few evenings lying in there with them, just touching the wrapping paper, when he should have been in bed.

He heard her make three trips from hall to front room, and then close the doors. She clicked off the kitchen light, and her footsteps came up the stairs. Mark lay down again, awake now, ready for his door to open.

He heard her close the bathroom door, then flush the toilet; heard the click as the landing light went off and saw the bright line vanish from the foot of his door. Heard the definite closing of her door and the sound of the springs as she got into bed.

He waited. Nothing.

He knelt again and looked out the window. No lights except the orange street lights. No sound in the house. No movement. No stocking. No little car, balloons, sweets, pencils. No kiss.

He sat now on his bed, looking at the door, going over it, making sure.

Out of bed, he pulled gently at his door, crept onto the landing; pushed at Angela's door. The room was illuminated by the same fizzy orange light that shone through his own curtains. Angela was asleep, and lying across the bottom of her bed was a big plastic sock-shaped bag. Mark stood still and looked at it for a long time. He tried to see in his mind's eye a similar shape on his own bed. He wondered. He crept back to his own room and looked again. Nothing.

Back by Angela's bedside he reached out and touched the bag. The red and white plastic was stretched tight over a box shape, then looser over some smaller things. There would be toys – girls' stuff – and sweets. Mark suddenly wanted more than anything – more than a kiss from his mum – some chocolate. Angela's chocolate.

Slowly, he pulled the opening of the bag round till he could reach and feel inside. The big box was a Selection Box, and he thought he couldn't open it – because she'd know. Then he thought he could. She was only six, she wouldn't know.

He tried to open it with one hand, but it kept moving, so he put two hands inside the bag. But the box was fastened with a piece of sellotape, and as he pulled at the cardboard either side it tore suddenly. The stocking bag split, Mark slipped and jarred the bed. Something rolled onto the floor.

Angela sat up.

'Is it Christmas? Has Father Christmas been?' She darted across the room to the light switch, and everything changed as the ceiling light came on.

Mark, cold now, and scared of what she would do next, punched her hard on the back as she jumped back on to her bed to examine her stocking. She didn't cry or make any noise, but looked slowly surprised, finding that things weren't as they should be.

'Leave my stocking alone. You've ripped it. Give me my stuff. I'll tell dad.'

She was getting louder with every sentence, indignation growing.

'Shut up,' said Mark.

'Go back to your own room.'

'Shut up,' he said again.

'You're not allowed. I'll tell dad.'

He punched her again, on the shoulder this time, and this time, she took a deep breath and yelled with pain and fright and frustration.

'Give me some,' he said desperately. 'Let me have some.'

She was lying over the heap of stuff now, trying to stop him getting it.

'Go away!'

Mum and dad were in the room, pulling Mark off the bed, shouting: 'What's going on?' putting arms round Angela, picking little presents off the floor.

Mark lay on the floor and kicked at his mother's legs.

'Where's mine?' he whined.

Dad grasped his arm and pulled him up.

'I'll give you where's mine. Get yourself back to bed.'

The pain in his arm from dad's grip loosened Mark's temper.

'It's not fair. Where's mine? She gets everything. It's not fair. What about me?' He was screaming now, and making lunges at Angela, who sat on mum's knee, snivelling and smirking at the same time.

The room rocked as dad's hand connected with the side of his head.

'That'll do, Les,' said mum.

Smack. Rock. Black. Light.

She got to her feet, dropping Angela on the carpet.

'I said that'll do.'

Dad's hand gripping his arm again.

'What you going do about it?'

Mum's voice, shaky, shrill: 'Leave my son alone.'

Mark was on the floor, in a heap. Angela kicked him and he kicked her back.

Dad's voice, full of hate: 'I pay for his bleedin' keep, I can do what I bleedin' like.'

Dragged to his feet by his pyjamas, dragged into his bedroom.

Picked up and thrown on the bed; head banged against the wall.

Mark looked at dad with the realisation that this hate wasn't just for when he was bad, it was there all the time.

'And stay there.'

Mark stayed. He knew when he was beaten.

After Angela was tucked back into bed and the lights went out again, he could hear the argument from the back bedroom. As he dozed off, the familiar phrases became part of his dreamscape.

'Little shit.'

'It's not his fault.'

Then, reasonable: 'Theresa, I'll keep him in food and clothes but you can't make me like him.'

'Just go easy on him.'

'When he behaves himself, praps I'll go easy on him.'

'Les –'

'That's enough. I've had enough. Go to sleep.'

Mark too, goes to sleep.

I read this out, even though I only wrote it this morning. There was nothing to do at home. Matt slept till midday, Don was occupied with his puzzle book and music, Kez had done all the shopping, and cleaned and cooked enough to keep us going for the rest of the week. The builders had the hall floor to lay, before they started on the living room.

I tried to look busy but then I gave up and sat with Don, writing to the sound of some seventies greatest hits.

'Ouch,' says Judy, when I finish.

'Better,' says Jerry. 'Coming along, I think. Now Joan, have you got something to cheer us up with?'

She reads a poem about a Greenline bus, which sends John and Jim off down a memory lane of trolley buses and the junction at Tramway Avenue. 'You could be sitting there late for work while they got their poles to put the thing back up again.'

You don't have to be as old as them to remember that, I think, and then I feel cross that because I can remember that, it puts me in the same basket as these old codgers.

At coffee break, I tell Jocelyn and Judy why I've missed two weeks, and they make sympathetic noises and tell me about accidents they have known.

Later in the pub, I have the same conversation with the men. Jeff is especially interested in the woodworm.

Across the pub I see a face I recognise – Shelley, a young woman I used to work with. I duck my head and turn half sideways so that if she does see me, at least I don't have to see her. We were quite friendly, but I don't think she'll approach me. I listen with deep attention to Jeff telling me about dry rot.

Don is fretting to go back to work, though his collar bone is slow to mend and has set in a slightly crooked way, so that they are talking about breaking and resetting it. 'In their dreams,' he says.

And my house is not my house any more. For a while, it was like being on holiday, exclaiming at the view, but now I feel bereft all over again.

I dream about tablecloths. I investigate whether there is a cure for woodworm, so that I can blame Kez and Don for not using it.

I look in charity shops at similar old people's vases and ornaments, even though mine haven't gone. They are packed in newspaper and large boxes at the back of the garage: 'So that you can go through them, mum, in your own time, and decide what you want to keep.'

I am only sixty, and I am being treated like an old person already.

I can't bring myself to look at them, because if I did, where would I put them? Except back in the box they came from. She didn't think of that, did she, when she was carefully packing them away, feeling like she was being so nice to me. Bloody daughters.

It reminds me of clearing my mum's house, sifting through the plates and tea towels and sheets and clothes, like a museum, but one where I had memories to attach to every teaspoon.

Not many ornaments though. Nan and Peg were the ones who all the ornaments came from. Just about the only ornament my mother had when I was a child, before she cleared my nan's house, stood, or rather, reared on the front room mantel piece.

I was forbidden to touch it, go near it, breathe on it, and must only look at it from a distance wider than the hearth rug. And my mother, knowing that she was heavy-handed and prone to break things, obeyed the same rules. When she dusted in the front room – not often, she wasn't much of a housewife, and as she said, we never used it so it couldn't need doing every week – when she dusted the mantel piece, she used two hands, her left hand holding it down, her right with the duster flapping at things. Then she'd blow on it, still holding tight, before taking her hand away slowly and backing off, eyes on it as if it was alive.

It was made of glass – a horse made of glass, rearing on its hind legs like Champion the Wonder Horse, and it was hollow and filled with liquid the colour of Lucozade.

The tips of its ears, the very tips, were empty, as the liquid had settled. Otherwise you might think it was solid orange glass. Where or who it came from, and what its meaning was, I never knew and never asked: it was just one of the immutables of life, but it seemed to be mum's most precious possession.

When at last she went into a Home, it was one of the items she debated whether to take with her, as she had doubts as to whether paid cleaners would manage to keep it intact for long.

After several times phoning me at work to discuss it, she finally asked if I would look after it for her 'for the time being.'

I said I would of course and didn't tell her I wasn't convinced it would survive family life – this was when Matt and Jay were still kids and missiles were still hurled in our house.

But what happened was worse than being collateral damage in some sibling conflict – worse, because Mum was there.

I was clearing the front room; she was directing me. Three categories of stuff: going with Mum, going to my house, going out.

I should say about mum that she was scared of almost everything. Mice, spiders, bangs in the night, lightning, unexpected knocks at the door; so she brought me up to be brave.

'You go, Pat. Catch it, Pat. Get rid of it, Pat. Come and sleep in my bed, Pat. Take the plug out of the wall first.'

But this thing of leaving her home and all her things and going somewhere without me, she was brave about that.

'That can go out,' she kept saying, and sometimes I would say, 'No I'll keep that,' because it felt wrong to get rid – even to a charity shop – of things I had grown up knowing.

And then we got to the orange horse.

'Careful with that,' said Mum. 'I'd do it myself but I

can't reach with this blasted thing.' (The blasted thing was her walking frame.)

I grasped the glass horse round its middle and lifted. It did not lift. I lifted with more force.

'What's up?' said Mum.

'It's stuck to the mantel piece,' I said.

'Well it's never been moved before,' she said. 'You have to give it a bit of a pull.'

So I did, and it suddenly left its position and reared into the air for the last time, leaving its glass base still stuck to the mantel piece with fifty years' worth of grime.

The orange liquid – which was probably only water – dripped off the tiles and on to the hearth, making a surprisingly big puddle, and my mum said, 'Well, after all that,' in an offended voice, as if I'd done it on purpose.

At Easter, Katie comes for a visit with both boys.

Oh joy. Well, joy and disappointment both.

Alfie doesn't really remember us very much. He goes to school now and is mostly interested in the design of his trainers and the strangeness of being five.

He is though, very keen on Matthew.

'When you were five, could you ride without stabilisers?'

'Can I look at the bottom of your trainers?'

'How many friends have you got?'

'Do you know my brother?'

Jay is as polite and charming as he has ever been, but

less forthcoming.

Yes, he likes university. No, he hasn't decided what he'll do afterwards.

But when Katie has to go home to go back to work, Jay stays behind for a few days, and he and Matt sit together in his room, comparing Ipods.

Alfie stays too, and I get to the point of wishing he didn't, because it's wearing you know, having a five year old asking questions and telling you things all the time.

Anyway, he and I are down the High Street, when I see Jean going into the Pound Shop. I never imagined her going in somewhere like that, but it goes to show you can never tell about people. Big swish car and buys her washing powder in the Pound Shop. Well, why not?

'Hello, Jean.'

She blanks me. Really – her eyes sort of de-focus, and she looks past me.

I try again. 'How's Julia?'

She turns and hurries away.

'Who's that lady, Nan? Who?'

'No one,' I say.

I find that I am remaking the encounter as I wish it had been: 'This is my grandson Alfie.' 'Oh he's a very handsome boy,' Jean would say. 'I broke my arm,' he'd tell her, pulling up his sleeve to show the plaster cast. 'I miss you at the writing group,' I'd say. 'I miss Julia too. Is she doing anything else?' 'Started work.'

I walk home through a fog of Alfie's chatter.

I am a bad mother, a bad grandmother. I have been a bad friend, a bad social worker, a bad wife. I wasn't a bad daughter, most of the time, but I stopped being a daughter ten years ago, more.

I remember caring about my mum, even when she was pretty much past caring about anything herself, but I don't know what I did with the caring capacity after she'd died. You'd think it would be transferable but I don't think it was.

'Nan.'

I'm peeling potatoes and wondering if I've bought enough for all the mouths I'm feeding.

Jay leans against the draining board, nonchalant. His lovely black hair is hidden under a strange woollen hat like a swollen beret, and he keeps his eyes focussed on our garden that he's staring at through the window.

'Can you tell me anything about my father?'

'Have you asked your mum?'

'Of course. I wanted to know what you could tell me.' His voice is cool and under control.

'Well he was very young, that's what I always think first about him. Younger than you are now.'

'Of course I knew that,' he says. 'But it's still strange to think about.'

'There's only one photo of him, as far as I know. I mean that we've got.'

'I've seen it.' He's sounding a little impatient now. 'You can't see his face in it really.'

That's true. His face was hidden, bending over baby Jay. The photographer – that would be me – taking the opportunity to do him a photographic favour.

Not that Murad was ugly – nothing that some early surgery on the squint, and a dental brace wouldn't have sorted out.

I mean it, his eyes, taken separately, were beautiful, and he had nice thick black hair. He wasn't very tall, about the same as Katie, but he was well put together, neither slender nor stocky.

'But what was he like? And what about his family?' He doesn't say "my family" but those are the words I think he wants to be able to say.

We just don't know. After Murad and Katie stopped seeing each other, the contact with Jay continued, but less and less often.

Even before Katie and Jay moved to Bristol, it was a rare occasion when Jay would see his dad or his Yemeni grandparents. There was talk, even then, of them leaving London and going to some other EU country. I remember Holland was mentioned.

But Jay knows all this and I can't think of anything else to say.

'We liked him, granddad and me. He was a gentle boy, very sweet-natured. I never heard him argue or get irritated. He was as proud of you as it was possible to be.'

I don't tell him about the off-colour remarks about girls' bodies, or how he was unreliable about keeping appointments or paying the pittance of maintenance. What was the point – he was a seventeen-year-old, not very bright boy, who worked in his uncle's kebab shop until two in the morning, and dreamed of joining the army if only his family would let him.

'But too young. No one could have expected the relationship to last.'

'I expect that's just what I did expect,' says Jay, just a little bit sharply. 'Anyway, mum's explained all that to me, the break up and all that.'

'I don't know what else I can say. It's so long ago that it's hard to remember that he was ever anything to do with you.'

'Not for me, it's not.'

'So. Have you tried to get in touch with him?'

'Not really.' What does that mean? But I don't ask. I drain the peelings and tip them into the bin.

'But Nan, it's like, I don't know who I am.'

'That's just your age,' I say. 'Everyone feels like that at your age.'

'No, it's always been like it, all my life. You look at Alfie – he's got heroes, there's so many footballers look like him, one week he thinks he's Theo Walcott –'

'Don't tell your grandad that –'

'– and he thinks because his middle name is James he's related to David James and he's going to be a goalkeeper.'

'Isn't he a bit old to be a hero?'

'I know that, but to Alfie, he plays for Bristol City and to Alfie, Bristol City is Barcelona. But listen Nan – when did I ever have a footballer that looked like me, or a singer, or a tennis player, or anyone?'

'But you're you.' I say desperately, because I don't understand anything except that I can't help.

'There isn't even a category for me, did you know that? I'm "any other mixed". What do you think that feels like? I might as well be a packet of seeds.'

'You're unique.'

'Tell the police that,' says Jay, and his voice is beginning to catch, just a little. 'Ever since – you know – they just pick on you all the time. I might as well be a fucking West Indian. Girls as well.'

'Well,' I say, trying to move somewhere else, 'there'll be girls who fancy you. '

'Oh yeah, like Kezia.' He flicks his fingers, dismissing her. 'Anyway, look at him. A Muslim policeman. What's that all about?'

Which left me wondering which side he was on. And how many sides there might be.

I have at least managed to keep on writing. Oh yes. Going to see Theresa has opened up new avenues, and they are much easier than writing about Rita. The thing is, Rita's life was so far removed from mine, and her sisters' lives are much more understandable to me. So I'm imagining what Theresa's life must have been like, with Les, and how her children must have been.

Rat trap

Angela was doing her homework. Her maths text book and homework book were already closed and piled neatly on her right.

She was now shading in a map of Europe, showing coalfields, iron ore deposits, fishing ports and different sorts of agriculture, using as many of her coloured pencil crayons as she could.

The evening air was warm and the back door stood open. They could hear the children next door playing in their garden.

Angela's dad sat facing her across the table. He had just laid out his hand of Patience for the third time; slither and flap, face up, slick and flick, face down.

'What's that?' said dad, pointing to a tiny mark on the corner of her maths homework book.

'Nothing.' She tried to hide it, but he reached across and picked it up. It just says:

A. P. Loves J. H.

'Who's J H?'

'No one.'

'You don't want to start with boys.'

'No, dad.'

'You know where that'll get you.'

'Yes, dad.'

'Keep on being a good girl, Angie.'

'Yes, dad.'

She went back to her careful shading. Brenda next door called her children in. A moth flew into the kitchen and Angela got up and closed the back door on the evening.

There was a knock on the front door, a heavy metallic sound, a man's knock.

'Get that, will you?'

She had an idea before she opened the door. It had happened before. It was still a shock, though, to see Mark standing between two policemen.

Their car, with its lights on, stood at the kerb. She didn't look at Mark. She knew what he would look like. His blue eyes would be both blank and filled with tears. His lips would be pressed tight in what looks like a grin, showing his dimples.

'Your mum and dad in?'

'Dad.'

'Can we come in?'

They filled the kitchen. Dad stayed sat in his chair. She went back to her chair on the other side of the table. But she began to put away her pencils and books because she knew she wouldn't get it finished tonight.

Mark had been picked up running through back gardens with other boys. Most fine evenings, and some wet ones, this was what they did; it was a game called Delavio. A bit of

Angela wished she could be out there, chasing and calling through streets and jennels and gardens, but she was a good girl – she stayed in with her dad and her books.

The police knew Mark – he hadn't needed to tell them where he lived; they'd brought him home before. Tonight, there had been some damage to someone's greenhouse and fence.

'Have a talk with him, Mr Plant,' suggested one as they left.

Angie wanted to leave the kitchen and she wanted to stay. She wanted to look at Mark and she didn't want him to see her looking. She knew what was going to happen and she wanted to watch. Dad was going to paste Mark and Mark deserved it.

It started as soon as the front door closed behind the two policemen.

Mark was standing between the table and the sink, just standing. He twitched, as if to move towards the door. Dad stood up. He put his chair tidily under the table, without hurrying.

'Go to bed, Angie,' he said.

She went to the door, stood there, and watched.

Dad stood looking at Mark, then brought his right arm up so fast she didn't see the movement, and hit him round the side of the head with the flat of his hand.

For the first time in all the times she'd seen

this, Mark didn't fall over. He rocked, he staggered and grabbed hold of the edge of the sink. If it was me getting hit, she thinks, I'd lie down and pretend to be unconscious. That way he'd stop sooner. But Mark always went on getting up, as long as he could. And this time, he hadn't even gone down.

She saw dad pitch forward and knew he'd been kicked. Mark got hold of a saucepan off the cooker and lay about him wildly with it. Water hit the floor with big flat splats. Dad struggled to get it off him but as he did Mark had got the grill pan above his head, holding it with both hands. He brought it down on dad's head. After three times the handle broke and the pan flew across the room in her direction. She was still standing, watching.

Mark was getting closer to dad, punching doggedly, face screwed up like a little boy's, saying nothing, his breath coming in great sobs as if he'd surfaced after too long under water.

Dad was hitting back, but not hard; he was hurt.

Mark pushed him – a big shove in the chest that sent him backwards, and Mark was past him and out the back door. His breath and his footsteps faded out of hearing.

It must have been gone eleven when mum came in from work.

'What you doing still up?' was the first thing

she said. Then she saw dad sitting in the arm-chair instead of at the table.

'What's happened? Where's Mark?'

Dad's forehead had a big cut on it, with an awful flap of skin, sticky with blood and hair, that was hanging down until he pressed it back in place. He was still holding a wet tea towel to it. He had another wound on his shoulder, where it joined his neck, a gaping cut from the edge of the grill pan, with raised, bruised edges like lips. His right arm was bruised from elbow to wrist and he couldn't move his fingers.

'Mark did it,' Angie said. She was proud that she stayed to watch and stayed to help.

'Go to bed,' said mum.

She stood in the kitchen as if she didn't know what to do, then she crossed to dad and lifted the bloody tea towel. 'You should get that stitched.' He didn't speak.

'Go to bed,' she said again, to Angie.

She was in bed, but trembling too much, now that it was all over, to go to sleep, when she heard the car stop, the footsteps, the knock at the door. She was at the top of the stairs when mum opened it.

'Mrs Plant?'

'Yes.'

'Can I come in?'

'You can talk to me here.'

'Are you the mother of Mark Edward Plant?'

'Yes.'

'I'm sorry to tell you that Mark's been arrested.'

'Oh.'

'We need you to come down to the station with him, with him being only fourteen. We need you there when we charge him.'

'What's he done?'

'Damage. Resist arrest. Assault PC. Actually, love, he's been chucking rocks at cars off o't railway bridge. He's hit a few as well. It's a miracle nobody's been killed. Then we've had to chase him all across allotments, and he's kicked and punched my mate something terrible.'

'I'm not coming.'

The policeman saw Angie, further down the stairs now. 'If you need someone to stay wit' little lass, I can radio for a policewoman.'

'It's all right. Her dad's here. But I'm not coming. I'm not having nothing to do with him.'

'Look, love, he's got to have someone with him. What about his dad?'

'You want to see what he's done to him. No. We've had enough. That's it.'

The policeman gave up. He backed away down the path. Now Angie was in the hall, looking out of the door. Neighbours were standing at their open doors, looking. In the back of the police car, she could just see a head of floppy fair hair, bowed.

'And don't bring him back here,' said mum, quietly.

The policeman heard; lifted a slow hand to Angie's mum. He got into the driver's seat and drove away. It was the last time Angie would see her brother for nearly five years.

'Back to bed, you.'

Later, when she was lying awake, she heard noises from her parents' room, creaks and wordless moans. She knew what it was. She'd heard Brenda and Dennis next door often enough, but she'd never, ever heard her parents at it before. After they were finished, and silent, she lay awake still, wondering what excuse she could give Mr Long the Geography teacher for not finishing her homework.

I don't know where that came from. It may even be true, or true-ish.

Anyway, I read it out the first week back after Easter and it's gratifying that I see Jocelyn flinch when I say the bit about Les' head. It's true – he does have a scar just at his hairline.

We have begun to live a different kind of life. Matt is living with us, apparently content, quiet but improving, in his old room that he used to share with Jay, long ago.

He has appointments to go to the hospital but will soon be discharged: just a matter of time and waiting to see how he goes on. He uses his time in trying to reconstruct his old life as contained by his phone, each new contact giving rise to another, and another. Busy on Facebook too: searching, befriending, getting himself back into the mix.

Kez stays too, in the bedroom that she used to share with Zoe. She works, sometimes with a theatre company that goes into schools, sometimes with a circus skills project, mostly youth clubs and holiday schemes. She seems happy, and is seeing the young policeman who came to tell us about Matt's incident – as Jay seemed to know well before I did.

Goodbye

Theresa takes a bus from Liverpool Street. She wears a black coat of her own and a black polo neck and skirt she has borrowed from Angie.

Ever since she received Val's letter, she has felt scared and excited, like stage fright. As she has travelled farther from home, she has felt less and less anxious about Kim, left to the care of Angie; until now, looking out of the bus at the half-familiar street corners and municipal park gates, Kim and Angie have no longer any way of pulling at her. Their great hawsers that have kept her tethered to Les, now slip from their bollards and trail behind her through the water, visible if you care to look, but useless.

There is the wooden kiosk on the pavement selling papers and magazines; it has proved more lasting than some of the brick buildings.

There is the road down to the bus garage, where in Theresa's childhood, the trolley buses often came to a stop when the poles fell off the wires at the junction, and a man had to come and patiently try to get them together again. Little blue sparks darted out, while the passengers rubbed the condensation from the windows to look out at the public toilets.

Here are the roads that lead to where Theresa lived with her family, but where the house is now empty. Theresa has only the slenderest of ideas of what has happened to them all.

After she left home, she heard nothing from them. After Les' mum died, only a year or so later, she heard nothing from anyone. Some years, feeling hopeful, she sent a Christmas card to her parents; once or twice she sent a birthday card to Val.

For nine years, nothing. Then a Christmas card signed "mum". It was like a spirit message: 'To Theresa and family from Mum.' It was a way of telling her that her father had died. Since then, a card has come each year, but only, always, with the same message.

Theresa kept them all, until last November, when she gave them, she didn't know why, to Kim to play with, so by the time Christmas came – with no card, they were cut into many small pieces and thrown away.

Theresa has never been to a funeral before. She worries that people will notice her bag, which has to be bigger than a handbag, to accommodate her nightie and a change of clothes. She has only a vague idea of where the crematorium might be and has to ask the bus driver where to get off.

And she's on the wrong bus, so has to walk through the streets to find it. She's still early.

The first person she sees, as she stands sheltering from the wind under the porch-like structure of the chapel, is Alan. She can't help smiling.

'Theresa?' In his late thirties, he is still boyishly unfinished. Colourless, twitchy, overweight, relying on the goodwill and pity of good people. She is still smiling. She can't speak.

And she can't remember his name. Before they work out what to do, other people start arriving, to wait in the waiting room for the family and the coffin. These are people Theresa doesn't know, neighbours; distant relatives.

She is confused by their faces, uncertain whether she might know them or not. When her sisters and brother arrive, she knows them, of course. At least, she knows Rita.

Rita looks like Theresa might have looked but doesn't. A lot of glossy hair, wide shoulders, impeccable make-up. Specially bought black outfit. Rita looking at home, born to lead the mourners at a funeral.

Kay has put on weight, more than her sisters, but she still has lovely skin and wide grey eyes. No longer impudent, her rebellion confined, like Theresa's, to a little unlucky teenage sex.

And Val. She wouldn't have recognised Val. Val doesn't seem to recognise Theresa either, doesn't even seem to see her.

Theresa stands well back, against the wall of the waiting room, watching and trying to breathe. No one except Alan has noticed her.

When they begin to move into the chapel, she

keeps to the back. Rita, Kay, Val and Tony, and two girls who must be Kay's daughters, one older and one younger than Angie, fill the front pew. Tony vanishes from sight among the females.

Seeing the coffin, Theresa feels for the first time that this is a funeral and that she is here after all to mark the death of her mother. But she said goodbye to her mother so long ago. It no longer carries any weight.

The girl who cried through many nights for homesickness, and who screamed for her mum during labour: that girl is a stranger to Theresa. That girl is buried under debris, silenced, not dormant but dead.

The front pew though, are truly upset. Rita stands through the hymns, and tears splash on to her hymn book. The two girls sob loudly and Kay and Val each put an arm round a girl's shoulder. Tony sniffs and blinks and blows his nose, but no one takes any notice of him. When the coffin rolls silently through the little red curtain, the younger of the two girls begins to cry even harder and her sister turns away from Val and they cling together as the mourners file out into the Garden of Remembrance to stand shivering in thin January sunshine.

Theresa is wondering, What should I do? Shall I speak to Val? Where do we go next?

Then Rita approaches. 'How did you get here?'

Theresa doesn't know whether to say: 'on a bus,' or to tell her that Val sent a letter.

Rita is not crying now, and she is not softened by grief or the occasion.

Theresa recognises, though she finds it hard to believe, that Rita is still angry with her. After twenty years, she is no different from the sister who once went to their father and told him that Theresa had stolen not only Kay's boyfriend, but hers as well, who moved out to their Aunt Ginny's rather than continue to share a house with her, who screamed after her as she left the house to get married to Les: 'I hope your baby dies.'

These are only memories to Theresa; not even painful any more – cold ashy memories that happened to someone else. To Rita, the pain is still hot. Kay's head is beginning to look round, to seek out Val, to ask for some decision or other.

'Alan.' Theresa thinks, that's right, Alan, I remember now.

'Can you look after Theresa?' She takes him to one side and whispers. He nods. As Theresa, hurt, bewildered, embarrassed, turns to go, Rita has one more thing to say.

'If you thought you'd see Malcolm, you won't. He's away on business. He won't be back till tonight. So.'

'Come on,' says Alan. By the time they arrive

somewhere – and she doesn't at first notice where – she is trembling with the shock. For Rita to behave like that – Rita was never like that – she and Rita always got on. She says nothing, and Alan takes her, walks her, through little cold streets to the only place he can think of to take her.

As they approach, of course she begins to realise that she recognises where she is. The curve of a street corner, the look of a wall, the way a street can tell you: 'that's the way you went to school': they all come back to her. People have changed their gardens, put up carports, bought their council houses and put in UPVc windows, but it's still the landscape that she knows, without knowing she knows.

'I can't take you to my house,' says Alan. 'My mother's not well, she doesn't like people coming in. She's gone a bit funny as a matter of fact.'

'Well then –'

'It's all right. We can go to your mum's house. I've got a key.'

Theresa realises she doesn't even know how her mother died.

'I haven't heard from her for years you know,' she says.

'She used to talk about you. She wished you hadn't gone so far away.' His voice is mumbly and indistinct, as if he doesn't talk much to

289

people. 'Why didn't you send a picture of the baby?'

Why didn't she? Because everyone hated her, they would rip it up, and because she never possessed a camera. She once thought she would send a school photo – of which child? She forgets now – but never got round to it, or else, or else –

'I don't know,' she says.

He lets her in through the back door. The kitchen is cold but there's no smell yet of mustiness or disuse. Alan looks round sadly, proprietorially too.

At the funeral, he was nobody, not family, not entitled to recognition. Back on his own ground, he can claim his share in the story of Theresa's mother's death.

'I used to look in every evening, when I got home from work. I'd pop in here before I went next door to sort *her* out.' He indicates with his head in a way that lets Theresa know that his own mother is difficult and doesn't deserve the attention she gets from him. 'Then later on, after I'd got *her* settled, I'd pop back and have a cup of tea with your mum. I'm going to miss her – well, I already miss her.'

Theresa is looking round the room. The big table, that seven of them sat around at every teatime, has gone and she can't even imagine how they managed to fit it in.

There's a fridge, and a washing machine – they weren't there when she was a child – and the old coke boiler has gone. The walls are painted a pale lemon colour.

'I did that for her,' says Alan. 'She wanted to pay someone to do it, she said she couldn't manage a ladder any more, but I told her I could do it – it only took me a day or two.'

Theresa does not notice that the paint has been smudged at the join with the ceiling, and at the door frames and skirting board, there are yellow feathers of paint spoiling the white.

'Wait here,' says Alan. 'I'll pop next door and get some milk and make you a cup of tea.'

When he returns, she's still looking round the room. Everything in it, it seems, has changed, but she feels, or wants to feel that it's the same; it's home. She moves to the sink to fill the kettle and notices with gratitude that the old push-button tea caddy is still fixed to the wall. Empty though.

'Tea bags in the tin,' says Alan. He fusses about, straightening things she has touched and moved, turning the mugs so that the handles face the same way.

It's quite dark outside now, as they drink their tea. 'Are you staying tonight?'

'I don't know. I thought Val might ask me. My ticket's for tomorrow.'

'You can stay here. The heating's been on, an

hour every day, to keep it aired. You can sleep in your mum's bed – there's not another one made up.'

'She didn't –?'

He doesn't know what she's asking, and she can't say it, but she thinks to herself, Well, when he's gone, I can sleep on the settee.

'Look,' he says. 'I've got to go back and see to mother. I'll pop back later, shall I? Have a look in the cupboard. You'll find a tin of soup or something.'

She's sitting in the front room, by the gas fire, just sitting, looking, when she hears the back door open again, and goes into the kitchen just as the light is switched on. The man gasps, then tries to cover his fright by laughing.

'I didn't know anyone was here. What are –?' Pause. 'Theresa?' He has recognised her before she has properly realised that he's not Alan.

Malcolm has filled out from the skinny boy she knew, to a big man.

His hair doesn't fall over his eyes any more, but is combed straight back, in defiance of thinning temples. He still has the eyes, the smile.

'Why aren't you at the house with the rest?'

'Rita –'

'Oh, Rita.' He dismisses Rita. He explains that he's been away all day; missed the funeral, hates funerals anyway, phoned Kay on his way home. She asked him to stop by her mum's house and pick up her jewellery box. Theresa doesn't ask why.

They are still standing in the kitchen, the cold air from the open door stirs around them. 'You haven't changed.'

She laughs.

'I have.'

'Well, not so much as Kay has. You've kept your figure. How many kids?'

'Three.'

'Les treat you all right, does he?'

She doesn't answer, unsure how to.

Malcolm steps forward, touches her hair. She smells cigarette smoke and beer.

'I'm sorry,' he says. 'It has to be said. I'm sorry for what happened. But what could I do?'

She feels him touch her hair, feels her insides move, feels her vagina move, knows she would let him if he wanted her again. Doesn't see Alan at the back door.

'What about my boy?' he says. 'I know it was a boy. What did you call him?'

'Mark.'

'Mark.' He's pleased with that. 'How's he getting on?'

If she could lie she would, wishes desperately that she'd prepared a story. 'I don't know.'

'What do you mean?'

'He ran away.'

'When?'

'A while ago.'

'So where is he?'

'I don't know.'

He turns away, disappointed in her. Turns back and tries again.

'What's he like?'

She's defiant now.

'Bad. He was a bad boy. Very violent. Got into trouble.' She doesn't say how good-looking he was, how affectionate to her, how quick and clever, how she misses him.

Malcolm's upset now, visibly. This is not what he wanted to hear, not what he expects his world to contain, he wishes he'd never asked.

'Bad parents make bad kids,' he says shortly and, this time, leaves.

Alan steps aside to let him pass, then comes inside and closes the door.

Now Theresa cries. Cries and cries, for everything. For Mark and for Malcolm, for her mum and dad, for her lost sisters and her lost self. Cries and cries, sitting on the edge of her mother's armchair, rocking, her head in her hands, taking no notice of the cup of tea Alan has made her, taking no notice of Alan as he tries to put his arm round her.

She cries and cries, ignoring the box of tissues he offers, letting the tears run down her hands and wet her sleeves, wiping the snot from her nose with her sleeves. When she begins to slow down, and looks with surprised disgust at the slimy mess she's made of Angie's jumper, Alan is still there.

'Take it off,' he says. He's maybe surprised and maybe not, that she only has a bra underneath. Who knows what he knows about women? She shivers.

'We'd better get you to bed.' Theresa has no will anymore and allows herself to be taken to her mother's bed, in the room where as children they were hardly allowed to go, allows him to undress her.

Alan is excited by the wetness and the abandon of her tears, and as he takes off her skirt, he's more excited, and surprised, by the wetness of her knickers.

Who knows from when he was planning this, or whether he was planning it at all, but whether or not, he gets into bed beside her (taking his trousers off but leaving his shirt and socks on) to warm her and comfort her, and fuck her. Not expertly, but eagerly, (though it's all the same to Theresa) and several times, through the night.

Well that's another one I'm not going to read out. Honestly, I don't know where this stuff is coming from, I don't even know if it's true, it just came to me, and I just wrote it down.

Today I got the letter.

Of course Don knows: the whole business would have been difficult to keep from him if I wanted to – well, I did want to, but it just wasn't practical. Anyway, he is what they call 'supportive,' which means he never mentions it unless I do, which means that we don't talk about it.

What happened was that I let a child get injured. I didn't do my job properly, I made a mistake, I was sloppy, I allowed other things to get in the way of my judgement and because of it a child ended up in hospital, a young woman ended up in court and without her child, a whole family has to live with the knowledge that they didn't stop it either. I could have stopped it happening.

Tasha Jervis. The name means nothing to me, and why would it? She's about eighteen, hair pulled tightly off her face, little eyes caged by eyeliner and spikes of mascara. She'll be fat one day. We've had a complaint from a neighbour. My piece of paper from the Referral desk says 'Neighbour wishes not to be identified or contacted. Child cries most evenings until about midnight. Thinks it might be left unattended.'

I explain that I've come from Social Services and that

I want to talk to her about her child.

'She's not here,' she says, and there's a slight note of triumph in her voice, but she lets me in anyway. I've been in this flat, or one like it in this block, a hundred times. I know it will be bare: it will have a big telly, which will be on, a heap of tangled toys, a buggy in the corner, possibly with the baby asleep in it, a packet of fags on the arm of the chair, a mug with a cartoon hedgehog or pig on it.

She's OK, Tasha, she shows me the little girl's room, and her cot, which is clean, she speaks of her with affection, she tells me that her grandmother has taken her out to the shops, and right on cue, the door is opened with a key from outside and Linda Dickinson comes in, pushing Sahara in the buggy.

The sight of Linda knocks me back. Fifty-five years of knowing her, forty-four years of knowing that I said that thing to her and neither of us have ever mentioned it. But I've thought of it every time I've seen her skinny figure – gaunt as she got older – pushing its constant pushchair – children, grandchildren, now great-grandchildren – round the shops, and I bet she has remembered it too.

And it knocks her back too, seeing me. Of course I realise later that she possibly – probably – had no idea I was a social worker.

She is puzzled, confused. There she was, in her familiar pond, and here am I, the wrong sort of fish.

She doesn't say anything and I say:

'I've come from Social Services.' I can tell we've entered into an agreement not to be the two people who are slight, though old, acquaintances, but to keep to our assigned roles.

'I'm Tasha's nan,' she says.

Professionally, I am reassured by Linda. She is a grandmother, I am a grandmother, we keep an eye on things; we care about these little children. We are mature and not swayed by the same sort of impatience and boredom and flightiness we might have had when we were younger. We can be trusted.

And she lifts Sahara out of the buggy, and when the little girl toddles straight to Tasha, I'm confident that I can make a note in the file that "attachment appears secure". It's a great feeling.

Nothing wrong here, apart from poverty which I can't do anything about. She's off our books, she's off my list, that's a 'No further Action': move on to the next one. For me, what swung it was Linda Dickinson. I had known her for years. Hadn't she brought up babies? I knew they hadn't turned out to be hard-working upstanding community stalwarts, but social services is concerned with visible damage, not nebulous possibilities.

Linda's kids were fine, healthy, not ill-treated, not neglected. It was the fathers I blamed. Linda couldn't pick a good man, she just couldn't. When I went back to the office and read the case file, only out of interest because I had closed the case of Sahara Jervis – I could see that Linda had battled on, having babies, raising children, looking after the children of her children, baby-minding, picking up pieces, contributing a bit here, a bit there, fetching kids from school, having them for weekends and holidays.

Linda's first bloke was a baker's roundsman called John. He turned up at Aunt Peggy's funeral and I remember him solemnly shaking Leslie's hand. Later, I think he went to prison. She had two sons by then, and later, there were more relationships and more children, mostly boys.

From the file, I learned that Tasha was the daughter of James, and he didn't seem too bad at all, though Tasha's mother had departed the scene quite early on in her life, and he'd had to bring up Tasha and her two brothers by himself, though doubtless with a lot of help from Linda. There were names in the file that I recognised, though of course not one of them was called Dickinson.

What happened later that week – and why should I be able to predict it from what I saw? – was that Tasha went out for the evening, leaving Sahara in her cot but not, as it turned out, asleep.

And this evening, it was more than constant crying that alarmed the neighbour; it was something banging, and then a period of screaming, so that the neighbour, quite an old lady, gathered up her courage and went and knocked on Tasha's door. No one answered the door, but the screaming went quiet for a short time and then started again, even louder with pain and panic. From this, she rightly guessed that the child had been left alone, and she called the police, who broke down the door and took Sahara to hospital, in front of an audience of everyone in the block.

She was hurt. The police got there only just in time to prevent her suffocating herself with the bedding she was tangled up in. She had overturned the cot and caught herself in the bars and underneath the mattress. There was bruising consistent with this and a dislocated shoulder. There was also, according to the X-ray, evidence of a previously broken rib, although nothing on her medical record explained it. Tasha returned to find her gone, and herself under arrest.

And I went to work the following day to find that it was my fault.

At first, I expected this letter every day. I looked on the mat inside the front door every time I passed; going upstairs or down, going out, coming back in. I began thinking about it on my way home. By the time I was at the corner of our road, I was visualising it – A brown envelope? A white one? – waiting for me.

Every day I picked up the letters from the mat, not knowing if the one I was waiting for was among them. There were a few birthday cards in October, a whole slew of cards at Christmas, there were bank statements and letters offering us a good deal on a new car or a phone package. Bills for gas and electric, water and phone, broadband and council tax, reminders about TV licence and road fund tax and eye tests.

Sometimes there would be a letter face down, and I would walk past it few times thinking that this was it but not going to pick it up. When I did – getting a grip, holding my breath, all that – it never was.

You can't live for long in that kind of suspense. I found myself forgetting to wonder as I came through the hall to go upstairs, will it be there? I could pick up a scattering of mail and sort through them as if it was a casual event, and slowly it became in reality a more casual event.

I could still wake in the night and wonder when it would happen. I could see myself – more vividly in the dark – in front of the men in suits. The words Public Enquiry looked at me from my alarm clock when I pressed the button to find out that it was 3.37 a.m. One night, the letters danced and sparkled and rearranged themselves to read High Court. Men in wigs.

And now it's here. In my hand. Unopened. The image I had of being alone in the house to open it has vanished. Don is sitting in his chair reading the paper. Matt, only just out of bed, is doing something with his phone. Kez is bending to plug in the sewing machine to alter a costume. Music is playing. Bright blue and orange ribbons have fallen in a heap on the floor. I am walking into the room from the hall with a handful of letters.

Neil Young was singing at the time, telling us it's only castles burning.

Nothing is ever as you think it will be. Since Christmas, we have lived through plenty of drama and change. Accidents and incidents, shocks and hospitals. My letter might be the worst of all. I dare not even hope it will deliver me from the long desk, the solitary chair, the men – there'll be one woman – in suits.

There is a letter from the hospital for Matt, but he is deeply interested in sending a text, hunched away from us and turned towards the window. His bare feet on the rung of the chair have a semi-circle of grime round each heel. I give Kez a stiff square white envelope and wonder if I can hide mine somewhere till later. She opens it – I can see it's a wedding invitation – with a cry of what is at first delight and then something else.

She hurries from the room saying 'Scissors', though I can see them next to the sewing machine. Matt's phone beeps and he jumps as if he was not expecting it, and dashes to the kitchen.

'What's going on?' I say.

Don doesn't look up.

'Spurs Wigan,' he says. 'Should beat them but you never know.'

I slide the letter into the magazine rack where it will smoulder and tick until I can come for it with a steady hand and heart.

When I do, it is inviting me, not to anything too formal, but to a meeting with my manager. I'm not retired, although that's what I told the people at the writing group, and my children, and anyone else who asked.

I'm suspended. I was suspended ten months ago, last July, the 5th of July if we're going to be exact, at 2.37 p.m., after a meeting with the same manager that lasted twelve minutes. And now I have to go back and walk through that open plan office again, and some people will look up and smile or wave, and some people will pretend they haven't seen me and some will make it clear that they have seen me and they don't care if I – they even want me to – notice what they think about me.

It wasn't my fault. I didn't mean it to happen. Anyone else would have made the same mistake – there was nothing to suggest – well, only the report from the neighbour – but everything seemed OK. Maybe a referral to Sure Start, but she looked fine: no visible bruises, there were toys, there was evidence of attachment, there was family support, what was I meant to know? The thing that happened hadn't happened yet. I want all these excuses written on a banner that I can display without having to say anything.

It is at this moment, me standing in the kitchen with the letter in my hand, music playing as always, Matt upstairs, Kezia who knows where, that the phone rings, and it's Rita.

She said she said

The guests climb out of the big black cars, and enter the house. Mark and Theresa are almost the last of them.

Kay stands inside the open front door. She is a small woman, whose plump face sits on top of her solid bosom like a child peering over the back of a sofa. Two daughters stand with her, one either side, protecting her and keeping her in the background. She should be at the centre of this event, but she lets, she encourages her daughters to step forward to greet and guide the guests. Of course, it's natural that they know most of the people – Guests? Mourners?

Mark has never been to a funeral before.

The daughters seem a bit unsure about how to deal with Theresa, but the sight of her moves Kay into action. She comes forward, looking almost excited, and hugs her.

Theresa doesn't try very hard to hug her back, but she gives a little laugh, and begins to cry again.

One of the daughters puts an arm round her and takes her to sit down. It's not a funeral where emotion is encouraged, he can see.

Kay turns to Mark now. She lays a hand on his arm and whispers to him.

'I couldn't put you in the car with us. Malcolm would have wanted it, but people would notice.'

The younger (taller, blonder, harder) of the sisters looks curiously, wondering what Kay can have to say to someone she's never met before, who's only here because he gave his mum a lift down, who has nothing to do with Malcolm.

Mark nods in a way that he hopes conveys something appropriate, and moves into the big sitting room.

The sun shines through the picture windows at the front of the room, and at the back, the patio doors have been slid open. It's warm, and some people have already taken off their jackets, so the proportion of black in the room is much less than it was in the church, and the mood correspondingly less sombre.

A moderately lavish buffet is laid out in the dining area of the room, and people are emerging from the kitchen with cups of tea and glasses of beer.

Some are venturing into the garden. Conversations are beginning.

Mark has no one, except his mother, that he knows, and he stands shyly, hands in pockets, listening.

'...M1 as far as Stevenage...'

'...wasps near the buffet...'

'...last Christmas I think it was. Or the one before...'

'...Debbie's little girl...'

'...somewhere near Watford, I think...'

'...You could have come with us...'

'...Well, it hasn't sunk in yet...'

Mark sees that his mother is talking to a man of about forty, whom he guesses from his looks might be her brother.

That would be Tony, then. Or maybe not.

How can Mark know? Theresa has never talked about these people, though they're her family.

He knows only their names, and two photographs, which lie in the kitchen drawer in his mother's house, unregarded and getting year by year more grimy and crumpled. One of his Aunt Val aged about thirty, all big hair and a sullen expression, standing on a doorstep, and one of the three eldest sisters, Rita, Theresa and Kay, on the pier at Southend, all wearing white winkle-picker shoes, so that the bottom of the picture looks as though someone has taken scissors to it.

They know no more of him, he has to assume. He's either a gatecrasher or a ghost.

Last week she phoned him.

'I've got a favour to ask.'

'What's that, mum?' He thought it would be something to do with Sean.

'Can you give me a lift to London?' She always calls it London, though it's twenty-five miles from the Thames.

'What for?' He'll need time off work, doesn't

she realise that it's not always easy?

'It's a funeral. And can you come to the funeral with me?'

'Who's died?'

'Malcolm. My sister Kay's husband.' She said it, he thinks now, without a quiver.

'Isn't dad going?'

'No.'

Not a surprise. He and Angie knew, even if they'd never been told, they knew in the way that children know things about their parents, that their dad didn't get on with Theresa's family.

The reasons weren't far to look for – he'd got her pregnant, her parents maybe opposed the wedding; wanted her to have the baby adopted.

Mark and Marie have talked about it so often, and drawn the comparison between his parents and their own story. It's only a few weeks since they tried to make Angie understand what it must have been like for her, but Angie doesn't do feelings; she didn't want to know.

'All right then. I'll clear it with Terry and let you know.'

And now he's here.

The younger of the daughters, Stephanie, comes over to him with a bottle and a glass.

'Would you like a beer?' she asks.

'Thanks. Look, I'm sorry about your dad.'
She'll never know how hard that was for him to

say.

'Thanks. It hasn't sunk in yet. Here, come and meet some of the family.'

On an immense, pale leather sofa, sits a version of Theresa in black silk:

'This is Rita.' And next to her is a woman whom he would not have recognised as the Auntie Val of the photograph. 'And this is Val. This is Mark.'

He holds out his hand. Rita, as she takes it in her cool dry hand, notices the tattoo on his knuckles. She says nothing, but it seems that the temperature of her fingers drops noticeably. He sits down between them, and Stephanie sits briefly, before seeing something that needs dealing with, and returning to the crowd.

'Have you spoken to my mum yet?' he asks.

'We don't speak,' says Rita, and turns to talk to someone on the other side of her.

Val speaks confidentially, much as Kay did.

'It's not very nice for you, getting dragged into this. But Kay would have it. She and Rita have fallen out over it. I've been backwards and forwards between them all week.'

She looks him in the eye for the first time.

'Did Theresa tell you?' she asks.

'Yes.'

In the car, coming down the M1.

'Mark.'

308

'Yes, mum.'

'There's this thing I've got to tell you.'

Long silence.

'Go on then.'

'I don't know how to say it.'

'Just say it.'

'Well, first of all – look, if I tell you, you won't crash or nothing?'

'Course not.'

'Well, look, your dad – Leslie –' Long silence. 'He's not your real dad.'

First feeling – relief. How he'd always hated him.

'Come on, mum. You've got to tell me more than that.'

'Are you all right?'

'Yeah, I'm all right.'

Pull into inside lane, slow down a bit, pull back away from this big truck. Steady.

'What about Angie? Is he her dad?'

'Oh yes.'

'And Kim?'

'Yes.'

'And Sean?'

Long silence.

'No.'

'OK.'

Long silence.

'Go on then.'

'What?'

'What do you think? Who is my dad?'

Long silence.

'Don't you know?'

'No.' But he does. 'Not Malcolm?'

'Yes.'

'Oh, great.'

Mark and Theresa drive on for seven miles in silence. Then he pulls into Newport Pagnell Services and parks.

'Mum.' He looks at her. She's been crying. 'Tell me.'

'Nothing to tell.'

Long silence.

He knows she won't speak, however long he waits. He has to try to work it out for himself.

'And now he's died and I never even met him.'

'You look like him.'

'Oh great. Will anyone notice, do you think? Mum, this is weird shit.'

'You won't swear at Kay's, will you?'

'Mum, I know how to behave. Look, we've got to get on. We'll be late. You might have told me before.'

'Kay wanted you to go down while Malcolm was in hospital. She wanted him to see you.'

'Why didn't you tell me?'

'I didn't know what you'd say.'

'You could have asked.'

'Val and I talked about it. She didn't think Kay

knew what she was doing.'

'So now I'm going to be stuck in the middle of my own dad's funeral, that I've never met. Fucking great, mum.'

'You won't swear though, will you?'

'No, I won't swear.'

Val seems nicer than her grumpy photograph. But the camera lies, doesn't it? Mark has had pictures taken of him that didn't do justice to the complexity of his whole self, just as the name and number underneath didn't adequately describe who he was.

'I don't suppose you know who we all are,' says Val.

'No.'

'Does Theresa talk about us?'

'No.' Does Theresa talk?

'Shall I tell you?'

'Please.'

'Most of those –' She gestures towards the garden, where voices are raised cheerfully and un-funereally, '– are friends and business people of Malcolm's.'

'What did he do?'

'You don't know? He had his own business. Shopfitting. Well, he knew everyone, got on well with everyone. Steph took it over. She went into it straight from school – good business head on her shoulders, Steph. You saw Debbie when you came in. She's a teacher.'

'My sister's a teacher. And her husband.'

'Must run in families. That's her husband over there with their daughter. She's ten.'

Mark is grateful to this nice woman for her considerateness, but these people, to him, at the moment, are not the point.

'What about Malcolm? What was he like?'

She almost winks. 'Well, he was lovely, Malcolm. Everybody liked him. Bit of a ladies' man though. Poor Kay had her moments with him, till Steph went to work in the business and kept an eye on him. That cramped his style a bit, I can tell you.'

'Did you know him when –?' he falters, not knowing how to say: *when he was shagging my mum.*

'Well, I was quite little, so I wasn't told all the details. Rita knew him first, you know. They worked together in Pearson's – big department store. It's John Lewis's now. And she brought him home, or to a dance or something, and then he and Kay started going out.'

'And Theresa?'

'She was dead jealous.' She puts her hand to her mouth, and looks round to make sure no one has heard her say the word "dead". 'I do remember that. I remember her crying on her bed and kicking her feet on the wall like a two-year-old, and she said 'Who's prettiest, Val – me or Kay?' Well, she was, even I knew that, but she thought – well, so I think now – that being pretty gave her the right to any boy she liked. She couldn't stand it that Malcolm liked Kay better. I don't know, because Kay's never talked about it, I don't know how it's been for Kay all these years, knowing Malcolm had another child. I don't know what Malcolm thought about it either.'

'He knew then, did he?'

'Oh yes, he knew. The whole street knew, what with the weeping and wailing that went on. Our mum and dad were very respectable, you know, and it wasn't done then to have babies out of wedlock, and to have two together, and then find them fighting over which one would marry him –'

'Proper fighting?'

'Oh yes. Theresa used to go into her room at night and carry on screaming at her, and they used to come to blows, and I'd run downstairs and get my dad and he'd have to come up and send Theresa back to bed. Funny, that, being grown up and pregnant and being ordered back to bed by your dad.'

She looks at him, wondering if she's said more than she should have.

'Shall I get you a drink? You look a bit shell-shocked.'

'I think I'll go in the garden for a bit.'

Outside, the sunshine warms him and the

noise of the people recedes. From the far end of the well-groomed garden, he looks back at the house.

They are all strangers to him, and his mother rather stranger than the rest.

He lets himself out of a gate at the end of the garden and finds his way, by means of alley-ways, to where he parked his car that morning.

He is twenty miles up the M1 before he pulls into Toddington services, and sits for eighteen minutes, staring at the back of a silver Toyota, before turning back south to pick up his mother, and say his proper goodbyes.

I wrote that after I saw Val. That's what Rita phoned me for, to say would I go round to Val's, she couldn't go, something terrible had happened, she was busy with the girls, Val needed someone who knew Kay.

It was only afterwards that she told me Kay was dead.

Val's house is not far from Kay's, but much more modest, with a front garden so small that the gate bangs into the doorstep as you open it. When she comes to the door, she looks perfectly composed, and looks behind me to see if I am on my own.

Then she pulls me into the house by my elbow, shuts the door and begins to cry noisily. I pat her on the shoulder, and she hugs me uncontrollably. I steer her into what must be the kitchen and fill the kettle while she gets clean mugs from a cupboard, still sobbing. At last she says:

'Rita couldn't come then?'

'She's with the girls, she says.'

'It was Deborah who found her.'

It's worse than the heart attack that I'd been imagining had carried Kay off. She had killed herself.

'When?'

'Some time yesterday, we think. Deb called in on her way home from work and found her.'

We sit with our coffee, which I've made without even remembering that I dislike it, and Val wipes her eyes and rubs at the mascara smudging her face.

'I can't even think,' she says. 'Rita's done everything, she's been amazing. I just go to bits and pieces as soon as I open my mouth.'

'Well,' I say. 'I won't ask you anything. I'll just sit here and you can say whatever you like, or nothing at all. It's up to you.'

So we sit for a while in silence until she starts to cry again and says:

'This is no good. Just ask me stuff. I can't sit here wondering whether to say it or not. Go on, just ask me.'

So we become more natural, and even gossipy, and I have a few tears for poor Kay as well, and Val opens a bottle of wine although it's not long past midday.

And I pop along to the corner shop and buy sandwiches and call Don to say I won't be coming home till late, and later in the afternoon Val and I go for a little walk round the neighbourhood, passing the end of Kay's road but not looking along it, and by then I'm sober enough to drive home, and Val is sober enough to start another bottle, and she feeds her cats and we sit in the front room and talk about Rita.

'She's on these adverts in the TV magazines, for loose covers.'

'Really? I would have thought that's a bit beneath her.'

'Oh, with Rita it's all about money isn't it? She's not doing so much of one sort of work – you know, the finance stuff, so she's filling up the coffers with something else. She wants to have a comfortable old age.'

'I should think she's pretty safe.'

'No, I mean really comfortable. So she says but I don't think she'll ever change her lifestyle, do you? She won't go and live abroad or anything. Do you think?'

'I don't know.'

'I thought she might talk to you.'

'We're still friends,' I say. 'I just don't hear from her much anymore.'

'Nor do we.' She means herself and Kay. 'She remembers our birthdays, that's about all.'

'Mine too. I wonder if she remembers Theresa's.'

'Not a chance. She won't hear her name. Still, you know all that. You were there. I was just a little girl. I didn't really get what was going on.'

'Strange how it all comes back to that, every time.'

'Nothing good has happened ever since.'

Kay's funeral wasn't like Malcolm's. It was May, but a grey, cold day, the greyest May can be, with the trees thrashing about in the wind and spits of rain in the air.

The daughters had organised it, but grudgingly, it seemed, and I was only included because Val insisted, though as it turns out she didn't manage to insist on Theresa.

I drive out to the Crem on my own and I sit at the back of the room on my own, with empty seats between me and the family. Steph and Debbie, and Debbie's husband.

Not the granddaughter, who is away on a holiday with school, and no one has thought it necessary to bring her back to see her grandmother laid to rest.

Val and, yes, Rita. But no Aunt Ginny. No friends or neighbours, none of Malcolm's family, no cousins of her own, though there'd been several on Ted's side at least.

It looks as if the daughters are so ashamed of what Kay has done that they assumed no one would come if they asked them, so they didn't ask them.

The usual duty vicar, who has to consult his notes for Kay's name. No hymns, which I am glad of, because half a dozen people can't fill even a small crematorium room with sound, not unless they know each other well, and no one here seems to know each other at all.

The coffin slides through the curtain – there is one squeaky roller – and that's the end of Kay.

There is a sort of half-hearted invitation from Debbie to 'come back for a cup of tea', but no one takes her up on it, and I find myself standing on the forecourt next to Val and Rita, watching Steph, and Debbie and her husband, whose name I never knew, drive away in separate cars. Val wipes her eyes, Rita looks like stone.

'Well then,' says Val. 'Pub lunch?'

'I'll drive you,' I say, and we follow Rita's car (something black, sleek and sporty) to The Pied Bull, still a nice pub, in spite of the nearness of the M25, and sit looking at each other in a state of wonderment. How have we got here?

'Let's get a bottle,' says Val, but we both defer to Rita in the choosing of it, calculating, I guess, that she'll pay for it. And we study our menus until the wine is poured and then we lay them down, as one, and look at each other again, and Val says:

'I'm so angry I could spit.'

'It wasn't right,' I say.

'What did she expect?' says Rita.

'Who?'

'Kay.'

'Reet, it's not about what she would expect. She wouldn't expect anything. She would expect to be put out with the wheelie bin, but what about us?' She takes a big swig of wine and hides behind her menu to sniff a bit.

'I mean,' says Rita, a bit softer now. 'She brought those daughters up and they never had a good word to say for her then. They bossed her about as soon as they could talk and they were always on their dad's side. Since he died, she's been an inconvenience.' Anyone would think to hear her that she'd had weekly contact with Kay, inconvenient Kay.

'Well it's not how I want to remember her,' says Val. 'That was like some pauper's funeral. It was like hanging her at the crossroads as if she was a criminal.'

'At least she got a proper funeral. Suicides never used to.'

'It's not a crime. It's probably the most sensible decision she ever made'

I say, 'Do you know, I thought you told me that she seemed a bit more cheerful lately.'

'She did. I'd go round and she'd be talking about the future a bit, as if she might have one. You know, she said she would try to lose a bit of weight and she didn't say no when I said I'd take her to see Theresa. I didn't expect this.'

She has nearly finished her glass of wine and she

pours herself some more, without including me or Rita. 'I feel so guilty now that I put off going to see Theresa. It might have made a difference.'

'I don't think she would ever have gone,' I say, and I really do believe that.

Kay would never have felt up to it, however many springs came and went with new promise, but maybe, and I don't say this, maybe it was the thought that she would never go and see Theresa again that made her decide there was nothing to live for.

She didn't leave a note, or any indication at all of what was going on for her, except that she did choose a weekend when Debbie and her family were on a visit to her in-laws in North Wales and Steph was on holiday in Sharm-el-Sheikh, when Val had already made her weekly visit and wouldn't be expected again for a few days.

She made sure – Paracetamol and a bath and a knife to the wrists. Belt and braces.

A waitress comes for our order and we all go back to the menus, choosing, possibly at random, but when the food comes, we eat as if we are starving.

Rita, I notice, has placed herself with her back to the room, but the waitress – not a young one – has clocked who she is and I can see her telling the girl behind the bar who they've got in today, though it looks too as if she is having to explain a bit too much.

'You know,' I think she's saying, 'she used to be on that programme that was on after the news, years ago, and then she was on in the afternoon, some sort of talk show. No, I never watched it myself, but my mum used to like it.'

Val orders another bottle of wine and Rita raises her eyebrows – not at me, more to herself – but says nothing.

'Poor Kay,' I say. 'It's like she never got to grips with the modern world.'

I'm thinking about the world we grew up in, of hair rollers and American Tan stockings and pale pink lipstick and black and white TV and the Light Programme. You washed your hair on a Thursday evening and let it dry and slept – or didn't sleep – with your rollers in, and that had to do until the next Thursday. So your boyfriend never saw you on a Thursday, at least not until he was fairly steady and could be trusted not to go off you. I don't think anyone ever saw Rita with her hair in rollers. And Kay never even used them at all. If you tried to do her hair or tidy her up, she just pushed you away and laughed, loudly, like a boy.

But those times were the times that Kay belonged to, and everything since – hippies, punks, women's liberation, riots, wars – seemed to have passed her by without leaving any mark.

Since she married Malcolm on her sixteenth birthday, she never made a decision. He did all that: house, furniture, holidays; the lot. She never complained, never seemed to notice his infidelities, never cared that she was only a housekeeper. Never had a job, never learned to drive, never had an opinion.

Never sang again, as far as I know. Just grew fatter, a

big layer of fat like armour against the world. Kay, looking out of her big fat face with fifteen-year-old eyes. Still in a world of phone boxes and coal delivery lorries, where only deaf people walked around with bits of plastic in their ears. In her world, Elvis was still alive – good god, *Alma Cogan* was still alive – police cars still had bells; men went to work on bikes.

None of us actually, none of the girls I knew, except Rita, ever had any idea of a real career. We all wanted to get married. All our older relatives ever asked us was: 'Are you courting? Are you engaged yet?' but we all got over it. We changed with the times, we took exams, we had jobs and we moved up ladders, and we didn't think having a husband was the be-all and end-all.

Just Kay, stuck in a Mills and Boon world of little wife and powerful husband, saw her daughters become women but never knew how they did it, just Kay. She never grew up.

Val has been drinking more than me and Rita, but you wouldn't know it. I guess she must be a proper alcoholic. Leaving aside the black clothes, we are all wearing, we are an ill-assorted trio. Me, big and dowdy, Val sombrely dressed but brightly made up, Rita slender and delicate and elegant, a different class of being altogether. She has eaten a large salad but says no to dessert, and while Val and I ponder over cheesecake or treacle tart, Rita takes out a smartphone and goes through her messages.

When I've finished eating, and the waitress has taken the plates, Rita turns to me.

'I'll get the bill,' she says, 'if you want to get off now.'

It takes me a moment to realise that I'm being shown the door.

'I'll wait for Val,' I say. 'I said I'd take her home.'

'I can do that,' says Rita, then, turning to Val to exclude me, 'I need to talk to you about the will.'

Now, I don't expect to be included in family business – no, actually I don't mean that, I don't expect to be included in the will, of course not, but I do expect to be part of this conversation, having been almost part of this family for so many years.

I realise as well that Rita has hardly addressed a remark to me personally all day. She has been polite, as if to a stranger.

I have known her since she was six. That makes ten years of calling for her every morning so that we could go to school together, dragging Theresa along with us, and later cajoling Kay along as well, promising her sweets which we had no means of providing, if she would only get a move on and not make us late.

That was one of the bonuses of getting into the grammar school, that Theresa and Kay, when they left primary school, went in the opposite direction to us. They went on foot, while we walked only as far as the High Street to catch a bus. Bus fares were two pence for children – I mean two old pence, for decimalisation was ten years or more in the future.

Rita and I had two ways to get school and back – two buses at 2d each = 4d, or one bus and a walk = 2d profit. In the mornings, we used two buses, to be quicker, but after school there was no hurry. We might walk with Merle or Barbara, or others who went that way, and buy sweets with the left over twopence. Rita always had the exact money, but my mum was less organised and would quite often give me 9d for the day, or occasionally two sixpences, and then we would buy actual chocolate. Other days we'd get cheap stuff – blackjacks four for a penny, or gobstoppers or bubbly out of the machine. And talking all the time – hours and hours of my life and hers spent together talking and giggling and gossiping, and even when we reached the corner where she went to her house and I went to mine, we would stand and find more to talk about.

Years later a woman recognised me as one of the girls who used to lean on her garden wall, pulling leaves off her privet hedge and talking, sometimes until it was dark. And now Rita won't address a word to me.

When I say some of this to Don later, he doesn't share my hurt – well, why would he?

'It's just time isn't it,' he says, and that's supposed to be enough to make sense of it all.

I dreamed that I was in some sort of lost property office. 'A room of colour,' said a voice, and it was, clothes piled up everywhere, children's, ladies', all colours, soft and clean and new, but tangled and jumbled.

There was nothing I needed in the way of clothes, but I picked a bag off a shelf, a brown leather square with a shoulder strap and some pattern on the leather, what they call tooling I think.

And I undid the zip and it was full of stuff: money and papers. I took out a little bunch of receipts, held together with a clothes peg and at the bottom of the bag, I could feel keys.

'But how will she get home?' I cried out, before I woke up.

Don had no idea – and neither did I – why I was so distressed by this. He hates me telling him my dreams anyway. He looks away and waits for it to end, so all I could do was to try to forget it, and of course I did.

Two weeks after Kay's funeral, on a fine Tuesday evening in late May, I read out the story of Malcolm's, to an audience who don't seem to know what to make of it.

'So?' says Joan. 'This boy never knew who his father was? Didn't he ask? I think I've missed something here.'

In the pub afterwards, Jerry and Jeff are more encouraging – more than Joan, and more than usual.

'Not bad,' says Jeff. 'Understated.'

And Jerry says: 'Coming along, coming along,' which I believe is what he's paid to say, though I haven't had my fair share lately.

We are approaching the last class of the year. Jocelyn is off to Addis Ababa on more research for her family book. In Judy's absence, we sit together and she promises to email me.

'How's your son?'

'He's fine. Really, he doesn't seem to have any long lasting effects. Quieter than he used to be, no that's not

really it, he was always quiet, but he seems a bit more –
together, I suppose.'

'More cheerful?'

'That would be asking too much. But looking forward. Talking about going to college.'

'That's what they do nowadays.' This is John inter-
rupting. 'Two days a week, call it full time, media
studies nonsense. Needs a proper job.'

I wait for him to recommend national service, but he
goes back to talking to Jim about the closure of the post
office.

'Not media studies anyway,' I say to Joss. 'He's thinking of some kind of metal work, maybe silversmithing, I
don't know where he got that idea, but he could be good
at it, you never know.'

'Good that he's a bit more upbeat,' she says, and I
have a horrible memory that I said that about Kay, just
before she killed herself.

It's not even dark as I walk home. Some sort of bird
is singing from a roof top – I'm lying, I know what it is,
it's a blackbird, just like the one on the White Album –
and the air is soft and warm, though full of petrol
fumes. As I approach the corner of my road, a car
passes, stops and parks and as I come level with it, the
passenger door opens and someone gets out.

My first thought is that I'm about to be attacked,
mugged and left for dead. My second thought is that it
is Jean, and I don't have any other thoughts, because it
is Jean and she clearly knows it's me.

'Pat.'

'Hello Jean.'

'It's nice to see you.'

'Is it?'

She knows what I'm talking about.

'I'm sorry. At that time I couldn't face talking. I'm sorry.'

'It's OK. How's Julia?'

'She's doing well, I'm thankful to say. How's Matthew?'

'He's fine as well.' Then, hold on a minute, she doesn't know Matthew, where's this going? Where's it come from?

'We heard – from Jocelyn – that he'd had an accident. I was worried that it would set Julia back, but she seems to be over it all now. She hasn't tried to get in touch or anything?'

'Jean, I'm sorry, but you're not making sense. What are you talking about?'

'Matthew and Julia?'

'What about them?'

She sighs. 'You don't know, do you? We thought you did. That's why Julia wouldn't come to the writers' anymore.' I suppose something is dawning.

'Matt and Julia know each other?'

'They were at school together.'

'So?'

'No that's not all. They went out together, for ages. Over a year.'

'When was this? It's the first I've heard of it. I never knew Matt had any girlfriends. Honestly, boys.'

'He never told you about it?'

I try to make it light but it comes out bitter, out of embarrassment. 'Matt doesn't tell me about anything. He doesn't talk to me at all, really.'

'He was a lovely boy,' she says.

This is the first good word I've heard about Matt since he was in junior school and I want to hear more, but the car driver – presumably her husband – sounds the horn.

'Look,' she says, 'I've got to go. We're on our way to pick Julia up. I'll ring you.'

'You didn't find him a bit...?'

'Quiet? Mmm. A bit grubby too. But sweet. So good for Julia. Such a shame.' And she gets back into the car.

'Did you know someone at school called Julia?' I was intending to say that to Matt as soon as I get home, but something stops me. Something about the way he is bending over what he is doing – texting of course – in the way he has done from being a small boy, that same angle, that same neck, makes me back off. The gap between us is still too wide. And I can't tell Don either while Matt's there.

Then the phone rings – though it's nearly eleven – and it's Zoe, with some complaint about Grace's day nursery and do I think it's all right for children to bite each other. I take the phone upstairs and ask her straight out. If she doesn't know about this, then no one does.

'Of course I know about it,' she says, crossly, as if either I should have known, or else should never have found out.

'Why didn't someone tell me Matt had a girlfriend?'

'You never asked.'

'Did Dad know?'

'Oh I think so, at least the beginning. He knew about that.'

'So what else is there to know? What was the end?'

'Mum, don't ask me, ask Matt. It's not my business to tell you his problems.'

'What do you mean, problems?'

'Don't ask me anymore, I've said too much now.'

'No, Zoe...'

'Bye Mum, I think I hear Grace calling.' I know that's a lie, Grace has never woken in the night since she was six months old.

Not only do I not know what my kids do, I don't know what messages fly between them through the digital networks. Next morning, Matt has already gone to sign on when Kezia appears.

'So, Zoe says you know all about Matt and Julia.'

'Well I wouldn't say −'

'I always thought he should tell you,' she says. 'But Katie and Zoe said not to.'

'Why ever not? What's wrong with me? Was it such a big secret?'

'Oh mum, it's just no one wanted to upset you. We know what you're like about abortions and Matt was so...'

'What did you say?'

'Oh sorry − you didn't know that bit. Oh god. I've let

it out now.'

Once again, it's Kez who is explaining my own life to me. Matt was Julia's boyfriend, Julia got pregnant, had a termination. They split up, she had a bit of a break-down. It happens.

'Well you didn't want Katie to have an abortion, did you?'

'That's not true. I did want her to, of course I did.'

'No Mum, she told me, she said at the time that you were dead against it. You said she mustn't let people put pressure on her to.'

'Yes that's what I said, I didn't mean she shouldn't, I just...' I'm helpless to explain all the things I meant.

'And Katie said that you told her that you and Rita once had this big row when she had a termination.'

'Well yes we did, but that has nothing to do with it.'

'But you told Katie. You were telling her that you would have a big row with her.'

No. No of course not. Too late now.

It was in the middle of the night that I had this thought about Matt and Julia's baby: 'We would have had a white grandchild.'

I couldn't decide if I was allowed to have that thought, or what it said about me, or about Jay, Alfie and Grace, my non-white grandchildren, or even about my daughters. I wondered, if I said it to Don, what he would say, and what it would reveal about how racist we could be.

I'm back at work and it's hard. Not the remembering what I have to do, not the dealing with my colleagues who have all been supportive – though I can't help feeling that I could have done with the support over the whole of the last year, not just when the coast is clear to be nice to me.

But it's hard, getting up in the morning, remembering to shop or take things out of the freezer, finding time to make the bed and vacuum the floors. But I have got a job again. I have got away with it. 'I could not reasonably have known etc. etc.'

I've agreed to an inconvenient job move – that's my punishment, and a small one beside Linda's, which is that she's lost her great grandchild, and maybe Tasha too, I suppose.

I found out that it was Linda who had got me off the hook: her testimony that things were all right that day.

Don is back at work too, and Kezia has had an offer of work in Bristol and is staying with Katie for an undefined length of time. Matt is still at home but mostly in his room. But this Friday, I'm having a day off and going on an excursion.

I never thought I'd be driving up the M1 again so soon, and not in this silky Jaguar either, and not with Val if it comes to that.

The Jaguar was her idea. 'I just wish I could be there to see their faces when they open that garage and find it gone.' "They" being Debbie and Steph, and in the case of the Jaguar especially, Debbie's husband. 'He's had his eyes on it ever since Malcolm died.'

I did wonder – Don and I had a conversation about it – whether the car would still go after so many years locked in the garage, but Val has surprised me by being quite familiar with the inside of a car engine and she had checked and changed all the things that could be checked and changed, and taken it for a run round the M25 at two in the morning when she couldn't sleep for excitement.

And now we're on our way to see Theresa.

'We can't send a letter,' Val said. 'Les could get hold of it and she might never get it. And it will take her a while to get her head round all this. She'll need us to be there.'

'Are you sure you want me to come?'

'I bloody am sure,' she said. 'For one thing, you're there to sort out Les if he starts. And for another, you're as near family as makes no difference.'

It's August, and a strong wind is tearing the poor leaves off the trees by the roadside. Rain clouds on the horizon, like the rolls of dust you get under beds. Litter from cars and lorries is whipped about, and liable to land on the windscreen. Specks of rain fall and a downpour threatens, but Val and I are light-hearted, even frivolous.

We phone Theresa from the motorway in the after-noon and she tells us, as we hoped, that Les is not at home.

'How does she sound?' I ask, from behind the wheel.

'A bit bewildered I think, but pleased we're coming.'

So we're heading north, Val and me, nervous and

ecstatic at the same time, in this big smooth car.

'I can't keep it,' she says, to convince herself. 'Where would I put it? But at least I can sell it and get something better than mine.'

'But why,' she says later. 'Couldn't Kay have given it to me years ago? She knew I was down to have it. Didn't she? Do you think?'

Later, she asks if I'd like to take any of Kay's furniture, to replace mine that has had to be thrown out.

I think about it, and I'm tempted – there are one or two nice things in there, but then I think what Don would say, not to mention our daughters, and I – regretfully – say no.

'Well you know best,' she says, and then, 'Oh I am absolutely scarified, aren't you?'

There are still privet hedges around here, busy with sparrows. Where I live, everyone has torn up their hedges so that they can park their cars, but here, in this frankly grotty bit of Sheffield, the streets are wider. There are fewer cars and the hedges still exist, mostly unclipped and entwined with white bindweed. The smell takes me straight back to summer holidays from primary school, on those damp cloudy days you sometimes get, that hold the smells down at pavement-level. Makes me remember being ten, kicking around the streets with Rita, looking for something to do.

As we turn into the street, little groups of kids turn and look at the car and us. I know this sort of street and this sort of kids. They'll be nosing and poking around as soon as we're inside the house. Some of them will have big brothers and some of the big brothers won't mind scratching a car like this, or worse.

'We don't want to be twocced,' I say. 'Let's take it back to the main road and ask if we can leave it in the petrol station.' So we do, and arrive at Theresa's on foot.

First, of course, we have to go over Kay's death, and life, and the funeral, for Theresa.

The daughters never even told her, as I suspected, but Val has told her all about it since.

'I always thought Kay was the lucky one,' she says.

'How do you make that out?'

'Well, she got Malcolm. She had that nice house, and Malcolm, and plenty of money. I know he died and that must have upset her, but she wasn't badly off, was she?'

'She was never lucky,' says Val strongly. 'Malcolm was awful to her. He'd go after anyone in a skirt, you know that. He never changed. And Kay knew, I think he even told her all about his women. She even knew about Rita.'

'What about Rita?' This is me, not Theresa – she's looking a bit stunned by the force of Val's feeling.

'Malcolm had a thing with Rita. I thought you would have known about it. A long time ago, but Kay knew all about it. He paid for her to have a termination, didn't he?'

Theresa seems to accept this without question – what kind of life must she have led? I want to know every-thing Val knows about this, but I know I can't say any more, not in front of Theresa.

Anyway, we are here for the big occasion, which is to

tell Theresa that by the conditions of Malcolm's will, she has inherited Kay's house, and all her money.

When I first heard this, I thought how annoyed Deborah and Stephanie would be, but thought that they would at least inherit the shop-fitting business.

I was wrong about that though. It turns out that most of that belongs to Rita, and has done for some years. Steph runs it and makes a good wage, and she and Deb have some sort of part ownership where they take some of the profit, but basically, it's Rita's company now.

Theresa takes her time to understand all this, not helped I would say by Val's erratic explanations, which keep taking us up interesting but fruitless gossipy alleys.

Theresa sits at her kitchen table, looking at Val as if she suspects it's a trick, or a dream, and then she stands up and says:

'Right then, I'll go and pack.'

It takes us a while, Val and me, to realise what Theresa is talking about.

She is prepared to leave, there and then, and come back with us to Kay's house. She's not going to think about it, she's not going to sell Kay's house, or do anything, except give up her life in Sheffield, with Les.

'Stop a minute,' says Val. 'We're not going back tonight. We're not driving all that way without a night's sleep and a bottle of wine. If you want to come with us tomorrow, that's fine, that's lovely in fact, I couldn't ask for anything I'd like more, but think about it. Sleep on it.'

'I don't need to sleep on it,' says Theresa, but she agrees to wait till tomorrow.

What we have to do tonight, therefore, is to go and see her children and let them know what's going on.

We go to Mark's house. I once met Mark, very briefly, at Malcolm's funeral, when he looked both baffled and enraged, but now he's quite different. A big, placid, take-life-as-it-comes sort of man.

His wife is Marie, also big, but less placid. You can tell who runs the show. Their children are there only as photographs in the hall: fair-haired, cheerful, with a definite look of Malcolm.

Theresa's other children arrive separately. Sean I've seen before, and he's no more communicative this time. And Kim I've met, though I'm not sure whether she really remembers me or whether it's just the professional polish.

But Val hasn't met them, so there are introductions and explanations. I've never met Angie before, though Val has: she's a wiry, energetic-looking woman, with the face of an intelligent and kindly terrier. I can see Les in her.

'You'll have to look after your dad,' says Theresa, and Kim says that she already does.

'Don't worry about him,' says Mark, and Sean nods his head vehemently.

'Someone's got to,' says Kim, but Angie says:

'He'll be OK. But will he know where you are, Mum?'

'He'd better not,' says Theresa. 'You can all know. You can come down and see me, but I don't want him

336

coming near me. Don't tell him, will you?'

It's strange how they all seem to accept this new state of affairs, rather like Theresa did, easily, accommodating into their lives without any fuss.

Not much is said. We drink tea, until Val and I get up to leave.

'Will we give you a lift back?' and I'm thinking: Is she going to spend the night in the house with Les, knowing that she's leaving him in the morning?

And she clearly is. She'll go to work tonight, though she's late for her shift, and give them Val's address to send her wages on, and then she'll go home, and in the morning, she'll pack her things and Val and I will pick her up and load the car and take her away from her life.

And Rita and Malcolm. It's been chewing at me all evening and as soon as we're alone, I have to ask Val about it.

'I thought you would have known,' she said. 'I thought you knew everything about Rita.'

'Did she tell you?'

'God no. Kay told me. Malcolm told her. I think, you know, he got some kind of kick from telling Kay things like that. He was charming, wasn't he? I mean, if he was nice to you, it was hard to resist —'

She's not looking at me as she says this, and it occurs to me that Malcolm has maybe notched up the whole family, and I feel disgusted, and quite jealous. How come I was left out?

'Anyway,' she says. 'He was a bully. Not a bully like Les, but a bully all the same. He made Kay what she was.'

'I don't want to be nosy, Val, but I can't help wondering – did he try it on with you?'

'Well, there was the odd kiss under the mistletoe, that kind of thing, but Kay told me to tell her if he tried anything. And she said she'd know anyway and I believed her, so – '

I don't know if I can trust what she's saying, but I can't really push it, can I? So we return to Rita.

'I thought she'd be strong enough to stand up to him?'

'Do you? I'm not sure. She's not so tough as she makes out.'

'She did always fancy him, from when we first met him. We all did. But I thought she had more sense.'

'Well,' says Val. 'We all do stupid things, don't we? We can't help it in the heat of the kitchen, you know what I mean. You just get overcome with it, don't you?'

Well no, I think.

I dissuade Val from a second bottle, reminding her that we have to get on our way early tomorrow. Though Theresa has promised to be ready at ten, and assured us that Les won't be there, we can't be sure it will work out as she says.

But it does. When we arrive, Les' van is not outside and Theresa is standing, looking out of the front door. Inside one suitcase and a number of plastic carrier bags from Lidl are lined up.

'Is this all you're taking?'

She looks at me as if it was a silly question, and I guess that this is more or less all she's got.

'Have you left him a note?' asks Val.

'No,' she says calmly. 'Let him sweat.' I feel sorry for him now, but I'm not going to argue with her.

'Have a last look round,' I say. 'Make sure you've got everything.' And we accompany her round the house, feeling – at least I do – tense as wire in case Les should return before we get away.

It's a very bare house. The front room reminds me of the Doughty childhood home, chill and bare, but with no suggestion that children ever played here.

The bathroom is clean but old-fashioned in a very unluxurious way – bath, basin, toilet, no shower, cold floor, one toothbrush in a mug, thin towels on a rail.

No wonder Kim went and found a life where the water was hot and the towels were thick, and the air was scented with something other than toilet cleaner.

Two of the bedrooms are empty except for a bed and a wardrobe, no sign – again – that children ever lived here.

The third is the marital bedroom: very tidy, every-thing put away or packed; thin curtains at the window with a marigolds print, candlewick bedspread, no mirror, no ornament.

'It's a good thing,' says Val to me. 'That you didn't want Kay's furniture. I never thought she'd want to come and live in the house.'

She's said this so many times over the last seventeen hours. I'm wondering how Theresa will cope, living in

339

Kay's upholstered, thick-curtained, cushioned, cosy house. Will all those sofas and curtain ties and bath mats and cupboards full of sheets and towels keep her safe from the ghost of her sister? And the ghost of Malcolm. But then, of course, she's finally got what she always wanted: what Kay got to have before her.

You get the same sort of feeling from Theresa as you got from Kay, that they were arrested in time, never grew older, just shrivelled as girls, as if Malcolm was some kind of witch-prince who cast a spell. And Rita too?

'You know,' Val said to me last night, in our twin-bedded room at the Premier Inn. 'When Theresa left home, I really missed her, more than I missed Rita. We shared a bedroom, didn't we? And we used to whisper when we should be going to sleep. You know?'

'I never had a sister,' I say.

She is elated to see Theresa in the car, travelling south. She keeps looking across at her. I'm not so sure. We travel on, suspended, in Malcolm's car, south.

I'm exhausted when I get home, in the early afternoon.

The driving, the explanations, the people, the emotion. It's all taken it out of me. I can't do more than tell Don it all went off all right, before I fall asleep on the settee. Later, Don cooks for us.

Matthew has gone out. I lean back in my chair and reach for a cup of tea. Don doesn't ask me about it. I can tell him later, or tomorrow. I'm content to be home, and safe.

The sound of the doorbell does not alarm me.

The person who comes into the room is Rita. She is looking hesitant, if not downright timid, but I still know from looking at her that this is not a friendly call. Don hasn't noticed though.

'I'll be in the kitchen if you want me,' he says, and goes off to listen to the football phone-in on Five Live. I pretend to be hospitable.

'Sit down,' I say, waving a hand at a chair, and feeling thankful that we have complete floors again now. 'Can I get you a drink?'

'No,' she says. 'I've just been talking to Val.'

This doesn't seem to need replying to, not until I know what has been said.

'I know that Theresa is back,' she says.

She sounds as if Theresa is some sort of threat to her, some sort of interloper, something like an escaped wild animal, something that has emerged from hibernation to hunt Rita down. A bear. Not something like a small elderly, bewildered and beaten woman.

'She's left her husband,' says Rita. 'And you knew all about it. And you didn't say anything to me. Why didn't you tell me?'

Does she want me to answer? I will then. 'What difference does it make to you?'

'What does that mean?'

Are we going to sit here swapping questions all evening? Evidently we are.

'What do you want me to say?'

She is sitting facing me on an upright chair, not the

341

one I indicated to her.

Now she puts her handbag down beside her, leans back and crosses one knee over the other. That will crease her nice black linen trousers. She breathes slowly and carefully, as if she is alone in a room, doing her exercises. She wants me to say something, and I do. 'I've just got back,' I say. 'It's been a long drive and I'm knackered. Am I supposed to argue with you? Have you come for a row?'

'Why would I do that?' Oh god, we're still asking questions.

'Well if you want to argue, go ahead.'

She still says nothing, still sits there looking at me.

I say, without meaning to, 'We used to be friends.' It comes out like an appeal, when I think I intended it as an accusation.

'We were friends,' she says carefully. 'When you were on my side. When was the last time you were on my side?'

'What do you mean?'

'You did nothing to help when Theresa took my boy-friend –'

'Not that. Rita, you didn't want him. You wouldn't want him now, nobody would, I've seen him. Even Theresa doesn't want him. Even his children don't like him.'

'I don't want him, of course I don't,' she says. 'I never did. But you weren't any help, were you? You weren't any help when I wanted to stay on at school. You could have stayed on with me. You could have supported me.

Emotionally.'

'Rita, this is all years ago.'

'I am not Rita.'

'Yes you are.'

She hesitates, decides not to go there, continues. 'You ruined my wedding. You ruined my bathroom carpet –'

'Have you been making a list? You're being ridiculous, you know.'

'You got yourself invited to my wedding and then you ruined it. And ever since, you have gone round to Kay's, year in year out, talking about me.'

'No I haven't.' Though I have, she's right.

'You sit here in your nasty little house and you're so smug with your husband and your children and your grandchildren – you only ever get in touch when you've got some new offsprog to gloat about, and you tell everyone you are my friend, as if that makes you something, and I could tell them what sort of friend you are, and now you've been plotting to go and bring Theresa back when she's the one I hate above all. And you don't even know that it's wrong.'

She hasn't raised her voice at all. Don won't have heard a thing. She's wrong, everything she's said is wrong: it's not the way it has been and it's not the way it is, and I don't know why, but I say:

'I'm sorry, Reet.'

'I'm not Reet.'

'Sorry.'

'Right then. Tell Theresa, tell her and tell Val, that I don't want anything to do with them. They are welcome to each other. I was going to buy that house from her. I would give her a fair price, she'd have a nice little nest egg, she could give up work, and stay up there, wherever –'

'Sheffield.'

'Wherever. I wasn't going to cheat her. She would have got what was hers. But I am not going to see her in Malcolm's house, that's for sure. I will never go there while she's there. You can tell her.'

I should say, *'Tell her yourself.'* but I say again, 'I'm sorry.'

'I'm going,' she says, standing up and shaking down her trouser legs. She looks remarkably elegant as usual and I think to myself that this will probably be the last time I ever see her.

'You don't have to go,' I say.

'No, I want to go.'

'Don't let me stop you then.' We are behaving like teenagers, I know. Then she goes, seeing herself out.

Now I can hear Don filling the kettle in the kitchen – he'll come in with three cups on a tray looking pleased with himself – and I think, well, it's just me and Don now, that's all.

The story about Malcolm's funeral is the last one. I can't think of any more. I won't be going back to the writers' group. I haven't even replied to Jocelyn's emails. Well, as I say, I'm back at work now. Life is a bit of a rush again and in the evenings, I collapse in front of the telly, like everyone else.

I met Linda in the greengrocers one Saturday. There was no hiding. I turned round from paying and there she was, her face about two feet from my face, and then she stooped down to pick up a child's glove dropped from a pushchair. You never see Linda without a pushchair.

Not Sahara of course, another child, another girl grandchild. Our faces practically collided. I think I smiled, although I didn't mean to, it didn't feel appropriate. She nodded. Then I walked away.

And I saw Rita the other day. Not in person. There was a revolving rack of birthday cards, the sort that take old photographs and put amusing captions on them. Some of them had been taken from knitting patterns – did I say that modelling knitting patterns was Rita's speciality?

So there she was, about twenty I should say, as pretty as anything but wearing a cardigan that we would not have used to be buried in: pale blue, with lacy stitches round the yoke and wrists. My nan had a bedjacket something like it, I remember, that she was very proud of.

But Rita was professional: there was no sign on her face that she found the garment laughable. She smiled demurely, lips closed, looking straight at the camera from her Jean Shrimpton fringe, there to make ladies of the age I am now believe that they could look like that if they got out their needles and spent three weeks doing slip one, knit one, pass slip stitch over.

That was about 1967 and that was the record of how

she looked, and it was wrong but funny. It made me laugh.

She looked – young of course. Unbelievably young, when you remember that we thought we were grown up. But she looked – sweet. I'd never seen that before, because I knew of course that she was not sweet, never had been. It made sense though. She always knew it. That was the way to get on.

I bought it to send to her. I would put a message inside about pretending to be something you're not.

But then I thought I wouldn't. I thought that Rita couldn't help it if her face did the pretending. If she looked open, open-hearted and approachable, welcoming and giving; if she looked like that, she couldn't help it when people thought that's what she was like.

She even fooled me, and I *knew* what she was like. But I was ready and willing to be fooled, and the pretending was all mine.

About the Author

 Susan Day has been making up stories since before she could do joined-up writing, but has only recently become brave enough to let people read them.

Who Your Friends Are is not her first book, but it's the first one to be allowed out of its computer file and cardboard folder.

If anyone is interested, she was born in Middlesex, has lived in Essex, Leicester and Paisley and now lives in Sheffield. She has a husband, three children and a garden.

Printed in Dunstable, United Kingdom

64203275R00201